NASHVILLE DREAMS

JULIE CAPULET

"All I wished for was to experience that spark you read about, just once. What I wasn't expecting was the Fourth of July and heaven on earth all rolled into one." ~ Stella

Bass player Kade Tucker is known as the Magic Man, and not only for his riffs. After breaking off a disastrous relationship, he swears off women. Only problem is, five minutes later, he might have just met the love of his life.

Stella Bell has always done what's expected of her. Until a secret letter and an unwanted proposal on the same day prove to be her breaking point. For once in her life, she's going to do something for herself. As fate would have it, that means taking a spur of the moment trip to Nashville.

A hopeless romantic, Stella has been hiding her true self for far too long. And when a gorgeous, mysterious stranger rescues her from a torrential downpour, she decides to go with it. The hot, dreamy Kade Tucker proceeds to enlighten Stella in every possible way, until she begins to realize that some dreams really can come true.

But will Kade's twisted ex and Stella's family secrets – and a very accidental pregnancy – get in the way of their HEA? Or is this a match made in Music City heaven?

Nashville Dreams is a sexy standalone rockstar romance starring a hot musician and a sweet & sassy dreamer who's the one he always knew was out there somewhere. Now that he's found her, he has no intention of letting any one of her dreams go unanswered.

Music City Lovers

Nashville DREAMS

1

KADE

"LET's go to Aspen for New Year's. Just you and me. By then we might have some celebrating to do. For something I think we both want to happen. It would be so fun, Kade. Can we?"

My girlfriend Carmen has been dropping some heavy hints lately. And I've been putting off the inevitable. I know that, as soon as I tell her how I actually feel, she's going to go ballistic.

It's a scenario I've been doing my best to avoid. But I can't avoid it forever. I should never have let things get this out of hand to begin with.

In fact, why the fuck did I?

I know exactly why. Because there's nothing I hate more than making a woman cry. It's my one weakness and something that grates on me like nothing else does.

My father used to make my mother cry, with his binges and his moods. It was his own inability to *stop* himself from making her cry that fueled his downward spiral and eventually took them both. And it made a deep impression on me, imprinting me with an absolute aversion to the tears and sadness of women, especially tears and sadness that are inflicted by me.

This hang-up runs so deep that I often avoid getting into relationships in the first place, even though every night of the week, I've got a thousand hopefuls trying to get close to me. Every time I *do* take the plunge—something I never take lightly—I'm always hoping like fuck that she's *the one*. That one stellar, star-stuck, meant-for-me true love that I'll fall head over heels for, that I'll never want to leave, that I can spend every moment making sure she's as happy and blissed-out as she can possibly be.

Deep down, I'd love to find that. I *aspire* to it. To me, it seems like the most beautiful dream there is.

But that's all it ever is: a dream.

The reality is totally different.

Now, as it happens every time, I'm about to end it. I steel myself for the gauntlet of tears and heartbreak that's coming—on her end, at least—and all the grating melodrama that comes along with it.

Things haven't been going well. I thought maybe she'd pick up on that vibe and figure it out. No such luck. Instead, she's fixating on rings and proposals and moving in together, when all *I* can think about is how to get myself out of this pathetic excuse for a relationship as quickly and painlessly as possible.

Carmen is all for creating scenes and feigning outrage even when the situation doesn't call for it. And when it does call for it, like what I'm about to do definitely will, things get ugly. Which is why the next twenty minutes is going to be a living hell for both of us. I'm about to give her a reason to cry the realest tears there are. Also why I've been putting this off.

I was hoping this time might be different.

I knew I wasn't in love with her from the beginning but I kept hoping that would change.

It hasn't.

That's my problem.

It never fucking does.

Every single damn time, the doubt creeps in almost immediately. I fight those thoughts. I try so hard to see the good, the beauty, the draw. To feel a real, perfect connection. But over time, inevitably, it gets harder to do. It takes more and more effort. I find myself forcing it. I feel the need for distance closing in.

Right now, I feel the need for more than distance. I feel the need for a total break from the hellscape our relationship has become.

She's dressed in a white jumpsuit that makes her look small and frail. I've tried to get her to eat a real meal but she never does. She's all about denying herself the good things in life. Food, loud music—it's ridiculous that we're even together, for fuck's sake—and the grittier, deeper side of lust that I haven't even brought up with this one. I keep everything about what we have fairly vanilla because she can't handle anything darker. Which is too bad, because that's where the most intense kind of pleasure is always found.

It's another reason this relationship was basically doomed before it began. I'm tired of holding back. I want to unleash the beast of my lust all over…someone. I don't know *who* yet but she must be out there somewhere.

She has to be out there somewhere.

There are only two things I want out of life. One, to play music, which has panned out for me and my brothers as well as anything ever could. We're rich and successful beyond our wildest dreams. Every song on our latest album has hit the top ten and at this point we have more money than we know what to do with.

It's the second part of the equation that's so damn elusive. The one I keep closer to my chest. To *feel* so hard for someone it's the only thing you care about.

That's my problem. I never do.

Carmen and I met at an after-party. She was cute enough, running with a crowd of people who are famous for the money they've inherited, their social media followings and their ability to market themselves, or whatever it is they do. She wasn't a groupie. She wasn't as grasping and needy as so many of them are, which comes with the territory when you're in a band.

I know what I look like to women. Edgy and mysterious, at least compared to my brothers, who are both outgoing and for the most part about as laid back as it gets. I'm 6'3" and built as fuck. I have blue eyes. Women are always gushing about the color of my eyes, which feels to me like false advertising. My eyes should be black. They call me the brooding one, the dark horse, the dreamer. I don't know if I'm any of those things. All I do know is that I live to channel my creativity into something real and to drink every drop of life like I'm starved for it. Most of all, to *feel* things. Deeply. To experience the kind of love that kills you and breaks you and at the same time lifts you into some higher plane of the chosen few.

I know I could do it justice, like my parents never quite did. For them, there was too much baggage. Happiness doesn't always come easily. And true love seems like the hardest thing in the world to hunt down, and to hold onto.

Carmen sidles up to me, blinking her pale eyelashes at me. We haven't been out yet today. Without the usual make-up she spends almost an hour on every morning, she looks colorless and washed out. "I was looking at some rings online yesterday…"

Here we go again.

Carmen is—to put it kindly—highly strung. Uptight, according to my brothers. A total bitch, according to my sister. As I watch her react to my silence, I try to remember what it was that drew me to her in the first place.

Her enthusiasm? The lithe little spitfire who knew what she wanted as soon as she saw me, and went for it with everything she had?

That was five or six months ago and my brothers and sister are right: I haven't been truly happy since that night. In fact, I've never in my life felt so low as I do right now. My blues have taken on layers of inky black that I can tell my family can see in me. They've been trying to talk me into breaking up with her since day one, and they're right. I should have. I guess a small part of me hoped there was something salvageable here. I'm about to turn twenty-seven and I've never been in love. Not even fucking close.

Both my younger brothers are head over heels, ridiculously besotted to the point where they've both moved at the speed of light to get their girlfriends to move in with them and to get rings on their fingers. They were practically on their knees before the poor girls—sisters, as it turns out—knew what hit them.

Maybe it's just not in the cards for me—which depresses the hell out of me. Maybe there's a glitch somewhere, and fate's scales are tipped too far in the wrong direction when it comes to me. Or there's a hole in my soul where the falling in love mechanism is supposed to live.

Whatever. All I know is that *this* isn't love, and I'm tired of putting off what needs to be done.

"About that…" I begin.

"About what?" The pissed-off scowl is already in place. "Kade? Sweetie? I think we should talk about our future."

I feel nothing. No spark. No anger or even compassion. Just emptiness. And dread, over what's coming.

Fuck it. I decide I'm done with relationships. They never fucking work.

I wish like hell I could sleep my way around the city, like my cousin Gage used to do. Problem is, I don't have it in me to sleep around without it *meaning* anything. I'm always wishing it'll be *her*—the star-crossed girl I can never find—and when it clearly isn't, I lose interest. Another one of my hang-ups.

Even Gage has fallen hard, which we never thought would happen. I just got back from a few days away with my family over Christmas. I was ridiculously relieved when Carmen went home to her own family. I found myself telling my brothers and sister I'd already broken up with her, just so I wouldn't have to listen to them lecturing me about how she's all wrong for me for three solid days.

Both my brothers and all three of my cousins have found the one they want to spend their lives with. All five of them were all loved-up and starry-eyed the whole time

I was with them. Of course I'm happy for them. And it only cemented into place my resolve.

Because what Carmen and I have is a million miles away from loved-up and starry-eyed. For me, at least. As always.

I'm aware that I'm about to break her heart. I do it as carefully as I can. "I don't want to go to Aspen for New Year's. And I don't want to shop for rings. I'm not in love with you. I've tried to make this work but it isn't. I think we should stop seeing each other."

She stares at me sharply. Her ice-blue eyes well up, but the sadness is quickly overridden by hellfire and fury. "You're breaking *up* with me?" Her voice is shrill and abrasive.

"I don't want to hurt you, Carmen. But I can't keep pretending everything's fine when it isn't."

"How can you *say* that? Everything's been so good between us."

This is part of the problem. We're on completely different wavelengths. I don't know why I've been trying to bridge a divide that's unbridgeable. Maybe so I don't feel so damn lonely all the time. "No. It's not good. It hasn't been good for a long time. Maybe ever. It's over, Carmen."

"Kade. That's just not true! We're *perfect* for each other. Everyone thinks so."

Do they? Not in my world. Not that it really matters either way. "The problem is, *I* don't think so."

Her face is red and blotchy, the anger creeping up her thin neck like a stain. "And you're just *springing* this on me? Out of the blue? Why didn't you say anything?"

"I have said things. You just haven't listened. But you're right, I should have made myself clearer weeks ago."

"*Weeks?*"

"Or months. I've been hoping my feelings would change. But they haven't."

"But Kade…" Tears stream down her bright red cheeks. The sight brings back all the worst memories of my life in a jarring, horrible flood. "Is it something I've done? What's wrong with me?"

"There's nothing *wrong* with you, Carmen. I just don't *feel* anything, which isn't a good sign. You'll be better off with someone else. It's best this way."

"For *you*, maybe. It's so *easy* for you, you bastard! You can have any woman you want! Is that what this is? Is there someone else?"

"No." I wish there was. I wish like hell there was. "I'm just done."

"But I'm in *love* with you, Kade. I *love* you. I want to *marry* you!"

The thought of marrying this girl makes me feel darker and more rage-filled than anything has in a long time. Fuck, I'm an idiot, for letting this go on for far too long. "I'm sorry but I don't feel the same way. You're a beautiful person, Carmen," I tell her, even though I don't entirely believe that to be true. The more I get to know her, the more greedy and manipulative she becomes. "You'll find someone else. Someone who can give you what you want."

"*You* can give me what I want, Kade. *You.* Baby, *please.*" She clings to me and I have to physically stop myself from pushing her roughly away. I feel a sudden, violent aversion to her touch. All I want to do now is to get the fuck away from her.

I remove her grip and hold her shoulders, keeping her at arm's length, which is easy to do since I outweigh her by around three to one. I say it slowly, willing her to understand that I'm not playing games or fucking around. I want out. "I can't give you what you want because I don't love you."

"Stop saying that!" she screams. "You *do* love me. You have to!" More goddamn tears and it takes me right back to all the fights and sadness that broke my parents.

She raises her hand as though to slap me but I hold her wrist, making an effort not to break it. I so easily could. "Don't make this harder than it has to be." This whole thing is starting to piss me off. The black cloud hanging over my life has become heavier than I know what to do with.

"Then don't break up with me, Kade," she pleads. "*Please.* I'll make it better, I promise. I love you so much, Kade. Don't leave me."

I release her wrist. "It's not working. You must feel

that too. It's over, all right? Let me call my driver and he'll take you home. You'll be happier this way. You'll see."

She falls to her knees, clawing at my belt buckle. "I'll *show* you, Kade. I'll convince you. Please. I'll do anything. Let me make you feel good."

I take a step back. For fuck's sake. She's never done that before and it's a hell of a time to want to start. This was a major part of the problem. She's the most sexually repressed and unadventurous woman I've ever known. With her it's all missionary position or she's accusing me of being twisted and depraved.

She has no idea.

Fuck, I'm an idiot for not doing this sooner.

"Get up." I regret the past six months with a fury that's sudden and feral. I want her out of my life. I take my phone out of my back pocket and text my driver.

Her face is streaked with tears. "You *do* love me, Kade," she sobs. "You said it to me."

Once. To try it on. To see if saying it might make it feel like it was something that could potentially stick. But it had the opposite effect. It felt completely, totally wrong as soon as the words were out. All I wanted to do was somehow pull them back. To grab them out of the air and grind them into the dirt. "I wanted to love you. I genuinely tried. But I can't. I don't." It sounds harsh and it is.

And it gets a reaction. "You're incapable of love, you selfish prick! You don't know *how* to love. You're a cold-hearted son of a bitch who doesn't know the first thing about love."

It's the worst thing anyone has ever said to me. It confirms my deepest fears and makes my life feel more bleak than it ever has. *It can't be true.* Problem is, I think maybe it is. "Maybe you're right."

"Of course I'm right." She's on her feet now and the tears have given way to her seething, volatile temper. "You're an *asshole*, you know that?" She reaches for a book and throws it at me. It misses.

"Jesus, Carmen. Calm down."

"Calm down? *Calm down?* You know what you are, Kade Tucker? You're a commitment-phobic redneck with no heart!" she shrieks. "You're a selfish jerk who's too wrapped up in your own twisted head to get close to another person. You think you're all cool and deep, just because you're famous? Well, *I* know better. You're cold and heartless. You're nothing more than a self-absorbed wannabe, that's what you are!"

Wannabe? This almost makes me laugh. Better than tears, at least. And Carmen was never going to go quietly. I text my security.

She throws a heavy brass candle holder. I duck, and it smashes into the glass coffee table, sending a spray of shattered shards across the floor. "For fuck's sake."

"You arrogant hillbilly selfish up-yourself *jerk!*"

Four security guards enter my apartment. "Miss?" one

of them says to her. "Come with us, please. We'll escort you to the limo."

"Fuck you!" Nice. Carmen picks up a vase but the guards easily take it from her. She looks like a frail, angry little bird that just fell out of its nest, now restrained by the hulking guards. "Get your hands off me, you fucking meatheads!"

"Please, miss," one of them says to her. "We'd prefer to escort you without restraining you." They're polite but they'll do what needs to be done. I know from getting mobbed on a regular basis that these guys are good at their job.

I go to the bedroom and grab her suitcase. All those times she talked about moving in together that I brushed off. It makes it easier now. I've spent most of the past six months on the road anyway, so there wasn't time to settle in. Now, I'm grateful for that.

I hand her bag to one of the guards. Then I hold her coat out for her so she can put it on. It's cold outside. The guards release her and I help her get her coat on. As much as I want her to leave, I can't shake the protective instincts that are so ingrained in me, not for her in particular, but for anyone who's vulnerable for any reason.

At the gesture, her eyes well up again. "You're really kicking me out, Kade? Baby?" The word has always irritated me, come to think of it, because I was never hers. Now it has all the effect of nails on a chalkboard.

"You'll find someone else in no time, you'll see." At

this point I don't really care either way. About her, or anything at all. I feel completely, totally empty. It almost worries me how desolate the roadmap of my life has become. "You and me were never meant to be."

"You're wrong," Carmen pleads. "Let me stay, Kade. We can talk through it, I know we can. Please give me one more chance to change your mind. *Please.*"

I look down at her gently. "There's nothing left to talk about, darlin'. You take care of yourself now. You'll be okay."

"How can you *do* this to me? You're so mean!"

"I'm not mean, Carmen." My voice sounds husky and devoid of emotion. "I'm just done."

The guards lead her into the elevator and she follows, knowing by now they'll restrain her if she doesn't go willingly. As the doors slide closed she screams, "You haven't seen the last of me, Kade Tucker, you fucking bastard! You'll *pay* for this!"

Jesus.

That was just as gruesome as I expected, but it's finally over.

I walk over to the bar and help myself to a generous helping of Jack, which I tip back. I put on a cowboy hat, a long oilskin coat, and some sunglasses, even though it's raining, and I make my way down through the back entrance of the warehouse, letting myself out onto the street. My security won't be happy with me, but unless there are fifty thousand of them, I can handle the fans if it's smaller groups of them. I'm a lot bigger than they are.

I pull the collar of my coat up as high as it will go, to shield myself, if it'll make a difference.

I get a lot of publicity, more than a lot of bass players, for whatever reason. Travis is the golden boy of our band and the lead singer. Vaughn is the wild-child drummer. And I'm the walks-closer-to-the-dark-side, mysterious one. The enigma. Turns out just as many women prefer that type.

They study my lyrics. They swoon over the baselines I play. They scream and cry and cheer during my solos. With our last Rolling Stone cover, there was a spotlight on me with the headline, "Nashville's heartthrob bass player Kade Tucker's complex, catchy-as-hell harmonies will blow your mind and break your starstruck heart."

My looks get written about as much as my music. Roxie loves to show me the descriptions written about me online. "A soulful hunk," "a dreamy beefcake," "the sexiest mystery man in music," "a hot AF superstar whose emotion-drenched lyrics hint at a deliciously dirty mind that'll heat up your playlist and get your panties soaking wet."

Or something like that.

I don't pay much attention to it.

I get mobbed less than my brothers, maybe because I'm less approachable. But I get just as much fan mail and have just as many followers, or whatever they are, even though Roxie does all the social media stuff for me because I couldn't care less about that shit.

It feels good to be free.

I didn't realize how heavy the weight of an unhappy relationship can be. Especially when you're doing it because you think it's *supposed* to be making you happy, when in fact it's doing the exact opposite.

I'm done. Single. On my own.

And I intend to keep it that way for a while.

Making my way down Broadway, I pull my hat lower.

I have a gig tonight, which I didn't tell Carmen about. It's only a few songs, as a guest, but she would have complained, like always. The list of my crimes was endless. I wasn't home enough. I was too distracted to make time for her. My latest song wasn't about her. My newest tattoo wasn't her name.

As if.

Then there were the unbearable dinner parties with her pretentious friends, whose favorite topics of conversation revolved around how much of their parents' money they've spent lately and how many likes they've managed to get.

It was the *idea* of me that Carmen loved, I can see that now. *What took me so fucking long,* is what I'm asking myself. I'm a fool. A goddamn romantic who was looking for more than there ever was. The things she loved about me were all the worst things to love: I'm loaded, I'm famous, and all her friends wished I was theirs. What I didn't fully realize at the time was that the thing she loved most about me was that I was perfect for her image.

I have no intention of being fooled again.

I'm swearing off relationships.

I'll write music and clear my head. Take some time off from all the why-isn't-this-working and I-wish-I-felt-something-real-but-the-fact-is-I-fucking-don't.

I just wish I didn't feel so damn…*sad.*

It fucking sucks to feel lonely when you're with someone. It feels even worse to be lonely when you're genuinely alone. Because you never know if you'll ever *not* be alone.

My phone buzzes in my pocket and I glance at the screen. I'm expecting a barrage of angry calls and messages. But it's Gage, my cousin.

I almost don't answer it because I'm not really in the mood to talk, but he mentioned he might be coming to Nashville soon and I don't want to miss him. "Gage. How's it going?"

"Good." Gage and I are the same age, both the oldest in our families. We've always been close. "How's the rebound going?"

I told a small white lie to my family, that I'd already broken up with Carmen, just to keep them off my back because no one likes her. Now that the deed is actually done, it feels closer to the bone. My mood is dark, because I never actually envisioned my life as a lone wolf, which is clearly the hand I've been dealt. "I'm steering clear of women for the time being."

He laughs. "Sure. I give it five minutes."

"How's engagement bliss?" Gage proposed to his girlfriend Luna over the holidays. We never thought it would happen to the biggest playboy in the family but once he fell, he fell hard, like the people in my family tend to do. Except me, that is.

"It's surprisingly beautiful," he says. Falling in love is some powerful shit if it's got my staunchly cynical cousin all starstruck. I'd laugh at the unlikeliness of it all if I wasn't staring down the dark and lonely stretch of highway that's my immediate future.

"I'm happy for you, man," I tell him, meaning it.

"Thanks, bro."

"When are you coming to Nashville?"

"I have a client meeting there on Tuesday afternoon. You around on Tuesday night?"

"Should be. I don't leave for New Orleans until later in the week." I've got a few solo shows coming up. My focus for the past five years has been the band, but lately I've been taking on more side projects and doing a few more collaborations, which are gaining momentum. With my band, I play the bass guitar, but I also sing and play rhythm guitar. I recently recorded a solo album which has already started getting some serious traction. Roxie thought it would be a good idea to do a few shows and I agreed.

"Great. I'll make a reservation at Speakeasy. How's eight o'clock?"

"Sounds good."

"All right, Kade. Try to behave yourself until then."

"I'll do my best."

We end the call and as soon as I hang up, it rings again.

Carmen.

I ignore it, powering my phone off.

I make my way toward the bar I'm playing at tonight.

I decide I'll stay at one of my other houses until I leave for New Orleans. I own three in Nashville, because it happens to be my favorite place on earth and it's home. I use each house for different reasons, depending on my schedule and my mood.

The warehouse is where the band practices and records, and where we spend time together. No one else is there right now since our biggest tour yet just finished and everyone has split to take some time off. And after the break-up tonight I need some space from that place.

The twelve-bedroom house I own in the center of town, just off Broadway, is looked after for me by a couple of friends who are also musicians. It's a hub for local artists and it's where I hang out when I'm meeting up with my collaborators and performing different kinds of music with local and visiting bands, from blue-grass to rock to country to jazz.

And my house in Franklin is seven acres, with a brand

new house on it a friend of mine who's an architect designed for me. It sits up on a hill and has views of the pool and the treetops. I use it when I feel like getting out of the city for a break and some much-needed solitude, which, from time to time, I absolutely crave.

I also own an apartment in New York City, a house in New Orleans and a condo in downtown Austin.

The rain is really coming down now.

I'm about to turn the corner when I hear something.

It's a girl. "Hello?" she says. "Open the door. Come on. *Please.*" Her back is to me but I can see that she's soaked to the skin. She's pressing an intercom button by the door. "Hello?" She holds the button down for a few seconds, then gives up. "I can't believe this."

I stop walking. As she turns to look at me, I can see that she's crying.

Not again.

But I slide my sunglasses up. To get a better look.

She's cute, in a bedraggled, waif-like way. Her eyes are the brightest color green I've ever seen. Her hair is long and wet, hanging straight until it reaches past her shoulders, where it coils into loose, cheerful ringlets. Light smudges around her eyes give her a sultry look, and it's a sexiness she's completely unaware of. The wetness of her long eyelashes has created starburst patterns, giving her face a sweet, hot-mess glamour. Her lips are full and pink, perfectly-shaped, with a wet plumpness that hits me right where I live. At the sight of her soft mouth, without warning, my cock thickens. *Fuck.* Lately I've been so mired in my own unhappiness that I've been uncharacteristically… calm. But my calmness has suddenly and jarringly faded out. The shape of her rain-wet lips reawakens a revved-up lust in me that was—until right this second—trapped under the heavy weight of my own discontent.

I will myself not to *get a raging fucking hard-on*, but the tidal wave of relief and straight-to-the-gut bedazzlement she's hitting me with is the most forceful thing that's happened to me in a long time. Or maybe ever.

I'm alive, she's reminding me. *I'm hot and I'm overflowing with hunger and cravings that'll break every rule and ignite the kind of pleasure you'll never recover from.*

Damn.

She's achingly pretty.

It's a different kind of beauty than the one I've been closest to lately, which was hardened by anger or meanness or spite.

This girl has none of that pettiness behind her eyes, and the difference is sort of fierce and luminous. There's a purity to her expression that I feel somewhere in the middle of my chest. She's fucking gorgeous, cute but also sexy as hell. And she's *kind.* You can read that about her. She's quirky and empathetic, with a fun, eccentric edge. I don't know how I get all that with one glance but I do. There's an openness to her face that's riveting me.

"Are you all right?" I ask her, though clearly she isn't.

"I'm fine." She's wary. She's obviously not from

around here. Her coat is open at the front, and her wet clothes are citified and preppy, with a twist. You get the feeling she's a free-spirit confined by the invisible cage of family expectations or society's rules. She studies my look for a few seconds, and her wariness drifts. She notices my height, my build, my face. I'm rough-looking but there's something trustworthy about my eyes. I've been told this more than once and maybe she's tuning into that same vibe. "This is supposed to be my Airbnb. But they're not answering and the door is locked. It's just the cherry on top of what has been…a week. Do you happen to know of any hotels nearby?"

I think about recommending one of the many hotels within easy walking distance.

I've sworn off women, I remind myself. I'm taking a much-needed break. But I'm not quite ready to disengage from her layered, bright-eyed glow. She's fascinating me with all the different facets of her gorgeousness. The glittery emerald eyes that are so green they're surreal-looking, like she's half sea nymph or she just rode in from Atlantis on her unicorn. The sweep of her eyelashes. The cheekbones, with the slightest little hollows underneath, where a dimple quirks. Her skin is sun-kissed and healthy-looking, like she's been hanging out on a Hawaiian beach all day instead of here in the cold, wintery rain. The three tiny freckles across the bridge of her nose are shaped like a golden C chord. "I'm heading to a bar right around this corner for a drink," I hear myself saying. "We could get you out of the rain and you could call somewhere to see what's available."

She doesn't answer right away. But then the rain starts coming down harder, in an absolute torrent. Until it's dripping off my hat and off the ringlets of her hair, wetting her already-soaked white top, revealing a hint of lace, the fullness of her breasts and the outline of her taut nipples.

Damn it. Despite my attempts to tone it down, my cock hardens fully, throbbing hotly.

"I guess I won't be leaving a glowing review for this host." A hint of humor touches her mouth. Even standing here in the pouring rain, stranded, alone with a towering stranger she just met on the street, something about this situation entertains her. This detail does something to slay me, I have no idea why. She finds the fun in life, that twinkle in her green eyes is communicating. It's such a refreshing change from the girl who looks for the misery or the how-dare-the-universe-injustice-me-like-this in every situation, like the one I'm used to.

As she stares up at me, her full lips parted, I notice she has a small gap between her front teeth. I have this insanely savage urge to run my tongue along it. To sink deep into her mouth. To taste her. To feast on all that sultry lusciousness.

Fuck, it feels good. To *feel* so much.

I take off my coat and—carefully, so I don't scare her —wrap it around her shoulders. "You're getting wet."

We might as well be standing in a shower, the rain is coming down that hard. She smiles at the ridiculousness of the deluge of the rainstorm and that sweet quirk of her mouth makes my decision. There's no way I'm not taking her with me tonight. "And now you're getting wet."

Don't overthink this. You're coming out of a tunnel. You're not lovestruck, she's just the first pretty girl you've come across on the rebound.

I keep it light. "It'll be dry in the bar. How about that drink?" I'm wondering if she's even old enough. She looks impossibly young.

"A drink sounds fantastic."

I don't care either way but I want to know. "You're legal, right? Just out of curiosity." Because I'm asking the question for more than one reason.

She blinks at me, like she finds this funny. "I'm twenty-one."

I wouldn't have guessed that. She looks younger. Whatever happened to her this week to make it a crazy one, it just got a whole lot better. Because I'm about to make sure of it. I offer my arm for her to hold onto. "You ready, then? It's not far."

She takes my arm lightly, glancing up at me with those crazy-ass eyes that are charmed with bright light and warm depth, and green as all hell.

"I'm Kade." I hold out my hand for her to shake, and since her right hand is weaved around my arm, she holds my hand with her left and squeezes lightly. I hate that her hand is cold. It clashes with her sunny face and those jewel-bright eyes. I want to shield her and warm her. To make sure she's safe.

"Stella."

Stella.

Lost little rain-soaked glamour girl.

I don't bother analyzing the spin of my thoughts. I'm too mesmerized to worry about it.

You've somehow just proven me wrong.

2

Stella

Three days earlier…

"Wʜᴀᴛ ᴅɪᴅ you want to talk to me about, Dad?"

My father has called me into his office. As dean of the economics school at Princeton University, it's an impressive space, lined with mahogany shelves crammed full of thick books containing all the most important economic theories and practices, some of which were written by my father himself. A quaint window looks out onto the campus's stone buildings and the fresh snowfall.

"I've spoken to Theo," my father tells me. He's wearing his dark blue cardigan over a shirt and tie, his round glasses slightly askew from all the deep thinking he does. "He's going to make you his teaching assistant next semester. It's a role that can carry on into next year as you continue with your master's degree."

Theo and I have been dating on and off for around six months—if "dating" is even the right word for it. We usually go out on Saturday nights to a movie or to one of the restaurants in town. The rest of the week we're both too busy to spend time together. Which actually works for me just fine.

Our relationship is casual, more of a friend-zone kind of thing than a dreamy, sweep-a-girl-off-her-feet romance.

Theo's nice, in a gentle, academic cute-nerd kind of way. He's the same height as me and sort of lanky. He's the kind of boyfriend whose jeans would fit you—not that I've tried them on, and as it turns out, not exactly what I'm looking for in a man. His look is absent-minded meets preppy. You get the feeling he puts on clothes without really thinking about what he's doing. He's four years older than me and is an associate professor of English, a job he started a few months ago. I know my father played a role in getting him hired after we started sort-of seeing each other, putting in a good word for him with all the right people.

Theo is my father's idea of "a good catch." Theo's dream is to work his way up the English department ladder and eventually get tenure. He teaches a class on the Russian literary greats and he wrote his thesis on the works of Dostoyevsky and their relevance in modern society.

Yawn.

Not that I don't think Dostoyevsky is one of the greats. He probably is. I just have a hard time getting past page two without falling into a deep and dreamless sleep.

Like Theo, I'm also an English major. My father almost had a conniption when I announced *that* little gem, but I stood my ground. As much as he wanted me to major in economics, the truth is I don't have an economic bone in my body. I'm made entirely of prose and fantasy. Anything related to cost-benefit analyses or bullish markets makes me want to run for the hills. Preferably the kind of hills where you might find buff, possessive alpha heroes to fall in lust with at first sight.

I wasn't even entirely sure I wanted to go to college in the first place. I had dreams of traveling the world and spending long, lazy days with a random, beautiful stranger on a beach in Tahiti or somewhere equally as fabulous, learning to surf while writing escapist novels and generally enjoying my life, free from confining expectations that revolve around topics like professional aspirations and post-graduate diplomas. But my parents were adamant that I at least get my bachelor's degree.

I finally relented, and so did my father, once we reached an agreement. My grades were good enough to get me into Princeton (along with my name and my father's connections, obviously). I would attend Princeton —*if* I could be an English major. That was the deal.

My favorites are the Brontës, Shakespeare, the romantic poets and, of course, Jane Austen.

But the classics are a long way from where my heart really lies.

My true obsession is contemporary romance. The steamy kind. The kind where the characters' lust is entwined with their love, burning up the pages with their fiery—and fantastically descriptive—passion. The books I'm addicted to are the ones where the bedroom door is left open. Because it makes sense: hot sex *should* be woven into heart-felt love stories. To me, the best love stories are just as much about the physical relationship as they are about the emotional one. Whenever I read romantic scenes that leave the intimacy out, I feel like I'm missing half the story. True love *includes* sex. Exceptionally *good* sex. Mind-blowing sex, even. The kind that will change your life with its white-hot chemistry and orgasms galore.

Not that I would know about any of that first-hand.

I'm twenty-one years old and almost a college graduate. And I'm still a virgin.

Even worse, I've never even had an orgasm.

Not once.

It's embarrassing.

I'm a die-hard romantic addicted to love stories, yet I've never experienced anything beyond the occasional friendship-zone kiss.

I've had boyfriends and opportunities, but I could never quite bring myself to go there. Because each time it's been so very far from perfect.

Which is a problem.

Perfect doesn't exist.

Theo wants to take things to the next level. He brought it up one night after pizza and a movie and I said I'd think about it. I even went on the pill to prepare myself for what might be coming.

Crunch time hasn't happened yet.

I've been avoiding it. I'm not entirely sure why.

Okay, I do know why.

I *want* to have sex, more than anything.

But I want it to be romantic. I also want it to be…*hot.* More than hot. I want it to be amazing and beautiful and life-changing.

Of course I do. Who doesn't? I'm assuming I'm not alone in this since forty percent of the fiction market revolves around hunky (fictional) beefcakes and the lucky heroines who are on the receiving end of the kind of scorching pleasure that makes them fall so hard they're ruined for anyone else.

My problem is, I have no idea if that kind of romance actually exists in real life.

I haven't experienced anything even remotely close to that neighborhood yet. It's the reason I haven't jumped into bed with Theo or anyone else. I've never once felt "the spark" you read about, the one with such crazy off-the-charts chemistry that it changes everything about you because he's perfect for you and so drop-dead gorgeous all you want to do is get as close to him as it's possible to do.

The few times Theo kissed me softly...nothing happened.

No fireworks.

No white-hot chemistry.

No undying love.

You don't grow up reading Romeo and Juliet a thousand times without fixating on what all that insta-love would *feel* like. How two people could just *know*, so much that you're willing to do anything—even *die*—because being together in the afterlife would be far better than living without the one you were meant for.

Some days I'd even settle for a horny AF one night stand, just to experience that I-don't-care-about-anything-but-this-moment *craving* for once in my lifetime.

I want to get swept away by the man of my dreams.

Where is he? I keep wondering.

Maybe reality just isn't as orgasmic or intense or all-consuming as fictional love stories are.

Maybe I'm setting my bar too high.

I don't know.

What I do know is that I'm not in love with Theodore Cartwright IV. And I'm definitely not in lust with him either.

Maybe he *is* dream-man material. For someone else.

For a sweet, brainy scholar whose Kindle is loaded with Russian masterpieces.

Either way, Theo and I just aren't well-matched and it's the reason I've been planning to break it off with him for a while now. The only reason I haven't done it sooner is because—and this is a terrible reason to date someone —I know it will devastate my father. Theo is exactly the kind of man my father wants me to end up with. Theo's father went to Yale. His parents are stable, still married and live in a rambling old inherited-from-banker-grand-parents house on the water in Connecticut.

But I just can't continue to be with someone who doesn't provide any glimmer of a sign that what we have might grow into something more exciting and heartfelt and…*orgasmic*.

Yes. The elusive orgasm.

I've secretly thought about buying myself a vibrator, just so I can find out what all the fuss is about. But I haven't yet been able to bring myself to do it. Call me a dreamer, but what I'm really hoping is that a red-blooded *man* might do me the honors. For my very first one, I'd really like to be on the receiving end of a *human*. An extremely hot one, who's big and hard and so intense I fall in love with whoever he is because he's so freaking good at it.

And here I go again with my fantasies.

"Your grades are good enough to get you into the PhD-track program early," my father is saying. "I've spoken to Professor Hayworth about it. You can start working on your thesis in January, since you're ahead of schedule. Have you started thinking about a topic for your thesis yet?"

At some point—like now, maybe—I'm going to have to tell my parents what I actually want out of life instead of hiding it behind closed doors because my parents would never approve.

I'm starting to realize, though, that approval isn't everything. In fact, it feels less and less important every day.

"Dad, I'm thinking about taking some time off from school."

He's too immersed in his own agenda, he doesn't even hear me. Even though I still have a semester to go before I officially graduate, I have enough credits to finish now if I choose to. All those high school extension classes and summer school research projects helped me earn my degree in only three and a half years. Because I always do what my parents tell me to do. I take the extra classes and do the extra work.

My father wants me to start working toward my PhD in the spring semester, but I'm still deciding.

Actually, I've already decided.

"Isn't that wonderful news, Stella?"

"Dad, did you hear what I said? I'm thinking of taking some time off."

My father contemplates me with a stern, serious look

on his face. It happens to be his default setting and his only way of doing things: sternly and seriously. "What are you talking about?"

Arthur Hamilton Bell III, following in his father's and grandfather's steps before him. All Princeton men, all esteemed economists and professors of economics, all important scholars and some of the greatest minds of their generations.

I feel bad for my father sometimes. Like now. I'm sure he wished for a son of his own, to carry on the family tradition.

Instead he got me.

And then my sister, Summer. At least Summer is an economics major, much to my father's relief.

My parents had trouble conceiving a baby in the early years of their marriage. After many years of trying for a baby with no luck, my parents decided to adopt one.

Me.

It's safe to say I'm nothing like my parents, even though I've tried my best to be a good and dutiful daughter. They're amazing parents and I have no complaints. Except that I've spent much of my life feeling like a square peg trying to fit into a round hole. Most of the time I just go with it because my family is my family and I love them. But some days my own eccentricities feel a lot closer to the surface. Some nights I stare into the mirror and ask the same questions I've been wondering about my whole life.

Who am I?

Where did I come from?

Where are they?

Everyone else in my family has straight dark hair and dark eyes. My hair is chestnut-brown with natural red and blond highlights. The ends, where it curls, turn white-blond in the summer. I have olive skin that tans easily, and green eyes. It's not a huge deal to look nothing like anyone else in your family, but there are moments when the feelings of being *other* rise up, mainly because I have no clue about who my biological parents were or where I came from. All I know is that I was adopted from an agency located in Charlotte, North Carolina.

Once my parents were no longer so stressed about babies and pregnancies and whatnot, they conceived, out of the blue. Summer is two and a half years younger than I am. Their miracle baby. She's feisty but sweet, and very much my parents' daughter in the true sense of the word. I love her to pieces. She's been doted on all her life and is sheltered but also driven. She's an economics student— not at Princeton, though, which caused a major uproar in our household at the time. She insisted that she wanted to go to California. She's always hated winter and she wanted to follow the sun. My father finally relented when she got into Stanford. He would take that as a close second. She started last semester.

So this is my family.

And the plan that's been rolling around in my head

for a long time is starting to take shape. All the pieces have, just recently, begun to fall into place.

"Thank you for organizing that, but I'm not sure I'm going to do a PhD. At least not right away. That was never my plan."

The disapproving glower is one I'm used to. "Of course you should continue. You want to teach, don't you? What else would you do?"

"I thought I might travel, like I've always wanted to. And work. And, as I just mentioned, I'd like to write."

"Write? What are you going to write?"

"A novel." *A steamy one.*

He observes me for a few seconds, as though I've just reminded him once again that I'm an English major. English majors do things like write novels. "Plenty of people write *as* they study and teach, Stella. Theo is. He's editing a scholarly journal on Tolstoy that's already had an offer of publication."

I feel my eyes practically glaze over just at the thought. "Dad, I'm going away for a week. Maybe even a few weeks, since the semester is finishing. I'm leaving the day after Christmas."

"What are you talking about? Alone? Don't be ridiculous."

Summer is staying in California for the holidays this year. And something else has happened lately that's not only given me the courage to follow my own path, but has lit a fire in me that's completely new. And *hungry*, like a craving has taken hold.

After my sister left for college, I decided to do a search. For my birth mother.

Even a few years ago, I would never even have considered it, out of respect for my parents. I didn't want them to think they weren't enough. They are. But I also know that, deep down, I need to know.

I don't have delusions about a loving reunion. I don't even know if I *want* a loving reunion, or even if I want to meet the people who created me, at all. More than anything else, I want to know the story.

I want to know *why* they gave me away.

It might not be a happy story. It might be awful and sad. I'm prepared for all that. Either way, I want answers to the questions that have always burned bright. *How could anyone give away their own baby? To total strangers they know nothing about? How?*

The only information I have is the name of the adoption agency. *Children's Home Society, Charlotte, North Carolina.*

I've never even been to North Carolina.

Once my sister left for Stanford, where she'll no doubt excel and become exactly—or as close as he's going to get —what my father always wanted in a child, I felt myself starting to rebel, just a little. More and more. Like a chrysalis who has obediently remained wrapped in its shell for a long time, I'm finally feeling the need to spread my wings. Even if those wings happen to be a completely different color to the rest of my family's.

It was around that time that I googled the adoption agency's number. Without overthinking it, I made the call.

I received the reply this morning. A mailed envelope, sent to my mailbox on campus. I haven't opened it yet. I'm waiting until I'm alone.

"Stella, be reasonable. A PhD from Princeton will set you up for life. Why would you even consider throwing all that away on a whim?"

"A Bachelor's from Princeton will set me up for life, Dad, which I already almost have. Besides, it's not a whim. It's a plan."

"A plan? What plan?"

His tone is disparaging but I've already made up my mind. The decision has forged itself into something real and sure. Into something that won't budge. "Dad?"

"Yes?"

"I love you."

My father stares at me. We don't usually throw those words around casually. In our family, those words belong to special occasions or a heartfelt family moment. Not standing here in his office.

He's stunned and wary, like he can tell this is leading up to something. I keep going. "I love you and I appreciate you. You're the best father anyone could ever ask for. But this isn't about you. It's about me. It's something I want to do and it's something I'm going to do. I'm taking a few weeks off, or maybe a few months. I'm going to spend some time thinking about what I want to do next and what I want out of life. And you're going to be happy that I've achieved what I've achieved so far. You're going to allow me some space to figure out my own path because I'm twenty-one years old and it's time for me to do that. Okay?"

My father leans back in his creaky chair. He folds his hands in a sort of prayer position. He's quiet for a long moment. Then he says, "All right, Stella."

All right?

"You're right. You've worked hard and you deserve a break." It's possibly the nicest thing my father has ever said to me. But I sense that he doesn't fully understand what I mean by "a break." "And when you return you can step into the role of Theo's teaching assistant."

It's a start, at least. It gives me some time. "Dad, I have to go now. I'm meeting Theo and I'm already late."

He relents, possibly because Theo is his favorite topic. "Fine. But don't make any decisions until you've discussed them with us."

The new me is gaining momentum. "I've already made the decision."

My father contemplates me, like he can see the change in me and doesn't like it. "Why don't you and Theo come for dinner tonight. We can talk about it then."

"He was planning on taking me out to dinner." That part is true. And over a casual pizza—that's as extravagant as Theo gets—I'm going to break up with him. "I'll come by tomorrow, though, okay? I'll spend Christmas Eve and Christmas with you. We'll have a nice time together before I go."

"We need to talk more about this," he says again.

I walk over and kiss him on the cheek. "Don't worry, Dad. Everything will be fine. You'll see."

3

Stella

I GET BACK to the tiny apartment in town that I share with my roommate Piper. She's a business major and spends most of her time either at the library or with her boyfriend Dillon. He's a hockey player and a sweetheart with several missing teeth. The two of them have gotten serious over the last semester and, between that and the fact that she's applying to graduate schools, I haven't seen much of her lately.

I sit down on my bed and hold the envelope in my hands.

This is it. After all these years of wondering.

I'm finally about to get some answers.

Carefully, I open it. I unfold the letter.

It's from the woman at the adoption agency I spoke to on the phone.

Dear Stella,

This is everything we have on file for you. All of this information was given to us at the time of your adoption and we have received no further correspondence since then. It's not unusual for the information to be brief.

Your birth mother's first name is Madeline. She was seventeen years old when you were born. She has one sister who is two years older. Her parents' occupations were restaurant owner and administrative assistant. She has brown hair and green eyes. She enjoys writing and reading. At the time of your birth she was considering applying to college to study English.

Your birth father's name was not stated. He was eighteen years old when you were born. He has three younger brothers and one younger sister. He has dark brown hair and blue-green eyes. He enjoys swimming and football. His parents' occupations were factory foreman and bank teller. At the time of your birth he was planning to go to college and hoped to eventually apply to law school.

Your birth parents dated in high school, in Nashville, Tennessee, where both of them lived their entire lives to that point, and so did their parents. Your birth mother made a point of stating that you were a child born of love. They felt they were doing the right thing by giving you up for adoption, to give you the best chance for a stable upbringing, which they did not feel they had the means to give you at that time.

This is the extent of the information on file. We do not have surnames or contact details on file, I'm sorry to say. Again, this is not unusual and was a choice made by your birth family at the time of your adoption.

Please don't hesitate to contact me if I can be of further assistance, or if you'd like to discuss anything included in this letter. And please remember what I told you over the phone: it's a good idea to have support as you process this information. Getting answers to long-held questions can dredge up emotions you may not be expecting. Please consider me a part of your support system.

Warm regards,

Linda Clegg

Holy shit.

There are tears streaming down my face that I'm only vaguely aware of.

Madeline.

Green eyes.

Writing and reading.

English.

There's so much to think about. It's impossible to take it all in.

I sit there on my bed and I cry. Not just silent tears but deep, soul-wrenching sobs. I curl up on my bed, taking care not to wrinkle or smudge the letter. You don't grow up as an adopted person without wondering—every single day of your life—about who they were and why they made the decisions they did. My life is fantastic. I have no complaints. But it's a heavy thing, to feel like you've been abandoned by the people who were supposed to love you the most. Even if it's in the background, sitting there most of the time like a quiet, out-of-the-way shadow, it's still *there*. Every time you look in the mirror.

I feel myself let go, until my pillow is wet and the hitches of my breathing start to slow.

Wow. Linda was right. It does feel like dredging. Some deep well of my psyche, where all those questions have lived my entire life, has just been dug up with a big-ass shovel.

After so much wondering, I *know* something about them.

Nashville.

And I know where I'm going.

4

Stella

"Hey, Stella. How was your day?"

"It was fine, Theo. How was yours?"

"Better now." He stands up and awkwardly gives me a kiss on the cheek. He's typically disheveled in the way that means he's spent all afternoon mentally in a Russian gulag. His scent is of vintage, slightly moldy books. After all that's happened today, it feels harder to force the light-hearted blandness of my connection to Theo.

I slide into the red leather booth. "Sorry I'm late."

"No problem."

After my total meltdown, I did my best to make myself presentable. I'm more sure now than I've ever been about what I'm about to do. And I don't want to put it off any longer.

"What have you been up to today?" Theo asks me, sliding in next to me.

Discovering a piece of myself, I almost say. But it's too close to home. Too new. I need to savor it and let it settle before I can talk about it.

The waitress arrives to take our order.

"We'll have a large cheese pizza and two Cokes," says Theo. Our usual order.

What I've realized is that I've been on autopilot in my own life. My parents make all the major decisions about everything I do. My boyfriend orders dinner. Now I'm wondering if I've allowed this because I felt like I was less of a person than everyone around me. Like I wasn't worthy of taking the bull of my life by its horns because I don't actually know who I am. Which is overdramatizing things, but a little piece of that *is* true. Or it was.

You were a child born of love.

It's absolutely crazy how powerful those words are.

"Actually," I tell the waitress, "could you please put pepperoni and mushrooms on half the pizza? And I'll have a glass of wine."

Theo glances at me, like he doesn't recognize me. But then he says, "You're right. It's a special night. Make that two glasses of wine. Let's live a little."

The waitress brings our glasses of Pinot Grigio and Theo clinks his glass against mine. "There's something I've been wanting to ask you," he says as the waitress moves on to the next table.

"What's that?"

And right here in the booth at Roy's Pizza, Theo

reaches into the pocket of his khaki pants. "I know you've been holding out on me and I think I know why."

He pulls out a velvet box.

He opens it.

Inside, there's a small white-gold diamond ring.

Wait, what?

"Stella," Theo begins, like he's been practicing what he's about to say. "Since the first day I met you I've felt like we're a perfect match. We're alike in so many ways and we both want the same things out of life. Now that we'll be working side by side, it makes sense for us to seal the deal. Stella, will you marry me?"

I'm so stunned I can't even answer him.

"I know it's sort of sudden but it feels like the right time," Theo says.

"Theo…"

"You're the one for me, Stella."

"Theo. No."

His smile fades. "What do you mean 'no'?"

"I mean I can't marry you, Theo." I don't want to hurt him, but the thought of marrying Theo Cartwright is just totally wrong. I should never have let this get so out of hand. "Theo. I like you. A lot. You're a nice person and a friend. But I…I can't *marry* you."

"Why not?"

"Because. I don't love you, Theo. I'm sorry. I don't feel like we're well-matched at all. I actually came here tonight to tell you that I think we should stop seeing each other."

"Stop seeing each other?"

"Yes."

"But, Stella, your father has given us his blessing."

"You asked…my father?"

"I stopped in at his office on my way here. He said you'd just left. He was so thrilled for us."

It takes me a few seconds to speak. "My father would be thrilled, yes. You're his idea of a perfect husband. But, Theo…unfortunately, you're not mine. It's sweet of you. Thank you. But I can't marry you. And I'm leaving for a while. I'm so sorry. It's over, Theo. I have to go." Heavy, insanely deep-rooted discoveries happened to me today and my emotions are on overdrive. And now this. I slide out of the booth. I need to get out of here. My whole life suddenly feels overwhelming and claustrophobic.

"Stella, wait—"

I turn. I'm annoyed that I'm crying again and I swipe the tears away.

"Are you all right? I didn't mean to upset you."

"You haven't upset me. I just need some time to myself."

He's holding out the small velvet box. "Take it with you. In case you change your mind."

"Theo—"

"Please. Just think about it for a while. Give it back

later if you still feel the same way in a week or a month or however long it takes you to think about what you want."

I take the box, because it's nice of him. It's hopeful. And even though it's not going to happen, I allow him his hope.

Then I rush out of the restaurant and make my way down the dark street and through the snow flurries. My tears freeze and burn, but underneath them, something else is happening to me.

A feeling that my life is—and already has—about to change.

5

Stella

Christmas morning arrives. Without Summer there to diffuse my pronouncements with her bubbly energy, the atmosphere feels more tense than usual. I'm relieved when Summer calls just after we've opened the presents and I sit and talk to her for a long time in a patch of sun on the window seat in the den. I don't tell her everything. I just confess to her that I'm taking some time to think about what I want to do next. She tells me what I want to hear. *Do it, Stella. Go for it. You've done everything everyone has asked of you and you always have. You've carried the weight of all their expectations for far too long. It's time for you to stop worrying so much about what other people want. It's time for you to live your own life.*

It is, after all, why Summer went to California in the first place. So she can do exactly that. She's been stronger than me about making her own decisions. "I'm applying for an internship with Enzo King," she says.

"I've heard of him." Some hot investment guru who owns half of Hawaii.

"It's so competitive but I'm going for it anyway."

"Good for you, sweetie. You'll get it."

She laughs. "I blame you completely for my overdeveloped sense of self-confidence, Stella. It's because of you that I never feel like I'll fail at anything. Now you need to apply that same outlook to yourself." She's right, of course. "And I know there's more to this trip than you're telling me. But I'll let you fill me in on all that once you get there."

I promise her I will.

"Love you, Stel. I miss you."

"Love you too, Mooch." I've called her Mooch since she was tiny because she always wanted to do, eat, have and wear everything of mine. She loved me so much it sometimes felt like she was my little twin soul, even though we looked nothing alike. Because of Summer, I've always felt incredibly *necessary*, and I was grateful to her for that. Even if I felt out of place sometimes, like I was never a perfect fit in my own family, Summer needed me. I was her role model, her therapist and her rock. Now that she's fully launched and living on the opposite coast, it hits me again that I don't need to be all those things anymore.

It's time for you to live your own life.

Something I've never, ever done.

I survive the day. My mother is one of those throwbacks to a different time. She's a housewife, with no aspirations aside from making her home into a shrine of perfection for the sole purpose of entertaining the economics department of Princeton. It's her career and her lifestyle. Not that I fault her for that. She loves her life. She loves order and domesticity and familiarity. Everything's in its place, picture-perfect and lifestyle magazine photo-worthy. Straight and narrow. Organized and pristine.

Which is all fantastic, if that's the way you like things to be.

I remind myself to feel grateful for my parents and for everything they are. How lucky I am that the tree is perfect, the house a Martha Stewart fantasy come to life, the Christmas music gently wafting from the surround sound and the snow perfectly falling outside the polished bay windows, like my mother somehow choreographed the weather along with everything else.

What I realize is that I'm looking forward to some *messiness* in my life. Some spontaneity and a whole bunch of unpredictability. Some *wildness*, where things aren't organized at all but instead they're organic and fun and scary and new and completely…*mine.*

I can't wait to get started.

The day after Christmas, before my parents are awake, as quietly as I can, I take my packed carry-on, with my laptop tucked inside, and load it into my car. I made a point of saying goodbye to them last night, after some heavy discussions that included tears (my mother's), bribes (my father's) and staunch refusals (mine) that surprised even me with their resoluteness. It's time for a journey of self-discovery that has nothing to do with over-analyzing all the mistakes I'm about to make.

I told my family I was heading to Nashville, but not why.

Most likely there will be nothing to find there. It's easy enough to predict what will happen. I'll spend a few days checking the place out, because if two generations of my biological family are from Nashville, I at least want to see what the city looks like. I'll feel lost and lonely and I'll wonder what the hell I'm doing. I'll look in the phone books and I'll reach a dead end because all I actually know is her first name and the date of my own birthday. It's not like I'm going to run into my long lost birth mother randomly on the street in a city of a million and a half people and strike up a deep and meaningful relationship. I'm not even sure I'd want that to happen.

I'll take a look around and I'll lay those old ghosts to rest. I'll probably end up driving somewhere else before the week is done. Maybe some beach where I can sit under an umbrella, sipping Mai Tais while I write the first chapter of my novel, which will most likely be terrible and confirm all my worst suspicions, that I should stick to what I know instead of pretending I've got a steamy and wildly successful romantic bestseller inside me waiting to break free.

I crank up the music and sing along to my favorite songs.

By the time I pass Philadelphia I've entered that traveling state of mind, where you wonder why it was so hard to leave because now that you have, everything seems wide open.

I drive all day. When it starts to get dark I stop at a roadside diner with one of those old motels next to it that looks like something out of a B movie where shady drug deals go wrong. I check in anyway because I need to sleep and it feels good to be outside my comfort zone.

I take a long shower, then get into bed to answer some of my messages.

From Piper, who's spending Christmas with Dillon's hockey-mad family of five sons in Minneapolis.

> Help me! I've learned more North Stars stats than I ever wanted to know. His mother keeps all their knocked-out teeth in a jar

From Summer, who's on a beach in San Diego with her new roommate.

Christmas in a bikini totally ROCKS! Love you sis xo

From Theo.

I hope you find what you're looking for.

Yeah.
So do I.

6

Stella

By the time I reach the outskirts of Nashville, the snow has given way to a steady rain. I try not to read too much into it—like it's a sign from the universe that I shouldn't be here and instead should have done with my week off what any normal person would do, like jetting off to Florida or somewhere the sun was at least shining.

But no. Stubborn, sentimental fool that I am, I can't quite ditch the urge to find out more about the people who gave me away like a stray puppy, without so much as a backward glance or a reason why.

Over the past few days, I've gotten used to letting the tears just have their way with me. As the letter warned me, these dug-up feelings are hard, and deep, and they won't be denied. For whatever reason, I've cried more in the last twenty-one hours than I have in the last twenty-one years.

Last night I booked myself into an Airbnb close to the center of the downtown area and googled a parking garage nearby. I don't bother cranking up Siri just yet, though. It's too rainy to walk around. I drive for a while instead, exploring central Nashville.

It has that squat brick feel of all central American cities, with the taller buildings clustered close to the river. The Batman Building with its distinctive double points rises over the others, casting a majestic feel over the scene.

I think about…*them*. The people who grew up in this place and who knew its landscape and skyline like the back of their hands. It would all seemed so familiar to them. Did they take in this same view as they made the decisions they made?

The Batman Building looks beautiful tonight. Oh, and by the way, I think we should give away that random baby we accidentally conceived to total strangers.

I promised myself I wouldn't fixate on the things I can't change. But now that I'm here, it's hard not to think about them. How it all happened. The backstory of their mistake.

I imagine I can feel their echo. The molecules of air they stirred up when they once walked these same streets. Maybe they're here today. Maybe that tall, dark-haired man with the black umbrella is *him*. His eyes might be blue-green. He might enjoy swimming and football, or once did, all those years ago. Maybe that older couple coming out of the hotel over there are the restaurant owner and the administrative assistant, retired now. I wonder if they knew about me, or ever gave a second thought to the loss of one of their own.

I drive around until the sun starts to set. The rain has settled in and the streets are shiny with the reflection of Nashville's colorful lights.

Finding the parking garage, I pull in and park in a long-term spot. I'm thankful my carry-on bag is one of those plastic shell ones that's waterproof. My coat, on the other hand, isn't. But there's not much I can do about that.

Using my phone to guide me, I walk toward the Airbnb. The rain wets my hair and my clothes but it's not far. I walk past a few bars and I can hear live music.

I'm in *Nashville.*

It didn't even occur to me until now that I'm in the country music capital of the world. I happen to be a fan, even though I don't listen to it all that often. Maybe I'll go visit the Grand Ole Opry while I'm here and do some sight-seeing. Yes, that's what I'll do. Immerse myself in some culture since I've come all this way.

I get to the address of my Airbnb. I check the app for instructions about where the key is or what to do when I arrive but there are no messages. I ring the buzzer.

Nothing.

I ring again. The rain is coming down harder now and I'm freezing and soaked to the skin.

No one answers.

Another sign, possibly, that I shouldn't be here. Icing on the cake of my disappointment at this point. What the hell am I trying to do? Why am I here, frozen and wet on a random city street so far from home? On some wild goose chase for people who *don't want me*. They didn't want me then and they don't want me now. Nothing about this place does, obviously.

I ring the buzzer again. Who doesn't answer their freaking Airbnb? "Hello?" I say into the intercom. "Open the door. Come *on*. *Please*." Shit. Again with the tears, which I haven't been able to turn off since I read that damn letter. "I can't believe this."

I notice then that someone is standing behind me. Someone *huge*. My heart is beating fast and I start to turn. If the rest of my day has been anything to go by, I'm probably about to get mugged. Judging by the size of his silhouette against the rainy, neon backlight of the city night, I'll be no match for him at all. I don't care about my clothes so much, but if he steals my bag, I'll lose my laptop. These are the panicked thoughts that are running through my brain as I look up at him. *Please. I just want to write my book*, I'm tempted to say. Or what if his intentions are darker—

He's wearing a cowboy hat. And sunglasses, on this rainy night. *Is he crazy? A drunk street person who's down on his luck and borderline insane? Oh God, how stupid am I to have gotten myself into this—*

He lifts his glasses.

Whoa.

His eyes are blue even in the colorfully-lit night, rimmed by long, dense lashes. These give him an edge of whimsical dreaminess that clashes with his rugged masculinity. It's a strange thing to notice, alone with him like this on a mostly-deserted street. That he's...*beautiful*, in a hot, romantic, mystery-dark sort of a way.

He doesn't look drunk. Or crazy. There's something reassuring about him, in fact. Lightly concerned. Calm. And...seriously good-looking.

His face is stunningly handsome, in a rough, swarthy kind of way. The strong stripes of his eyebrows are barely furrowed with a beguiled curiosity. He has a square jaw and his neck is corded and tanned. There's a glint of gold from a chain he's wearing under his clothes. His hair, under his hat, is longish, hanging halfway to his shoulders. It's dark but with lighter inflections, like he was blond as a child but the full grip of his virile masculinity has seasoned and defined him into...this. A big, sexy tomcat. I can't help thinking it but you can't *not* think it, it's too forceful: here it is, alpha male perfection in the prime of its life. He might as well have it tattooed across his forehead.

I should be afraid of him. His size and the broad span of his shoulders promise a honed, powerful strength. But I'm not afraid. There's a depth to him that's strikingly magnetic. And the look behind his eyes is steadying me.

He makes a crazy first impression. I already feel

drawn to him, like I want to know him. More than know him. *Feel* him.

My heart is hammering in my chest and my blood simmers with a primal excitement. His vibe isn't threatening. *Dangerous*, maybe, but it's a danger you *want*, not one you want to run from.

Okay, wow.

"Are you all right?" The deep, low husk to his voice causes the tiny hairs on my arms to lift. I feel his voice in my stomach, weirdly. He has one of those voices that's confident and calming, like a very smooth whiskey.

"I'm fine." Sort of. "This is supposed to be my Airbnb. But they're not answering and the door is locked. It's just the cherry on top of...a week. Do you happen to know of any hotels nearby?" It's pretty clear my hosts, if they could be called that, aren't home. And now, I'm glad. Something about this guy's look makes it obvious he's from here. And if this is the type of person you randomly bump into on a rainy night in Music City, then maybe this place isn't so bad after all.

"I'm heading to a bar right around the corner," he says. "We could get you out of the rain and you could call somewhere to see what's available."

His *voice*. All layered bass notes and controlled-yet-stormy depth. Like something brooding and full of dark promise is simmering underneath the surface of his offer. The sound is...insanely alluring. I try to steer my thoughts away but they don't want to be steered. I'm thinking about what that voice would sound like in the dark. *What he might sound like when he growls and groans.*

Stella. Get a grip.

The shape of his mouth is mesmerizing me. I have no idea why, but as I stare up at him, a low heat settles into the low pit of my stomach. And lower, where I become aware of a tingling, pulsing warmth.

Oh my God.

As we stand here locked in this intense little bubble of checking each other out, the skies literally open up. The rain is torrential, dripping off his hat. It's almost funny how ridiculously soaked I am. "I guess I won't be leaving a glowing review for this host," I joke, because even though we're standing on a dark street in the pouring rain, there's something wildly reassuring about his existence. *I found one!* Even if he walks away and I never see him again, at least I'll know that drop-dead gorgeous alpha men are real. Because here one is.

He takes off his long cowboy-style coat and gently drapes it around my shoulders. The coat is warm and comforting from his body heat. The gesture, along with a whiff of his scent, sends a shiver down my spine. Cinnamon, smoke, leather and something else, a spiced alpha-male elixir that mainlines straight to my core, where his flames lick me. *He'd fight for you and maybe even care for you. He'd be dirty as all hell and so thorough it would take you to the brink of what you could handle. And it's obvious that he would, you can see that as clear as day: he'd entirely ruin you for anyone else.*

Help.

The thoughts running through my head are crazy, and my fascination digs deeper, like his appeal is not only getting under my skin but its effect is barbed with hot injections of pure, uncut lust. *Holy shit. This is it. Lust at first sight. It's happening.*

"You're getting wet," he comments. *He can tell?* Oh. Right. The rain.

The rain starts to slow a little, but his shirt is now soaked. "And now you're getting wet."

He smiles—and *wow*, he's gorgeous. He has the bluest eyes I've ever seen. Movie star good looks that are tempered with a rough, animal sexuality. "How 'bout that drink?"

"A drink sounds fantastic." I'm not ready to let him go yet. I want to watch him and stare at him. He's proving to me that my fictional fantasies might actually touch on real life sometimes too. And even though I have no thoughts about what might happen beyond this moment, his offer is too good to pass up.

"You're legal, right?" he asks. "Just out of curiosity."

"I'm twenty-one."

A spark of dark-lit amusement makes his eyes even bluer as he offers me his arm. "You ready, then? It's not far."

I let my arm weave through his. There's something immediately reassuring about his big, sturdy presence. I'm aware of a secret, slippery thrill. He's huge. And hard.

His muscular arm, under the layer of his shirt, feels like warm steel. The heat of his body leeches into me, imprinting me with a blooming frisson of anticipation.

"I'm Kade," he says. *Kade*. The name fits him. Unexpected. Cowboyish. Strong.

"Stella."

His slow smile is understated but deep and I laugh a little because I was so not expecting him to materialize out of the blue. There's a relief to his presence. Because, somehow, he's already my hero. For saving me from this lonely darkness. And for showing me that he's real.

7

KADE

WE GET to the bar and it's crowded, despite the rainy night. Of course I know why.

The bouncer sees me and lets us through, clearing the way for us. The word is out that I'm joining in tonight. Gus, the owner of the bar and a friend of mine, shakes my hand, noticing the girl on my arm. He's subtle about the fact that she's not the girl he might have been expecting. I happen to be famous, for better or worse, and my love life gets talked about.

I don't bother thinking about Carmen, and how this news will no doubt reach her within minutes. It doesn't matter that she'll take this as a sign that I was lying to her about not having anyone else.

So my rebound happened a little sooner than I was expecting. It's none of Carmen's fucking business.

So this little stranger is your rebound now?

I don't know what the hell she is. An angel. A goddess. A sign.

Whatever she is, she's mine.

Everything about me is focused on her and the light pressure of her hand where she's holding my arm. On keeping her there. Part of me is worried she'll disappear, like a mythical creature who showed up at the exact moment I was sure she didn't exist.

She's *too* sweet, *too* tempting, *too* perfect.

I'm not entirely convinced she's even fucking real. Maybe I'm dreaming.

But I know I'm not dreaming. My brand new reality has just taken on a new layer. A star-dusted one. She's surrounded by a halo of my own blazing anticipation.

To a few of his staff, who have now noticed me and are gathering around us, Gus says, "Clear the VIP table for them."

I wouldn't bother with a table if I was here alone. I can't sit in the crowd because I get mobbed and it creates a scene.

The VIP table is raised and private, in its own little secluded nook with a tinted screen and a view of the stage. A few bouncers guard the staircase and I happen to know it has its own exit out to the back of the building, in case things get rowdy. Which seems to happen whenever my brothers or I show up in any public place.

I had planned to show up, have a drink or two with Gus, play the three songs I agreed to play, then leave. The band that's playing tonight is a group of local musicians who jam together from time to time. I've played with them before, although it's been a while since I joined in. I've either been busy or on tour.

"Haven't seen you around lately, Kade," Gus comments, patting me on the back. "Good to have you back, man." Carmen didn't like this place. It's too lively for her. Not expensive enough. "I'll let the boys know you're here."

"Thanks, Gus."

He's staring now, as though he can't help himself. So it's not just me she affects this way. I have this raging urge to shield her from his view and everyone else's, to keep her all to myself. I want her *safe*. Protected. I want to bask in her gorgeousness *alone*, without sharing her. I'm not sure where all these Neanderthal tendencies are coming from, but I feel like I've morphed into a fucking grizzly bear who wouldn't hesitate to kill anyone who wanders into my territory.

I hesitate before introducing her. "Stella, this is Gus. Gus, Stella."

Her name feels weirdly prophetic. I was just thinking it earlier today: *that one stellar, star-struck, meant-for-me true love that I'll fall head over heels for, that I'll never want to leave, that I can spend every waking moment making sure she's as happy and blissed-out as she can possibly be.* Her name feels like it's wrapped up in all those wishes, even if I can't be entirely sure this is...*her.* It could just be me doing my thing again, looking for connections where they might not exist.

Maybe my own twisted angst about the state of my life five minutes before she walked into it has warped my perceptions into a fantasy version of whatever this is. Maybe I'm grasping.

I don't know.

Oh, I know. Like I've never known anything in my life.

You don't "grasp" for someone *this* damn gorgeous. You move heaven and earth to make her your own and then you hold on to her with everything you've fucking got.

Even wet and flushed from the pouring rain—or maybe because of it—she's easily the most beautiful girl I've ever met.

"Nice to meet you," she says to Gus, her voice soft and enchanting. *Mine.* I don't like that Gus gets to hear it and get a share of it.

What the fuck is happening?

She's still holding my arm, still wrapped in my coat. Her hair is wet, her eyes that off-neon shade of emerald green, her eyelashes long and jeweled with tiny raindrops that catch the light. Her face has a young, dewy freshness to it, like you often see on people when they first wake up in the morning. It's the exact same effect that every woman in the world wishes for and every fashion maga-zine spends shitloads of money trying to recreate. The full, pillowy, candy-pink lips. The rosy glow of her skin. The graceful line of her jaw and the gentle curve of her cheekbones, all the details of her converging into some crazy, ideal pinnacle of beauty. The smudged make-up and the echo of her tear tracks don't detract from it at all. Instead they somehow manage to enhance it and drench it in vulnerability. She's lost, she's soaked and her eyes are wary, hopeful and beguiled all at the same time. I have this urge to pick her up and wrap my whole life around her.

"You want to sit down?" I ask her. My voice sounds low and rasped. Because of her. I care that she's okay. I feel the wild need to make sure of it.

She bites her lip, her small, neat white teeth barely sinking into that mind-numbing softness and it takes all the willpower I own not to kiss her right here in this crowded room, both to stop her from doing that and also because her lips are so ludicrously juicy and sweet-looking, pure and pink like a ripe, exotic fruit. The look of them is not only getting me hot as fuck but also making me feel strangely, fiercely addicted. *So this is what this feels like.* "Yeah."

She's noticing the way the crowd is watching us as we make our way up the small curved staircase to the secluded table. I purposely keep her as shielded as I can. There will no doubt be speculation all over the internet before we even get to our seats.

"Why's everyone staring at us?" she asks.

"Uh...they know me around here. I told them I'd join in."

"Join in what?"

"The band. They've asked me to play a few songs with them."

"Oh. You're a musician?"

In every situation I've been in for the past four years, since we started hitting the headlines, everyone around me knows who I am, where I come from and everything else about me. This is...refreshing. If she recognizes me, the bigger picture isn't registering yet. "Yes."

"Do you sing?"

"Yeah. Mainly I play the bass guitar."

She smiles, those crazy-green eyes otherworldly and spellbinding.

We get to the table and I take off my hat, hanging it on a hook. Carefully, I take her bag and set it next to her. I unwrap my coat from around her. I'm not sure why my protective instincts are suddenly on overdrive but her safety and comfort have become my most feral priority. She takes off her wet coat to reveal the damp white top underneath. The lush swell of her breasts and the lightly outlined tips of her nipples are fucking with my state of mind. I want to lift her wet shirt and put my mouth on her. I want to lick her skin and suck on her beauty. I want to take care of her. *I want to be inside her.* My cock hardens fully and this annoys me. I happen to be well hung as fuck and it's uncomfortable, almost agonizing, pressed up against the button fly of my jeans, straining and fully-packed.

Usually I can bide my time. I'm not a hothead. I don't rush because I don't need to. But right now my lust is a wild animal that wants to *feed*. She's not ready for my sudden, raging fascination. What she needs right now is warmth, a drink, some food and some reassurance that she's not lost anymore.

She's found.

Kade. Chill the fuck out, boy.

She's so damn *beautiful*.

As she reaches into her bag for something dry, I can't help comparing her to Carmen. But there's not much to compare. Carmen is pale and skinny-thin. Her hair, her skin and her entire outlook always felt washed-out. There was no vibrancy to her because she was always wrapped up in her own petty grievances. I can now see all this with painful clarity. Fuck, how I wish I'd realized it on day one. She was always trying to add color to her look and her personality, with make-up and hair dyes and a manufactured online persona. But none of it was remotely convincing.

This girl, on the other hand, is practically glittering with all the details Carmen worked so hard for but never came close to achieving.

Stella's hair is damp and there's a curl to it. It's a rich, mink brown with hints of deep red and honey gold. Her cheeks are pink with health and a love-filled, empathy-charged life force. Her eyelashes are impossibly long. I find myself wondering if they're real. Carmen used to wear those fake ones, which *looked* fake because they were. I always had the urge to rip the fuckers off because who wants plastic hanging off their face? Stella's eyelashes are sweeping and gold-tipped, matching her hair and her glow with a perfection that's life-affirming. It's good to know that nature is capable of creating such a divine, dazzling creature who doesn't need artificial enhancements or staged radiance.

Stella wakes up like this, you can see that. She gets caught in a downpour and it doesn't wash off. I don't know why I feel so goddamn happy about that.

I want to show this girl what heaven feels like.

She's slim but curvy, her body sweet and lush and so much more womanly than the one I've spent the last six months trying to feed. Carmen was obsessed with losing weight and fitting into clothes that made her look downright emaciated. No man enjoys that shit. We're hard-wired to crave curves to hold onto and softness to sink into, to grip and to own.

Easy, tiger. She's stunning, you're on the rebound and you're horny as fuck because you've had an abysmal sex life for a long time. But don't go twisting this chance encounter with a lost, pretty girl into some kind of fantasy about her being your star-crossed soulmate. You don't even know her. You've exchanged around a dozen words. She could be as crazy as all the rest of them.

Two waiters arrive at our table. "A bottle of Moët, sir,

compliments of Gus," says one of them, popping the cork, pouring two glasses and placing the ice bucket on a stand. "And two Jack Daniels on ice," says the other one, taking the drinks from a tray and putting them on our table. Gus knows it's what I usually order. "Will you be ordering food?"

"I'm *starving*," Stella says, without a hint of angst about it. To the waiter, she asks, "Do you have cheese-burgers?"

"Best in town," says the waiter. "Sir?"

Maybe this girl *is* my soulmate. "Make that two."

The waiters disappear. "They like you around here," she comments. "VIP seats and complimentary champagne."

I don't bother telling her the place is packed tonight because of me. "Gus is an old friend of mine." I clink my champagne glass against hers. "To freedom."

Stella smiles and takes a sip, like freedom is the exact thing she wants to celebrate. "What kind of freedom are we celebrating?"

I tend to tell things like they are. And for some reason it's a detail I want her to know. "I broke up with someone today. It's the best thing I've done in a long time."

"Really?" The sweep of her eyelashes really is something. The effect hits me right in the middle of my ribcage. "That's kind of crazy because I did too. Just a few days ago."

"Yeah?" What I want to know is why everything she

says seems to fit into some unknowable cosmic puzzle. The one that always felt like it had a lot of gaping holes in it. "Who ended it, you or him?"

"Me."

"Why's that?"

She doesn't answer right away. We're strangers, after all. But already, pieces of us, little tendrils of mutual fascination feel like they're reaching out, mingling and beginning to entwine. "I just wasn't into it."

"How'd you end it?"

"He took me out to his favorite pizza restaurant the night before Christmas Eve. He proposed to me. I wasn't expecting it. Not at all. I'd been planning to break up with him that night anyway. So I told him I couldn't marry him and that it was over."

"Ouch." I take a sip of my whiskey, not exactly sure why I'm so relieved to hear this. I make a mental note *not* to propose to her in pizza joint, as if I ever would. *So now you're planning to fucking propose to her? What the hell? Slow down, you lunatic.* "How'd he take it?"

"He told me to think about it for a while, in case I change my mind."

The grizzly bear in me—and he's a new development, but he's *fucking* sure of himself—growls somewhere deep inside my soul. It takes me a few seconds to realize that...I'm *jealous*. It's not an emotion I'm used to. I couldn't have cared less if Carmen went out with her vapid friends or spent the night clubbing when I was away on tour. I have no idea why I'm going all caveman over a stranger I've known for half an hour. *There's no way in hell you're changing your mind, darlin',* is what I feel like saying to her, but don't. My fists clench and my muscles tense. I've been working out like a madman lately and my body feels hot and hard—everywhere.

Chill. The. Fuck. Out. "What was wrong with him?"

She's quiet for a few seconds, her gaze lightly exploring my face. My eyes. My shoulders. My fist, which I make a point of unclenching. The word LOVE inked across the knuckles of my right hand. "He's the future I'm supposed to want. But he's not the future I do want." She barely shivers. I resist the urge to lift her onto my lap and wrap my arms around her.

I slide the glass of whiskey closer to her. "Have some of this. It'll warm you up."

She takes a sip.

And I can't help asking it. "What was missing?"

She looks into my eyes as she says it. "The spark."

Well, hell.

I can give you more than spark, darlin'. I can give you the goddamn Fourth of July.

"It would be settling for something safe and predictable," she continues. "I don't want safe. Or predictable. I want something wild and romantic. Something extraordinary."

I think I might be in real trouble here, because something in me shifts. And forges. "I don't blame you.

Nothing wrong with wanting a little excitement in life." *Just say the word, honey pie.*

She seems to read this, that I could do exactly that. Which probably sounds cocky but it's just the way it is. I *could* do that. And I'm going to, starting right now. I don't yet know how or why or what it means, but I'm already *all in.*

Flags of pink warm her cheeks. "I should probably try to figure out where I'm staying tonight. I'm sure there's a hotel nearby. I can google it." She pulls her phone out of the small leather bag she's holding. She sets it on the table. The screen is lit with several names. Her new messages. Piper. Summer. Theo.

"Is Theo the guy?"

There's a hint of a smile in her eyes and I feel it all the way down to my goddamn soul. It's none of my business but I don't mean it in an over-the-line kind of way. More in an I'm-here-if-you-want-to-talk-about-it kind of way. I try to dial down the I'll-kill-the-fucker-because-you're-mine-now kind of way that's also a part of my question, because I'm feeling it harder than I know what to do with.

"Yes," she says.

"There's a one-bedroom apartment in my building that's free tonight, which is just around the corner from here. I keep it empty for my sister, but she's in Galveston visiting friends for a few days, so it's all yours if you want it. It shares a balcony with my apartment but it's separate."

She's watching me. Gauging whether there's any danger in me. Whether she can trust me.

"There are other people in the building too, friends of mine. You can meet them if you want to. There's also a three-bedroom downstairs with only one of the rooms being used. If you'd rather stay in one of those, you can."

"You're...a landlord?"

This almost makes me smile. "No. I own the building and a couple of friends look after it for me. It's six floors. So you could take your pick."

"Wow. That's really nice of you but—"

"You were going to stay in an Airbnb. It's basically the same thing."

"I wouldn't want to impose on you like that."

"You wouldn't be. It's empty." I ask it, because it's still hanging in the air and I prefer to dig deep into what I want to know, instead of wondering about it, or leaving things unsaid. "What *is* the future you want?"

Her eyes take on all kinds of depth and it slays me more than I'd like to admit, that something about the question is emotional for her, and also hopeful. "One that's more about that freedom we were just talking about, and less about other people's expectations."

Another one of those cosmic puzzle pieces clicks into place. "I think I can relate to some of that."

"You and your sister are close?" she asks.

"Yeah. I have two brothers too. We spend a lot of time together." I don't bother mentioning the band. She's clearly not from Nashville and it's possible she's never heard of us. Even though we've got the top three songs on the national charts right now, with five in the top ten, we get less airplay in certain areas. My guess is she's from somewhere outside of our main zones.

"So, what kind of music do you play?"

"Rock, country, folk, blue grass, jazz. A little bit of everything."

"Is that the band you usually play with?" She nods toward the stage, where the band is starting up the first set. I'm not joining in until the second.

"No. They're not really a band, just a bunch of guys who get together sometimes."

"Do you have your own band?"

I love this. It's an unfamiliar feeling to be such a clean slate. It's so rare for me to have a conversation with anyone—let alone such a glorious little golden girl —where it's just us, without the hype or the fanfare. "Yes."

"With who?"

"With my brothers."

"Really?"

"Really."

"You must be close to them."

I smile, exhaling a laugh because she's so damn cute it's ruffling some inner sanctum that's usually untouchable. The one where my deepest fantasies live. "Sometimes too close."

"Is your sister in the band too?" I find myself spellbound—again—by her flawlessness. Even her eyebrows are fascinating me. They're full and lightly arched. Carmen used to pluck hers then draw them back in. I watched her do this once and felt sort of disgusted by it. Who the fuck *does* that? Yet another thing that pissed me off for no particular reason. I love that Stella clearly isn't worried about trying so hard. She doesn't need to. She's spectacular as is, without any effort at all.

"No. She's our manager."

I don't elaborate. I want to get to know her before she finds out about the fame and the money. I want her to connect with *me*. What's hitting me hardest, I realize, is that Stella is nothing like Carmen or any of the women who came before her. She's not fishing for clues or promises. She's not trying to get her hooks in. In fact, for the first time in my life, I'm the one with everything to lose.

So much for swearing off women. For her, I'm willing to make exceptions to every rule and then some.

She takes a sip of her champagne then touches her tongue to her insanely luscious lips. *Fuck.* I feel almost dizzy with need. I want to *slide my tongue inside* with a fury that's messing with my sanity. And I hate myself for thinking it. As dark and dirty as my thoughts are, what I really want to do is treat her like the goddess she is.

Another text lights up the screen of her phone.

Theo.

She doesn't pick it up.

I resist an urge to smash the fucking thing. What fool would let this little angel slip through his fingers? He must be the stupidest motherfucker on earth. "Does he know you're in Nashville?"

"No. I didn't tell him that part."

"Does anyone know you're in Nashville?" Something about her unpreparedness, her ruffled manner and her small bag make me think she's made a rushed getaway.

"My parents." That thread of something deeper makes her eyes darken to a deep shade of jade. "But I didn't tell them why I've come to Nashville."

I hang back with the obvious question for a few seconds. She's running from something. Or running to something. Just the name touches on some emotion that's painful and complicated.

The waiter arrives with our food and puts it on our table. "Gus has ordered some extra security," he tells me. "The place is really filling up."

"All right." It's nothing new. I just hope things don't get out of hand. I'm now regretting agreeing to do this tonight. Then again, if I hadn't agreed, I wouldn't have run into my brand new obsession in the pouring rain.

He tops up our champagne then leaves us to it.

"I'm a good listener," I tell her. "If you want to talk about it."

"Thank you, Kade," she says, all heartfelt sincerity and sweet, mind-blowing gorgeousness.

I'm horrified when her eyes pool with tears. One paints a soft line down her cheek and she brushes it away. The one thing that kills me the most. Tears. Coming from her, it's just the worst thing I've ever seen. She's too beautiful. She should never feel sad or lost. *I'm going to fix everything for you, baby*, is what I'm thinking. *Starting right now, I'm going to do every goddamn thing I can to make sure you're as happy in every way as you can possibly be. I'm here now. Everything's okay.*

"I'm sorry," she says. "I'm ridiculously emotional at the moment."

"Because of him?"

"No. Not him. In my mind I'd already left him. It's just...a lot has happened this week."

"It's okay." I can't help it. I smooth a stray curl back from her face. "You're okay. Tell me what hurts."

Another tear falls and I can't handle it. With my thumb, I gently wipe it away. Unthinkingly, because it may as well be a unicorn tear and at this point I'm already half in love with her, as our gazes remain locked, I lick my finger.

8

Stella

As I watch him lick my tear, I make a decision.

Tell me what hurts.

If the rescuing me from a torrential downpour didn't do it, if the wide set of his shoulders and the hardness of his lean, muscular body didn't do it, if his thick hair didn't do it or the shape of his mouth, those words finally did. It's even written on his fingers, like he's already been stamped and selected.

Either that or you're reading way too much into a chance encounter with a random ultra-hot guy. Seriously.

He's a different kind of man than the ones I'm used to. I've grown up with academic types. Preppies and scholars, who've spent their lives in quiet libraries and cavernous university lecture halls. This guy has just as much intelligence beaming out of his blue eyes than all those so-called intellectuals, or much more. Kade's is an intelligence that's freakishly perceptive and laser focused. On me. I don't know if anyone has *ever* looked at me with the kind of intensity he's giving me. Like he's...starstruck, almost. Like he genuinely cares about the things I'm telling him.

Only a few days ago, I admitted to myself that I wanted to know what it felt like. I remember thinking it: *I'll even settle for a lusty, horny AF one night stand, just to experience that I-don't-care-about-anything-but-this-moment craving for once in my life.*

Here it is.

A big, roughed-up alpha musician with magical charisma beaming out of his eyes, feverish lust radiating off his rock-hard warmth and, even worse, a genuine carefulness that feels more protective and sheltering than...well, than anything ever has.

I'm going to take him up on his offer. I'm going to go home with him and stay in his apartment with the balcony attached to his own. And if he offers to enlighten me—because there's absolutely no doubt in my mind he could do exactly that on at least a dozen levels—I'm going to go with it.

Are you crazy? You just met him! What if he's a psycho killer?

I don't care.

Okay, I *care*, but I don't think he *is* a psycho killer. Psycho killers can't possibly have the effect he's having on me right now. The very first time I looked into his eyes, I felt it. My panties went *wet*, for god's sakes. That's never happened to me before. Not even when it was supposed to.

And his effect is only getting stronger, and deeper. My body wants to lean in, like all the little strands of my DNA are tuning in to the raw male magnetism he's emitting. His biologically A-list pheromones are roughly equivalent to crack for my romantic soul. I can smell his scent, of rain and smoke and animal heat. His nearness is feeding me a sweet warmth that's igniting little sparks along my bloodstream, gathering in my nipples, which feel insanely sensitive. Damp heat pools between my legs, where I can feel a warm, blooming pulse taking hold.

Wow.

"Why did you break up with your girlfriend?" I ask him. It's too personal, maybe. "I mean, don't tell me if you don't want to." *But he licked my tear. It's inside him now. We're already connected.*

"I'll tell you anything you want to know, darlin'." The southern-sounding endearment has a crazy effect on me. Fresh heat coats my pussy.

Holy hell.

I almost feel like...*I'm close.* Like if he touched me where that soft pulse has taken hold, I might finally be able to *get there.*

So this is what white-hot lust feels like. Right here.

There's a beautiful honesty somewhere behind his

unflinching, manly staunchness. "I wasn't in love with her. In fact I didn't even like her anymore so I figured it was the right thing to do."

I take a bite of a French fry. "Had you been together for very long?"

"It was around five or six months. It felt like longer."

"So, you fell out of love with her?"

"I never loved her to begin with."

"Really?"

"No."

"At all?"

"Not at all."

I ask it carefully, because I really want to know. "Why did you go out with her if you knew you didn't love her?"

"Because I hoped I would fall in love with her. I wanted to fall in love."

"You did?"

"Yeah. I always do, but it never happens."

"It doesn't?"

Kade smiles at my curiosity. "No. It doesn't."

"Not ever?" I want to know more about the guy I'm going to have a wild one night stand with.

What the hell, Stella? You've known him for an hour. There's no way you'd be that reckless.

Wrong. Because when the universe delivers *this* much hotness into your evening, sometimes you just have to go with it. I've run away to a city I've never been to *just* so I can have a new experience that will rock my world. This beautiful stranger feels like he's been put here just for me, to do exactly that.

Behind his eyes there's a depth and a compassion I think I might already be a little bit in love with. He's a hero, you can just tell: that rare phenomenon where sexual prowess and a moral compass converge in perfect symbiosis. Not to mention the six-foot-something, beefed-up male beauty on steroids. And he's a bass player, no less. It would be a crime *not* to have sex with this guy. I feel practically obligated at this point at least to try. He might as well have stepped straight out of the pages of my most wishful Kindle fantasies.

"No," he confirms. "I've never been in love. Not once."

I absent-mindedly bite my bottom lip as I watch his face. He brushes his thumb against my mouth, disengaging my lip from the soft hold of my teeth, as though he's protecting it. His gaze seems almost mesmerized, like he's thinking about kissing me.

Do it, the new wanton and crazed wild side in me is urging.

"How about you, little unicorn girl. Have you ever been in love?"

Unicorn girl. "No. I've tried. But it didn't take."

"I guess we have something in common, then."

Maybe it's the champagne, which he's now topping up, because I hear myself confessing something I've never actually confessed to anyone. "I've never even been in lust, if you can believe that." *Until right now.*

His blond-edged eyebrows lift. "No?" It's a strange thing to consider but I love the colors of him. The rosewood hue of his suntanned skin and the lightly bleached ends of his hair, like he's absorbed sunlight, even in the darkness of this room.

"One day I'd like to find out what all the fuss is about." Oops. I probably shouldn't go there, but the comment is open enough to interpretation.

Hot, dreamy Kade is contemplating me, his eyes narrowing. Getting my drift. "Which fuss, exactly, are we talking about?"

I feel myself blush. "Nothing."

His smile deepens as he reads my thoughts. "Never?"

My cheeks blaze.

He laughs softly and...okay, to hell with it. His laughter is the sexiest thing that has ever happened to me. Ever. "Interesting," he comments lazily.

"What's interesting?"

He's still smiling, sort of smugly. "I'm going to go out on a limb here, but I think what you're telling me is that either you've never had an orgasm or you've never had sex. Or both."

God. He hardly needs to spell out my inadequacies in black and white like that. I'm about to protest. To brush it off and deny it. But something stops me. His interest. His ability to decipher my off-hand comment with such perceptive accuracy. "I just...no, I mean, I...I've never...neither." *Damn it. What the hell, Stella?* This is so awkward. I'm about to die of embarrassment.

"Really?" he asks, like something about my dismal love life is wildly fascinating to him.

"No." I twirl an end strand of my hair, wishing I could take back my confession.

"No wonder you didn't want to marry the guy."

"Yeah," I whisper, feeling sort of sad because it *is* sad, to be so in the dark when what you actually want is to bask in full sunlight.

He contemplates my face with such careful interest, I find myself gazing into his blue eyes like he's the answer to all my hopes and dreams. This man is *crazily* magnetic. "It's actually incredibly easy to do," he says, a glint of mischief simmering behind his smug allure.

I try to hold my question, but I'm wildly curious. "What do you...mean?"

Kade sits back, cocky as hell, knees apart. There's something so outrageously *male* about the way he moves, like a big jungle cat on the prowl, my lust sort of ramps up another notch. I want to jump his bones, is what it boils down to. New territory for me but I'm feeling it *hard*.

He says it slowly, his voice low and deep, "I could show you some of what all the fuss is about right here and now, darlin', if you want me to."

I stare at him for a few seconds. "What...?"

His beautiful mouth quirks. "Up to you."

I shouldn't even ask, but *come on*. I can't really leave this one up in the air. I whisper it, not that anyone could hear us above the music and up here in our little secluded candlelit cove. "Here?" Are we talking about the same thing?

"If you're curious. Your call, either way."

"But..." I glance around, but no one can see us. "...how?"

He takes my hand, weaving his warm, strong fingers through mine. "Just put my hand where you want it and I'll do the rest." The look in his eyes is hot and playful and...there it is. Not just a spark but a bonfire. The one I was starting to doubt is an actual thing. It's shining out of this almost-stranger's hypnotic intensity.

And he's doing it again, making me wet with the dark glint in his jewel-blue eyes.

His hand, which is holding mine, moves to rest on my thigh. Its warmth leeches into my body to center on that secret, wet, pulsing place and the tiny nub that's become so hyper-sensitive I *know* it's going to happen. His promise is fueling my fire, his touch stoking it. "You sure you're ready for this?" He's teasing me. He's hardly going to deliver on a promise like that *here*, in a public place, fully clothed, to someone like me. Clueless and totally inexperienced, that is.

Of course I should refuse—if that's even what's going on here. But I can't. Because I *am* ready. I'm so freaking ready I'll do anything he asks.

"What's your last name?" I ask him. If he's about to do what I think he might be about to do, I need to know.

"Tucker. Kade Tucker." Why does that sound so familiar? "What about you, unicorn girl?"

"Why do you call me that?"

"Because I think you might be magic."

This makes me smile. It's a good line. "My name is Stella Juliet Bell."

"Stella Juliet Bell. It's a beautiful name. It definitely has a ring to it."

I give him an ironic look, despite the fact that my body feels like it's made of molten heat. "Like I haven't heard that one before."

He laughs at his own joke. I *love* his laughter and the way his blue eyes get those yummy little crinkles at the edges when he smiles. "Very nice to meet you, Stella Juliet Bell. Where are you from?"

"New Jersey. I was born in upstate New York but my family moved to Princeton eight years ago."

"Princeton," he comments.

"I'm a student there. My dad's a professor."

He's still grinning at me. "What are you studying?"

"English. What about you? Are you from Nashville?"

"Born and bred."

"Have you lived here your whole life?"

"Yes, but I travel a lot. I spend time in Austin. And New Orleans. They both like to think their music scenes are better than ours, but they're wrong. And occasionally New York, mainly for the jazz."

"My dad listens to a lot of jazz."

"Yeah?"

"Yeah. It's his favorite kind of music. I never quite get it."

"It's all about spontaneity, vision, improvisation. Inventing meaning while letting loose. They call it musician's music."

"Maybe you can teach me." Not that I'm implying that what's going on here will last more than an hour, or a day, or a night. I just...if anyone can teach me things, I have a feeling he's the one.

His voice and his scent are ridiculously appealing. His effect is galvanizing. I want to breathe him in. I have this stunningly intense craving *to take him inside*. My body leans in without me meaning to and he smiles. "You ready?" he murmurs. "You want it now?"

"I..." What to say? *Yes. Yes. I'm ready.*

"Give me your mouth, baby."

Baby. Darlin'. Unicorn girl. Why does it already feel like I belong to him?

He leans closer and my lips part because I can hardly breathe. Without a doubt, I have never had a more intense experience than the one I'm having right now. The anticipation becomes everything about me. The heat of his promise infuses me with a feverish need that engulfs every reservation, every doubt, every inhibition I've ever had. I want him. More than that, I *need* him.

Very gently, one of his hands slides around the nape of my neck as the other releases the weave of my fingers. He eases my knees wider. His hand slides further up my thigh. He's big and ridiculously strong and this sends a thrill of quivering excitement to the slippery depths of my body. I can feel that my panties are saturated.

Holy hell.

His scratchy jaw brushes against my cheek. Then his lips settle over mine and exert a gentle pressure, opening me with the warm wetness of his tongue. With his other hand, his fingers glide over the seam of my leggings—*there*—sliding back and forth with extreme gentleness and absolute insistence.

Pings of electricity are blooming inside me. His tongue is warm and velvety, sliding deeper. Long, slow drags of his tongue against mine. He opens my mouth with his, hungry for more. I take him willingly, lust-drugged. *God, he tastes good.* Like mint and whiskey, like dreams and magic. His fingers press and swirl with expert precision, finding the exact rhythm to tease the heat in one forward direction.

Oh my God, it's happening.

His tongue pushes into my mouth as the curl of plea-sure he's working with his fingers reaches an almost unbearably high peak, then breaks into tight, shattering waves of pure, vivid ecstasy. He catches the moan that escapes me, whispering between kisses. "Gorgeous Stella. That's my girl. You're so damn sweet."

Kade works my pleasure unhurriedly, his mouth and his hands playing me like a goddamn virtuoso plays his instrument.

I'm drunk on him. I think I might be in love with him. My body is still spasming, the ripples long and lush. As the rapture slowly starts to calm, I let my fingers wander across the rough surface of his jaw. He kisses me with a tender need that feels almost like adoration, for a long time, like he's as drugged as I am.

"Kade," I say softly.

"Yeah?" His voice is deep and rasped.

"That was..." I can't even speak. I'm still riding the intense, lingering rushes.

"...a small taste of what all the fuss is about. It gets a lot better."

"It does?" I manage to gasp.

"Of course it does. We still have our clothes on."

Okay, wow, that's true. But with the ripples of my very first orgasm still surging through my body, I can't imagine that anything could feel better than what just happened to me.

Kade does that thing again where he reads my mind. "Trust me, it can," he says.

The band is coming back on stage, I notice, after taking a short break. The lead singer tunes his guitar.

Kade pulls his phone out of his back pocket. "It's

really filling up in here. I'm going to call my driver and make sure he's out back, ready to pick us up once I'm done."

His driver? Maybe he means an Uber. And I guess that means it's settled. I'm going home with him.

He powers his phone on and after the little apple glows on the screen for a few seconds, a barrage of message bubbles pop up. Carmen. Carmen. Carmen. Carmen. Carmen. "Fuck," Kade seethes.

"Is that...her?"

"Yeah."

I'm still reeling with sensation. My brain isn't fully functioning. And I sort of wish *she* wasn't crashing onto the scene when I'm still in the middle of this extreme endorphin rush. It's hard to get my bearings. "Is she upset about the break-up?"

"You could say that." He suddenly seems tense. His laid-back vibe feels twisted up.

"Kade?"

When he looks into my eyes, I see it then: the tension fades out by a degree. His expression softens and...he really is the most physically beautiful person I've ever met. It's hard to get used to how outrageously *hot* he is.

"Are you sure you want me to stay in your spare apartment? Because if you have things you need to talk about with her—"

"There's nothing I need to talk about with her. Our pathetic excuse for a relationship is over. Done. I made that very clear. I don't need to see her again or talk to her about it ever again."

"All right." *Yikes.* He's in a mood. Over her. "Are you sad that it ended?"

"Honey, I'm sad it ever started in the first place. Being with her was the worst decision I've made in a long time. My family tried to warn me but I didn't listen. I wish I had. I should have."

"You can't always know. There's nothing wrong with trying. There must have been something about her you liked in the beginning." I don't know why I'm even talking about this. I guess...I want to know how he feels. Especially if I'm going home with him, which I'm now wondering if I should. I don't want him to spend the night pining for her or wishing I was someone else.

"I wanted her to be something she wasn't. I wanted her to be the love of my life. But she was a million miles from that. I'm a fool. For hoping my feelings would change."

"I was always hoping for the same thing."

Kade stares into my eyes. "Yeah?"

"It's okay if you need some time to get over her. I mean, you only just—"

"Darlin', forget about her. The person I want to talk to tonight is you. We're going to forget about everything that came before we ran into each other on the street in the rain. I'm going to go down to that stage and play a couple of songs, then I'm going to take you home and we're going to talk about the reason you came to Nashville. Even if it hurts. Because sometimes when you talk about things with a person who's a good listener and who cares, the things that used to hurt don't hurt quite so much anymore. Okay?"

I'm starting to realize I don't have it in me to refuse Kade Tucker a damn thing, especially when he puts it like that. "Okay."

9

Stella

I'm still feeling slightly dazed after the monumental...*thing* that just happened to me when I hear the lead singer of the band down below say, "Hey, Magic Man, we know you're out there. Come on up and help us out. We want to wrap our sound around some of your sweet riffs."

"Stella," Kade says. "The very last thing I want to do right now is leave you. But I told them I'd join in for a couple songs. It won't take that long."

The crowd is chanting and the place is jam-packed by this point, I notice now. I listen to what they're chanting. *Magic Man. Magic Man. Magic Man.*

"Are *you* Magic Man?" I ask him.

He shrugs. "It's a nickname that's stuck for some reason."

Magic Man. They're not kidding.

"No one will bother you," he says. "I'll make sure of it."

He seems stressed about that point and I'm not sure why he would be. "It's fine. I'll wait right here."

Kade looks torn, but he stands—and I'm reminded again of how tall he is, and how big. *How ridiculously built.* His body is hard and sculpted, and his jean shirt strains at the seams. He leaves me, making his way down the small staircase and past the three bouncers that are standing there. The crowd is basically going insane, cheering and pounding on tables.

It seems clear that they're all here for *him.*

Kade Tucker.

The name does sound familiar. I feel like I've heard of him, and this must be why.

My phone lights up with another message. *Theo.* I'm actually surprised he's being so persistent. When we were dating, he spent most of his time distracted and immersed in the existential angst of Dostoyevsky or whatever.

> Just wanted to make sure you're okay.
> And to see if you've changed your mind.
> Call me.

No, Theo, I haven't changed my mind.

Especially after the cataclysmic shift my life has just taken.

I just had my very first orgasm.

In a bar.

This feels like a huge deal, after all those times I've wondered if there was something wrong with me or if I was doomed to live out my life in the zone of the incapable-of-getting-turned-on and only-woman-in-the-world-who's-never-*been*-there.

I've imagined what it might be like, of course I have. Practically on an hourly basis.

What Kade just did to me was...not even in the same ballpark. It was far, far more intense, by a magnitude of around a trillion.

His promise that things only get better without clothes on is both daunting and...*something I need to find out about.*

I want to have sex with Kade Tucker.

I'm going to cash in my V card with the Magic Man.

Tonight. If he lets me.

No one tells you a single orgasm changes everything. Not just your body but your entire outlook. I feel insanely *happy*. I'm not sure why I would. I just broke up with my boyfriend, I've gone AWOL from my life, I'm in a strange city on a rainy night and chances are I'm about to go home with and possibly finally lose my virginity to a guy I met on the street an hour ago.

And I can't ever remember feeling as happy as I do right now.

Maybe it's the endorphin rush. All that serotonin pumping its magic formula through my veins, changing the alchemy of my body and soul. Weirdly, the feeling reminds me of a book I read once (okay, more than once) where the people change into vampires and when they do, their blood forges into a different substance altogether.

That's how I feel right now.

But instead of changing into a vampire, I'm changing into...*an addict*. I feel wildly needy for more of the things Kade Tucker can freaking *do*.

Would you listen to yourself, Stella? You're going crazy.

Yes.

My blood feels hot.

It wasn't enough. I want more. Not just eventually or occasionally. *Now.* I want to act on all my basest urges and make up for lost time. I feel my heartbeat where my inner muscles still pulse and in the tips of my breasts.

The band plays a chord. Then Kade starts up with a solo on his bass guitar that...okay, I'm really starting to wonder if Nashville is actually a portal into another space-time continuum. One where super-hot alphas hand out orgasms on request and play country-rock music that's not just the most talented-sounding thing I've ever heard, but downright panty-melting.

Holy shit, he's good.

Girls are squealing and crying, standing as close to the stage as security will allow, yelling to him. They love him. They want to marry him and have his babies.

A low flash of heat thuds through my chest. It takes

me a second to identify it but, God, I think it might be...jealousy?

He's mine, is what I'm thinking. Which is sort of ludicrous.

But I can't help myself. He's going to take *me* back to the spare apartment that shares a balcony with his apartment. *I'm* the one who's going to tell him why I came to Nashville because sometimes when you talk about things with a person who's good listener and who cares, the things that used to hurt don't hurt quite so much anymore.

I found him on the street in the pouring rain.

And *I'm* the one who's going to find out if orgasms without clothes on are even better than the one that's still pumping its dopamine rush through my hyper-aware and practically-in-love-with-him system.

I listen to him play and I'm more awed by him with each dizzyingly agile note he plucks. He's clearly a genius at this. The song finishes and the crowd goes wild for half a minute before the lead singer of the band asks Kade to sing one of his new songs, which Kade has to be talked into as the crowd cheers him on. I watch and listen in spellbound fascination. He looks like a slightly roughed-up Greek god dressed in double denim. His voice is husky and layered and so damn beautiful my eyes sting because there's something deeply emotional about it all. His music isn't just loaded with his own flair, it's *touching*. And heart-felt. It hits you right where you live.

It's hitting his audience where *they* live too, because the wall of fangirling women is starting to overwhelm the row of beefy security men, they're *that* rabid.

Shit. This looks dangerous. The fans are going to rush the stage. The bouncers are struggling to hold them back.

Kade sees it happening. And just as they breach the line, Kade has already slung his guitar over his head. He drops it and jumps off the side of the stage, pushing his way through the crowd to get to the guarded staircase that leads to our private table. They're clawing at him but he's bigger and strong enough to push past them. He disappears for a few seconds, then he's suddenly here.

He grabs my hand and my bag, along with his hat and our coats, and pulls me toward a narrow hallway that's behind our little alcove. "Time to go, darlin'."

The crowd is screaming from below and there's a thundering noise as they start pushing past the guards and swarming up the stairs.

Holy fuck.

Kade pulls me along with him, rushing down a back staircase and out a door, where an expensive-looking but nondescript car with tinted windows is waiting for him in the back alley. Kade opens the door and carefully pushes me inside, sliding in next to me as he slams the door. The driver peels out, like he knows the drill and does this all the time. I look behind us through the back window and I can see the crowd spilling out of the bar's back door.

"Wow," I gasp.

"You all right, honey?" Kade asks me, drawing his thumb gently against my bottom lip. Like he did before. Like this is something he does now. It's calloused and slightly rough and reminds me of what he can do with his hands. *All* the things he can do with those hands. *Magic Man.*

I still can't believe what just happened. "That was so crazy."

"I was hoping things might be a little more low-key tonight but no such luck."

I suddenly need more information. "Who *are* you? What's the name of your band?" And what do they do if they *catch* him when they rush him like that? It's terrifying to even think about.

"The Tucker Brothers Band," he says. "Have you heard of us?"

"The *Tucker* Brothers Band? Of course I've heard of you." They're one of the few country bands who cross over into mainstream rock 'n roll and get played on all the major radio stations. "Kade *Tucker*?" Everything finally clicks. I don't know why I didn't make that connection before, except maybe because my mind was focused on other things and I wasn't expecting this. He's a superstar. They're one of the biggest bands in the world right now. They're played on the major rock and pop stations even though their music skews country because their songs are catchy and popular. They're a phenomenon that transcends genre and I remember reading somewhere that their music "appeals to everyone with a heartbeat." The line was memorable.

Before I can fully process that my alpha dreamboat savior is one of the hottest rock stars on the planet, the car slows to a stop near a building with a large arched doorway and a steel high-tech-looking door.

Kade opens the car door. "This is us." Still holding my hand, he helps me out of the car. He swipes a key card against the lock of the steel door, which clicks open. It's like some kind of fortress, but I guess I can understand now why he needs that.

We go inside and the door closes with a heavy thud, followed by a series of clicking sounds as the complicated security system bolts us in.

The foyer area is made of gold and black marble and has two elevators, on opposite sides. He pushes the button for the one on the left and the doors slide open.

I follow him into the elevator. Time seems slow-moving and heavy with dizzying, star-dusted anticipation. We're alone, sealed into our own little bubble, and his nearness is making me feel reckless. He's so much bigger than I am, looming and gorgeous, radiating his raw, heady masculinity. "You sure you're all right, honey?"

"I'm fine. Are *you* all right? They were grabbing you."

"Couldn't catch me, though." Grinning, like it was no big deal.

"Does that happen to you a lot?"

"We don't usually let them get that close. I didn't

know it was going to be so packed out tonight. I thought maybe because it was just me, things might be calmer."

"They all wanted a piece of you," I whisper, because it's crazy, that I'm *here*, in Nashville with him, one of the most famous people in music that half of humanity wishes was theirs.

He leans closer. Angling his head just slightly, his mouth is close to mine and I can smell his scent again, of cool rain and Nashville dreams. His eyes are the color of the tropical ocean on a sunny day. "I don't really care about *them* wanting a piece of me," he says, his voice low and sexier than anything has ever been. "What I *do* care about is if Stella Bell wants a piece of me."

Before I can attempt to breathe or answer him, the elevator doors slide open.

Still holding my hand, he smiles and leads me into...*whoa*. The place is unbelievable. It's huge and open-plan, with gigantic windows running the length of the to-die-for apartment. The city below twinkles colorfully, glowing with the oily tones of the rainy night, which are reflected in the wide, smooth expanse of the river in the distance.

The kitchen runs the length of the right side of the room. It has marble countertops, state-of-the-art appliances and an enormous island. There's a bar further along with glass pendant lights running the length of it and cow-hide bar stools. A long dining room table next to the window could seat an army. Beyond that, there's a lounge area with a huge square U-shaped leather couch. A TV hangs against an exposed brick wall that's the size of a movie screen. Outside the wall of cedar folding doors at the far end is a patio with swanky outdoor furniture, strings of decorative light bulbs, a spot-lit hot tub and a pool.

"Wow," I hear myself gasp. "Is this your sister's apartment?"

"No, this one's mine."

Along the wall by nearer end of the dining room table, there are six framed silver vinyl records and a built-in shelf with eight statues of golden horns. I walk closer to get a better look at one of the framed records. *The Tucker Brothers Band.* "Are these...platinum?"

"Our second and third albums went double platinum and the fourth is close to matching that."

"What are these statues?"

"Those are Grammys."

I stare up at him but he just blinks and does that thing again where he mesmerizes me with the color of his eyes and the sweep of those eyelashes that are blond-tipped and longer than any man's have a right to be.

Kade's thumb slides along my jaw. "I'm just going to tell it like it is, little unicorn girl. I'll take you to the other apartment if you want me to—it's just on the other side of the balcony out there. But what I really want to do is to pick up where we left off before things got out of control tonight. I want to peel off those damp clothes and taste every inch of that soft, perfect skin. I want to show you—really show you—what all the fuss is about. Both of those things you were wondering about. All of it. I want to enlighten the hell out of you all night long and all day tomorrow and maybe even the day after that until you're addicted to all the things I can do. I want to make you feel so damn good you might even fall in love with me. But I'm not going to rush you."

Is this real?

Like hell he's rushing me. I've waited my whole life for this moment and I don't want to wait a single second longer. He's *better* than any Kindle fantasy. Even my very favorite writers haven't been able to conjure up a man who looks, talks, swaggers, sings or plays the goddamn bass guitar like Kade Tucker can. *Or* who gives little swoony speeches that are the most romantic thing you've ever heard. Slowly—because I don't want to jar myself out of what I'm still convinced might be a beautiful dream—I stand on my toes to touch my lips to his. I gasp lightly because he's overwhelming me, already, with his man-scent and the promise of all the brutal strength contained in those big, flexing muscles. "I don't want to go to the other apartment. I want to stay here with you."

It's all the invitation he needs.

Kade's hand slides around the nape of my neck and squeezes gently in a way that communicates his power over me. Under his protective kindness lurks a dark, dominant possessiveness. As his mouth eases over mine, there's an edge to him. A hot, dirty volatility that I can *taste* as his tongue slides over mine in a silky, intimate plunge. A wave of soft, sexy warmth floods my entire body.

I've kissed other men before. Trying to feel something. It always felt sort of messy and overly-intimate and not particularly appealing. At the time I thought it was just me, doing things wrong like I always do.

This kiss is something else altogether. Kade doesn't just kiss. He feasts on my mouth like he's already inside me. There's a deep, darkly-playful *enthusiasm* to his kiss, like he's thinking the filthiest thoughts imaginable while his heart breaks with need.

Each thrust of his tongue pushes a new wave of lust through my body and I suck lightly on his tongue, trying to draw the drugging taste of him deeper. He makes a low, rasping groan like an animal growl and my inner muscles clench on a needy emptiness. I've never been so *turned on* in my life. My own hunger feeds on his until we're both in a quiet frenzy of hot need.

He's so gorgeous and so damn *good* at this, all I want to do is get closer.

And I don't question it.

For maybe the first time in my life, I'm not second-guessing. I'm just *feeling*. Because everything about him feels so good.

Kade lifts me easily, and it sends a thrill of anxious

excitement through me. *He's so damn strong.* "Time for phase one of the enlightenment process," he says.

I don't care that I only just met him. I want him. He's *mine.* I wrap my arms and legs around him and kiss him again. He's huge and warm and—*oh God.* I can feel the immense, rock-hard ridge of his arousal against me as he holds me. *Jesus, he's big.* "I want to see if you were telling the truth."

"About what?"

"If it gets even better."

"Oh, I was telling the truth, honey pie. But it's best if you judge for yourself." Kade carries me down a hallway that I vaguely notice is lined with framed pictures of him and his band, awards they've won and posters of their concert tours.

His room is palatial, with a wooden ceiling, a king-sized bed and a few sparse pieces of chunky furniture. The place hardly looks lived in.

He lays me onto his bed, crouching over me, holding his weight with his muscular arms so his long body is almost touching me.

Lying here in this darkened room with him, I'm still aware of my own...inexperience. "I don't know how to do anything," I tell him. "I mean, I've read a lot of books, but I've never actually done...well, anything. Just so you know."

Kade laughs softly. His eyes are watching mine and they're careful and so vividly blue. "You're already better than anyone I've ever met. And we haven't even gotten started."

He's hot and rugged. He's also *sweet.* "I'm not usually in the habit of going home with people I've just met."

"Me either," he says. "And I've already decided that I'm going to be completely straight up with you. I haven't always been honest with everyone I've known and it makes things more complicated than they need to be. So I'm going to lay it all on the line with you. I think you're someone I've been looking for. That means you're getting everything."

Everything? What does that mean? Fascinated by the burly strength of his body, I touch my hands to his flexed biceps.

The old me wouldn't have dared. The new me has a mind of her own. "Bring it on, Magic Man," I whisper.

The fire in his eyes flares and I'm aware of a sense of my own power. He's craving this as much as I am. Heat pours from his body in waves, I can feel it in the blazing space between us.

He lowers himself, pressing the full weight of his body against mine. The hardness of him is astounding. The rigid, colossal swell of his *gigantic* erection presses against me, demanding my body soften and cradle him. He grinds against my hyper-sensitive nub, slippery from his effect and the orgasm he already gave me. The pleasure is surreal, blooming in a furtive swell where his big cock, through the layers of our clothing, presses with measured forcefulness. "I'm going to start by peeling off your clothes because I want to see you and taste every inch of your sweet perfection. I'll take it as slow as you need, darlin'. You tell me if I'm going too fast or if it's too much or if you're scared. Okay?"

"Okay."

Kade takes my mouth in a lewd, brain-demolishing kiss. Then he stares into my eyes. "We're taking this fast," he says, "and there's no reason to slow it down when we want it this much and it feels this fucking good. But I want you to know that you're safe with me. I'm going to make sure I don't hurt you by getting you nice and ready for me. I'm big and rough and you're going to take all of me, because I'll make you feel better than anything ever has. Are you ready for me, darlin'?"

Wow.

He's cocky as hell. And he has at least one gigantic reason to be. "Yes." I gasp. It might be the truest word I've ever spoken.

"Good girl." Kade's hands peel off the top layers I'm wearing with ease.

He unclasps my bra and pulls it off.

Kade stares down at me with a quiet, hungry awe. "Gorgeous little Stella," he murmurs. He takes my breasts in his warm, rough hands, rubbing his thumbs over my nipples. The flick of his calloused fingertips sends darts of zinging sensation from my nipples to the low pit of my stomach. And lower. The strikes of his hot breath against my skin make the taut buds tighten. He sucks my nipple into his mouth and I moan, nearly weeping with pleasure. His teeth scrape and his tongue laves against the underside of the sensitive peak and I'm almost *there*. The wave is cresting and it's crazily intense. It's going to change my life.

The pulls of his mouth are greedy and sublime. He releases my nipple, moving to the other one, which he kisses and suckles. "You want it bad, don't you, sweet Stella?" His voice is growly and deep. "I'm going to give you everything you need, I already promised you that. By the end of the night, you'll hardly recognize yourself. Tonight you're mine."

Oh, God.

He peels my leggings down, his thumbs catching the lace of my panties, yanking them off, until I'm completely naked. He's still fully clothed and it feels unbalanced. *And hot as hell.* I'm totally at his mercy, vulnerable and exposed. Slick and lightly swollen, pulsing with my need for him.

"Jesus Christ. You're too damn beautiful for words."

Piper talked me into getting completely waxed not too long ago. Some of the guys on the hockey team were saying their girlfriends had done it, and Dillon mentioned it to Piper so she'd wanted to surprise him. She dragged me along for moral support and convinced me to get it done at the same time.

So here I am, bare and pink and more wet and turned

on than I've ever been in my life. His fingers trace over my slippery, delicate folds, exploring me, opening me, dipping barely inside. He glides his fingers over the lips of my pussy, squeezing them between his straightened fingers as his other thumb skates over my clit. I gasp for breath, because I'm going to come if he keeps doing that. I need more of him like I need air. Kade knows this. He's doing it on purpose. He can tell that I'm on the high precipice of a profound, earth-shattering climax. But he's not going to let me get there, not yet. Watching my eyes, he holds his hand up. His fingers are gleaming with my juices. *God.* He raises them to his mouth and sucks the moisture, licking his fingers with a reverent but feral glow in his blue-on-blue eyes. "I knew it. My unicorn girl is made of nectar."

He pushes my thighs wider and I let them fall open. I *want* him to see me. I want to offer myself to him.

Kade's eyes darken, reading this. His head lowers, his warm hands bracing my thighs, aggressively pushing them further apart.

And then I feel his *mouth*. Long, slow, delicious licks that delve and taste me. Eating into me. "*Oh, fuck*," he groans, "I've found nirvana."

He nuzzles and feasts like he's *starved.*

He's dirty as hell. His mouth sucks and licks messily. His tongue and his fingers dip and explore, *everywhere,* plunging and tasting. The stubble of his beard is rough and his tongue is velvet-soft and the combination makes me whimper because a gigantic bloom of pleasure is rising inside me. I grab fistfuls of his hair. I need an anchor. I need to keep him there.

"You taste so fucking good, baby girl," he growls.

His tongue begins to circle my clit, teasing. He licks, flicking with his tongue as he slides two curled fingers inside me, silkily rubbing some insanely sensitive spot as his mouth latches and sucks hard, tipping me over into a tidal wave of pleasure.

I come so hard I see stars. My body quivers and writhes as I moan his name. My pussy clenches tightly, over and over, milking his fingers in rhythmic pulls.

Kade's mouth gentles but he doesn't disengage. He just keeps on licking and sucking, spinning my orgasm out further, sending jolts of electric bliss from my clit to my belly, all the way to my fingers and toes.

When the ripples begin to calm, he licks my pussy gently, like he can't get enough. "You're the sweetest goddamn thing I ever tasted," he murmurs, kissing his way up my stomach, sucking on one nipple, then the other, giving my orgasm another little hit with the clever swirls of his tongue.

"Kade?" I feel lust-drugged. "Come here."

He climbs up and holds himself over me, kissing my lips. I can taste *myself* and it's the most intimate thing. "You're going to have to get used to me doing that twenty-four-seven, honey pie, because I just found my happy place."

I don't know if it's a rare thing for a man to clearly *love* doing what Kade Tucker so thoroughly just did to me. I think it might be. And it's the kind of detail that makes me want to wrap myself around him and keep him. To stay in his bed and live with him every day and night just so he can do that again whenever he wants to. It's the kind of thing a girl could get addicted to very, very easily.

My fingers touch the button of his shirt. "Take this off."

He straddles me, holding his weight, and pulls his shirt over his head, tossing it aside. *Whoa.* He's buff as hell, his chest and shoulders hard and sculpted. His skin is darkly tanned and warm-looking. There's a dusting of hair on his chest.

I let my fingers explore the remarkable textures of him. The toned, brutal hardness. I've never been so fascinated by anything as I am by Kade Tucker's big, bronzed, ripped body.

My fingers rove over the defined, quilted muscles of his abs.

To the dark arrow line of hair that leads tantalizingly under the low-slung waistline of his worn jeans.

His eyes are watching mine almost challengingly. *Do it.*

To the cool metal of his belt buckle.

My fingers delicately glide over the insanely huge ridge inside his jeans. *My God.* It's daunting. *Will it hurt?*

"I won't hurt you," he says, and I wonder how he's able to read my mind like that. I explore the outline of his hot, swollen shaft through the layer of his clothing. I feel him surge, and grow even bigger. Hotter. Harder. "You ready for me to worship you and take you higher than you've ever been, darlin'?"

Oh my God. "*Yes,*" I whisper.

He unbuckles and unzips his jeans, freeing his—*holy freaking hell!*—engorged, *gigantic* cock. I mean, the thing is...massive. A giggle escapes me. Seriously, it's like a goddamn work of art. Dusky and silky, with ridged veins along its thick length. The smooth, rounded head is broad and hot-looking, leaking a slick of milky moisture. I've never been up close and personal with anything like this and it's powerful. It's a strange thing to think about, but his cock is not only impressive as hell...it's *beautiful.* It's what womankind was put on this earth to crave, and the sight of him does something to me. It lights a fire of need inside me that's shockingly intense. My mouth waters and the wet, pulsing warmth of my core clenches lightly. *I need it.*

Kade notices my wide-eyed awe. "Don't be scared of me, darlin'."

I'm not scared. But I'm wondering how it's going to...*fit.*

"Don't worry, it will."

"Can I...touch it?"

He exhales a low laugh. "You can do any damn thing you want to it, sweetheart."

I touch my fingers to the wetness, smoothing it over

the silky surface of his hot crown. *Wow.* My new obsession. My fingers squeeze gently and another gush of moisture seeps from the slit. Watching his eyes, like he did to me, I bring my fingers to my mouth. And I lick his essence. It's salty and earthy and my new favorite thing.

His eyes are as dark as blue embers. "Right, you're asking for it now, baby." He pushes his jeans lower and kicks them off.

My knees are pushed wider.

He takes his big cock in his hand and rubs the crown against my slippery pussy. *Oh, Jesus.* My inner muscles spasm softly, my body inviting him inside. I'm not coming again—yet—but his big length is like a magic freaking wand. The slow glide of him against me is feeding a wild rush of pleasure into my body.

"*Fuck*, baby," Kade growls. "I want you like this. I want to be inside you with nothing between us. You feel too damn good."

"I'm on the pill," I gasp.

"Yeah?"

"Yeah."

"I've never done it bareback before," he says, groaning another low oath as the head of his slippery cock parts my intimate folds.

I don't know why this surprises me. Or why it surprises me that *I'm* the one this beautiful, world-famous, well-hung AF magic man wants to start with. *Not even with her?* I feel like asking him. But I don't. I understand why. He said he didn't love her, at all, even though he tried to.

And I *do* want him like this. I don't bother analyzing why both of us are willing to get closer to each other after only a few hours than all the people that came before, even with relationships and reality and familiarity thrown into the mix. It doesn't matter. All that matters is *taking him inside.*

I barely arch up to him, causing the head of his cock to open me and press against my clit. *Oh.* I am *this* close to coming already, and all he's done is touch me.

"You want me to fuck you real good, baby?" He presses more strongly against me. We're so hot and wet that the thick head of his cock glides easily into the tight constriction of my body. "*Hell.* You feel like heaven." His words are slurred with husky heat.

He doesn't wait for me to answer him. My *body* is answering him, arching and opening, quivering with anticipation. He pushes deeper, the stretching, slippery friction forcing a pleasure-pain overload that's way too much. He's so big and so thick, as he slides deeper, his cock rubs against my clit while at the same time rubbing against some wildly sensitive trigger inside me. It's happening. It *hurts*, but the pain only takes the pleasure he's feeding me with his body even higher. I'm tight but so wet, the stretching, slippery friction reaches a high peak, then shatters into an excruciating wave of nearly-unendurable pleasure. I'm moaning his name as my inner muscles clench hard and tight around him, over and over, drawing him deeper as he thrusts into each spasm. My body milks his drives lusciously until he's deep, deep inside me.

It's too much.

He's *huge* and I can feel every inch of him, stuffing me hotly as my body draws him deeper. He groans and erupts inside me. The bucking spasms of his release caress *everything.* Hot jets of his cum coax another wave of ecstasy and I come hard—*again,* before I'd even stopped coming the first time. Higher, this time. Harder. *Will I survive this? The rush of pain-provoked pleasure is too damn good.*

The waves are long and lush, gripping him, again and again, as his orgasm pumps his hot seed deep inside me.

We're locked into our quiet frenzy for a long time, until the ripples begin to calm.

We're both breathing hard, gripping each other as our slick, secret bond throbs and spills. He's gazing down at me, smoothing a strand of my hair back from my face. I can feel a trickle of moisture where I'm overflowing with his cum.

I just lost my virginity to a buff, beautiful almost-stranger and I think I might already be in love with him. After years of wondering what it feels like, I've just had three or four of the most intense experiences of my life and I'm still coming. I don't ever want him to pull out. I want to stay right here with him for the rest of time.

He half-grins at me. It's a look that's both hot and sweet and I really can't believe that I've found him, this perfect man who's starting to make me come again just with the *look* of him. "Well, it's official," he murmurs. "Nothing has ever felt as good as you feel, sweet Stella Bell." His voice is low and edged with that awe that we're both feeling. "That right there is the best thing that's ever happened to me."

"You were right." *It is even better without clothes on.*

His smile widens. I love the natural-looking whiteness of his teeth. The crinkles at the edges of his deep-ocean eyes. The blazing masculinity of everything about him. "Told you."

Carefully, he rolls us onto our sides, gripping me so he stays inside me. He pulls my thigh higher with his warm hand and I wrap my leg around him. We lay like that for a while, just staring into each other's eyes. It's outrageously connective. The quiet, calming effect of him and the thickening of his cock as he starts to get hard again are the only things I care about.

He runs the backs of his fingers along my cheekbone. "You're so damn pretty."

I notice then that he has a tattoo of musical notes running down the inside of his tanned lower arm. I run my finger along his skin, tracing the notes. "What song is this?"

"My favorite song. I wrote it for our third album."

"What's it called?"

"It's called Unicorn Girl."

I'm not sure why my chest suddenly feels tight.

With...disappointment, maybe. He must call all his women that. Maybe we're all unicorns to him.

He reads my expression, smoothing the furrow between my eyebrows with his thumb. "Do you want to hear the lyrics?"

"Okay."

"It goes like this." Kade starts to sing and the sound of his voice makes me basically fall cataclysmically in love with him, it happens that fast. Or maybe it already happened, hours ago when I first saw him on the street in the pouring rain. Now, it digs deeper. His voice has that smooth husk to it, deep and layered and perfectly in tune.

> I look for her in the faces of the crowd and
>> in every stranger's smile
> Every country road, every city mile
> I search for her in every golden sunrise
>> and in the purple dusk
> Always hoping she'll turn up
> For now, my unicorn girl is made of
>> dreams
> I fall to my knees
> I beg you, lover, please
> Show up for me

After he finishes the last note, he says, "She hated that song." *She.* Carmen, I guess he means. There's a lot of gravity in his expression. A soulful insinuation. "Because she was never the one and we both knew it."

He was waiting for me. But it's too much to grasp for. Too big a leap to make. It's crazy to think that he and I are somehow star-crossed lovers who have been searching for each other all along and have now finally *found* each other after a random meet-cute on a rainy night.

The craziest thing of all is that it's exactly how this feels.

10

Stella

KADE'S FINGERS twirl absent-mindedly through a lock of my hair. He's still deep inside me, now fully hard again. He's watching my face with a look of absorbed, careful interest. Which is almost as intense as the other major detail rocking my world right now. The one that has to do with the fact that, if he started moving again, I could come very easily. I *will* come, if he grips me, or touches me, or thrusts with the smallest amount of intent. I'm sore but it's a pain that's buffered by a heavy, laden pleasure. His big cock, with it's ridged veins and enormous, silky rigidity feels seriously *good*.

"Tell me about why you came to Nashville," he says. "Who are you looking for?"

You. I was looking for you.

"Besides me." We both laugh a little and—*oh, hell*—just that slight adjustment makes me sigh softly. *I'm so close.*

He has a knack for reading my mind. It turns out the wild infusion of endorphins pumping through my veins isn't just a happiness elixir, it's a truth serum. My soul feels wide open. With his big body wedged thickly inside me and his brawny arms wrapped protectively around me, I feel safe.

"I'm adopted," I tell him. "Which isn't really a big deal. Except that sometimes it feels like a big deal."

He waits a few seconds. Then he lightly kisses my lips. "Keep going."

"My parents were always open with me about it and it was a detail of my life that mostly felt normal, I guess. I've always known about it and there was never a day that they sat me down and sprung it on me. It was just there. It was a part of who I was. Eighteen months after I was born my mother got pregnant with my sister and it was a surprise to them, that they could have a baby after so many years of not being able to. So I'm the only one in my family who's not related by blood."

"I can imagine that would feel sort of heavy sometimes."

Here we are, having this deep and meaningful conversation while he's hard and hot inside me but also sort of comfortingly waiting there, filling me, feeding me warmth and anticipation while he listens to my most closely-held secrets.

He's changing me. With his patience. With his husky, easy voice and his blue eyes with all their complicated

layers of lust and compassion and kindness and enlightenment and hot sex.

I find myself telling Kade Tucker things I've never
told anyone. The gravity behind his expression and the
wild intimacy of this moment makes me want to. "It does
feel heavy. I've never met anyone else who was adopted
and it's not something I talk about with my sister or my
friends because they can't really relate to it. My parents
and I have talked about it over the years. But I never
wanted them to feel like there was anything wrong with
what we have or that anything's missing. They're good
parents, they always have been. So I don't like to bring it
up. But whenever I think about it, it always feels sort of
raw and overly-emotional. It sneaks up on me when I'm
least expecting it. Late at night. Or in random moments.
It'll just hit me out of the blue that I actually don't know
who I am or where I come from. I don't know anything
about the people who made me. I'll probably never know
why they did what they did, but for some reason...they
didn't want me. They gave me away. To total strangers. It
turned out to be great and fine and my family is wonderful. But how could they have *done* that? How could anyone
take their three day old baby and just hand it over?
Without having a clue about what was going to happen to
it? To *me*? I just...I don't know how anyone could do
something like that. And the whole thing has a way of
making me feel like I'm not completely whole, because
something sort of huge is just...missing. I wonder if they

think about me. If they wonder about who I am and where I am and what happened to me. I mean, I think they must. But I'll never know for sure. It's something I think about every single day. Where are they? Who are they? Who am I?"

I realize my eyes are overflowing with tears. One paints a warm line down my cheek. I didn't mean to admit all that and it feels painful but at the same time cathartic, to let it out. Kade's watching me and his eyebrows are furrowed in the middle, like he's deeply affected by my tears.

"Sorry," I say softly. "I always get emotional when I talk about this. That's why I usually just keep it to myself."

"It's good to talk about it." Kade wipes my tear with his thumb. "I can understand why that would feel incredibly hard sometimes. To not know." For some reason, this helps. His dark, masculine-edged empathy is filling a hole in me, where my loneliness lives. When it comes to this topic, there's a lot of it. It's lonely because I've never had anyone to gush to about it. Until now. "Do you think they might be in Nashville?" he asks.

"Yes. I did a search. I contacted the adoption agency. The woman I spoke to sent me a letter just the other day. There wasn't a lot of information on file." I pause because I still haven't fully processed my new discovery. But it's dreamy Kade who's asking. The magic man. And even though I just met him, because of the way he's looking at me right now, I know I can trust him with this piece of myself. He'll be careful with me. He'll enlighten me. He'll help me. He'll take care of me. *He'll make love to me as he's doing all these things.* So I keep talking. "My mother's first name was Madeline. She had green eyes."

"Like you." He seems as intrigued by this information as I was.

"Yes. Even just that one detail felt important when I found out because...well, my parents and my sister all have brown eyes. Practically everyone I've ever met has commented on the color of my eyes."

"Because they're incredibly green," he says.

"Both my birth parents were from Nashville, the letter said, and so were their families. So I knew I needed to come see it for myself, even though I'll probably never find them. There weren't any last names or contact details. Just a few lines about their hobbies and their parents' occupations. They were both young when they had me."

"How young?"

"My mother was seventeen and my father was eighteen."

"And you're twenty-one. So your birth mother would be thirty-eight now. Her name is Madeline, she has green eyes and she lives in Nashville. That's actually a lot of information."

I shrug a little. "I can't really wander the streets

looking for a green-eyed woman who's in her late thirties."

"What were her parents' occupations?"

It already feels like he's...invested. He's also actually...*fucking* me right now and *he's very hard and very deep* and the combination of all of the above is ridiculously intense. "Restaurant owner and administrative assistant."

Kade is quiet for a few seconds. "You know, I caught up with my cousin Gage and his new fiancée Luna over Christmas."

I'm not sure why he's bringing this up now but I wait to hear what he's going to say.

"They were telling me this story about how Luna's friend Josie had a one night stand with a guy one night in Key West where they own a bar and Josie ended up getting pregnant."

"Wow."

"With twin boys."

"Yikes."

"Yeah. They had this one night stand and then went their separate ways. And soon after that Josie found out she was knocked up. And all she knew about the guy was that his first name was Noah and that he was from California."

"Oh no."

"Luna and Josie searched online for weeks to try to find him but there are a lot of people named Noah in

California. It was like searching for a needle in a haystack."

I'm listening intently now, starting to get the gist of why he might be telling me this story. "What did they do?"

"Well, Gage knows this private investigator who's apparently very good at tracking people down. So they gave him all the information they had to see if he might be able to find Noah, so she could at least call him and tell him he was about to become a father."

"Did they find him?"

"The private investigator looked through all the bank statements from the bar Luna and Josie co-owned, because he'd had dinner there and drinks and so on. And the private investigator also checked out the hotel reservations over that weekend of all the hotels in Key West. He was able to narrow the search down to seven people, all from California, all named Noah."

"Really?"

"Somehow he was able to find out their addresses, phone numbers, drivers license photos, everything. He even knew what kind of cars they drove and what type of dogs they owned."

"Wow."

"So he sent all this information to Josie so she could look through this list of these seven guys to see if one of them was her Noah."

I can hardly breathe because by this point I want so

badly for one of them to *be* her Noah. "Was one of them him?"

"Out of the seven on the list he gave Josie, Noah was the sixth one."

"Oh," I whisper.

"It was him and he lives in Big Sur. He's an architect, he drives a Jeep and he has a dog named Whiskey."

My eyes are pooling with tears again because I'm just so happy to hear that she found him. It also gives me a feeling of wide-open hope. If Josie can find her Noah...then maybe I can find...*them*. And I think that's exactly what Kade is getting at. "What did she do? Did she call him?"

Kade pauses again to wipe my tears away. He gets an anguished expression on his face when I cry, like it hurts him. Like my pain is something he needs to deal with personally, and undo. And *damn*, I'm falling so hard and so fast for Kade Tucker, I'm starting to wonder how I'm going to walk away from him. I've known him for a grand total of five hours and I'm having a hard time envisioning my life without him. *He's inside me. He's wiping my tears. He's listening to my story and he's about to figure out how to solve some of the questions that have plagued my entire life.* Everything about him feels like...a match. Like some divine destiny crashed into my life today in the form of the magical Kade Tucker.

I'm not sure what to do with this life-altering revelation right now. First, I need to know how this story ends. "Did she call him?"

"She did. She called him and he answered on the third ring."

"He did?"

"He did. She told him she was expecting twins. And that she didn't expect anything from him but she just wanted him to know that in a few months he was going to be a father."

"What did he say? Please say he didn't hang up on her."

"No. He was happy to hear from her."

"He was?"

"Yes. A little shocked by her news of course, but he was glad she'd searched for him. And he went to see her in Iowa which is where she went because her family was there and she wanted to be at home to have her babies."

"He went there?"

"Yeah. He went to see her."

I'm trying not to cry more but something about this story is important. I want so badly for them to get their happy ending. "What happened?"

"They had a good time together. Luna said they'd hit it off right away when they first met which is why they got carried away in the first place. It was like that again the second time they met. They spent the whole night talking. He felt the babies kicking and he told her he was fully committed to being there for her in whatever way she needed. And at the end of their weekend together, he invited her to California where he has this house he designed in Big Sur, on a cliff overlooking the ocean. With a crazy-ass view."

I'm both crying and laughing now. "This is the best story I've ever heard."

"Right? And then once she got there they fell completely in love with each other. So now they live together in his house and they're going to raise their kids together and live happily ever after."

He laughs with me and my tears are pouring out at this point, with happiness for these people I've never even met.

Kade brushes away my fresh tears and kisses me softly. "Do you want to know why I told you this story?"

"I think I might know why you told me this story."

"Do you want to hear my plan then, darlin'?"

I know what he's going to say and my heart skips a beat at the thought of this. "Yes."

"Tomorrow I'm going to call Gage and get the number of his private investigator. And we're going to see if we can find this Madeline with the green eyes who's probably somewhere right here in Nashville, maybe not too far away from where we are right now. Is that something you'd want to do?"

I'm kissing him as I cry. "Yes. It is something I'd like to do."

"Then that's what we're going to do. I'm going to

help you. And if you want me to come with you once we find them, I will. Because sometimes it's good to have someone with you who cares and who knows the story. It can make it easier." Kade gives a hint of a thrust down below and *oh, holy hell*, I'm about to come. I'm right on the cusp and my inner muscles flutter around him. "But first," he says, his voice low and graveled with intensity, "we have phase two of the enlightenment process that needs some immediate attention. I think that should be our first priority. What do you think, unicorn girl?"

"I think...if you do that again, we're going to be in the *middle* of phase two."

His eyes crinkle at the edges. "Good. Because phase two is even more fun than phase one."

Kade's mouth takes mine as his arms wrap more insistently around me. He grips me with his strong hands as he thrusts again, ensuring complete, total possession. Each powerful thrust forces pleasure deeper and deeper into my body, until it blooms in a tidal flush that rises inexorably, coerced higher and higher by the aggression of Kade's need. He does it again. And again. Then, in a long, gasping moment, the pleasure peaks, erupting through my body in an explosive, all-consuming rush. The cascading spasms are too much. *Too* intense. Nearly unbearable in the sheer height of their ecstasy. My inner muscles clench around his thick bulk, milking strongly at the full length of him until I can feel the violent beat of his own release and the warmth of his seed pulsing in thick, rhythmic jets into my body. He presses his savage groan against my neck.

We lay still, our bodies still clasping intimately, locked in a secret, fluttering dance. Our gazes meet in a soul-touching link.

"My unicorn girl," he whispers. His kisses are slow and lust-drugged.

After a while he moves us, pulling himself from my body with a spilling gush. He adjusts me, moving me out of the wet spot, spooning himself around me, wrapping his iron-strong warmth around my body. A deep comfort overtakes me. I don't overthink it as I say it. I can't. I'm too sleepy and blissed out. "I can't believe I finally found you."

11

Stella

IN MY DREAM, I'm walking along a pathway through a wildflower garden. It's my favorite kind of day, warm and summery. Hazy humidity wrapping itself around me like a comforting arm. I'm wildly comfortable. The horizon is drenched with golden possibilities, infusing me with optimism. There's an unfamiliar lightness in my soul, like all the weight of my life's worries has entirely lifted. There are so many things I want to do.

I will do them. I *can*, I feel so sure of this.

I get to a picturesque pool with crystal clear water. I sit next to it and dip my toes into the water. As soon as my toes touch the surface of this magical pool, I can feel that this pool is alive. It's taking form, kissing my toes in soft, wet licks.

It moves up my legs, kissing and tasting slowly and deliberately. Each touch of the water creature's tongue alights my body with slow, deep heat. It feels *so good*, this touch. Sweet and molten, painting me with its lust.

It's up to my thighs now, parting them, licking the high skin of my inner thighs. My pussy dews and throbs. I can feel that I'm swollen and pink as he gets closer. My clit is his target, I know this. Its prize. The honey of my pleasure is what it wants. It's what he feeds on.

I moan as he forces my legs wider, pushing my knees open so I'm fully on offer. I'll give him everything. He'll take what he wants and I'll give it.

His tongue swirls over my sensitive bud, loving it with his teeth and his mouth, sucking and laving. I moan because I'm in ecstasy. He might kill me with this much pleasure but I don't care. This is my life now. Wild, wet, tumbling pleasure.

"You awake, baby girl?" the water creature murmurs. He sounds amused by my dreaminess and my total abandon. I need him to take me over this impossible edge, to the oblivion of rapture he's promising me.

He turns me, so I'm resting face down, with my cheek pressed against the grass that's so smooth it feels like cotton. The water creature is behind me, adjusting me so I'm on my knees and they're bent and apart. My backside is up, my head down, so I'm fully on display for him. He can see how much I want him. I can feel that he *loves* this, that I'm offering myself to him. I love it too. I'm his for the taking and this is all I care about.

His mouth finds the center of my world, eating into

me, exploring me. He licks me everywhere, finding the secret pucker of my ass, digging lightly with his tongue, swirling the moisture of his mouth with his fingers. His mouth returns to my clit and I'm riding the crest of a surreal wave.

I feel his skating fingers, which caress me in an insistent, synced rhythm. He's working my swollen, slippery clit and the cove of my ass at the same time. I feel the heavy weight of his enormous, magic-dipped cock press against me, opening me to his thick invasion. "You want me inside you, little Stella Bell? You want me to fuck you nice and hard and deep, just like you like it?"

Do it. Please. I need it now. If he doesn't give me that big cock right now I'm going to freaking *die, does he not know this?*

"You're so damn wet and ready for me." He teases me, pushing the tip of his broad thickness inside me, then withdrawing it. Torturing me. "You want me to fuck you real good, baby girl?"

"*Yes. Yes. Please.*"

He slides his huge, ridged cock all the way to the hilt. I moan, taking all of him, my body gripping his brutal plunge with clenching adoration.

I also, right at that moment, wake up.

Oh.

It takes me a few seconds to remember where I am—and who I'm currently getting very thoroughly fucked by.

Kade Tucker.

He's not a magical water creature at all, but a very large, very real, very buff, *very thick and very hard* rock star.

Who's right now tipping me over the crest of a delicious peak of pain-spiked pleasure that I have no choice but to ride as I arch and writhe against him, working him with my spasming body. I'm coming so hard I don't just see stars, I *feel* them, as they ignite an overwhelming bliss that radiates through my entire body in spiraling washes of hot pleasure.

My orgasm grips his thick length voluptuously, milking the pleasure out of him until he's fucking me like a big lusty animal, pumping thick ropes of his cum deep inside my squirming body.

We ride it all the way, until the spasms begin to ease and lengthen.

His body is fully wrapped around me, mounted and gripping. He's still pulsing out the final gushes of his release and my body answers with snug pulls, as though it wants to take every last drop of him.

I feel the bite of his teeth lightly on my neck. The touch of his tongue and the strikes of his heavy breath. "*Fuck.*"

He rolls us onto our sides and we just lay like that for a while, *feeling* everything, so much. I'm so high on sated lust, I'm dazed by it. Drugged and blissed out from the experience of being so thoroughly made love to, I can't think. I can only feel.

Thoughts whisper behind my mind. *I wish this one night*

stand never had to end. I am really going for it with this beautiful stranger and I'm glad. But I also wonder what could possibly come next.

Slowly, he pulls himself from my body. I'm sticky and spent. I can feel his milky cum dripping down my thighs. It feels *dirty*, in a primal and beautiful kind of way. Our overflowing bond. My basest urges are on fire with...happiness, maybe. Satisfaction. This hot rock star has filled me with copious amounts of his life force and I'm basking in my own languid, feminine allure. *I* made him do that. I made him lose his mind with his pleasure and fill my body with it.

Holy hell, Stella. But I can't bring myself to regret a single moment or question any of it.

He's kissing my skin softly, the roughness of his stubble a light, delicious torment. "You're so fucking beautiful."

I feel Kade's fingers on the high skin of my thigh, catching the dripping cum. Pushing it back inside me.

"What are you doing?" I murmur sort of dreamily.

"Keeping me inside you."

Wow. I let him do it. I *want* him to do it. I love the feel of his fingers as he dips and swirls.

I almost remind him that I'm on the pill but I'm too relaxed. The magnitude of this intimacy is so new to me —and him too, I think. I've never wanted to be so *close* to another human being before. Especially one I barely know.

In one very important way, I know him better than I've known anyone.

Kade goes into the bathroom and turns on the shower. Then he comes back and carefully lifts me and carries me into the steam-filled luxury bathroom. The shower alone is twice the size of my own bathroom. It's made of smooth sandstone and walls of glass. There's a wide cedar bench running the length of one wall and five or six shower nozzles sluicing water over us while creating wafts of warm steam. I'm exhausted and limp with the afterglow of back-to-back stellar orgasms, but Kade sits me on his lap and holds me against his broad chest. He washes my hair and my body. He holds a detached shower head intimately between my legs, bringing me to another languid, crazy-sweet rise.

"Tonight I'm going to hold you close all night long," he says. "Tomorrow I'm going to cook breakfast for you while we call Gage. You're going to stay with me here in Nashville for a while and we're going to figure out what to do about finding each other. Because now that I have, darlin', there's no way in hell I'm letting you go."

12

KADE

I WAKE UP.

For a second I wonder if I'm dead. If I've died and gone to heaven or some goddamn thing. I feel so fucking peaceful. Comfortable. Wildly...content. It's not an emotion I'm used to.

I'm fully wrapped around the person lying in my bed with me, our arms and legs tangled and my fingers weaved through her soft hair.

Softer than Carmen's.

Everything about her is softer than Carmen.

This isn't Carmen.

I never felt this good next to Carmen.

And I was never wrapped this tightly around her, because I didn't want to be.

I slept hard, and deeper than I have in a long time. But my subconscious was clearly on a die-hard mission to keep this girl close. My bear hug is as resolute as an iron cage of safety.

I drink in the details of her, getting my bearings. I'm in my city house, not the warehouse. I broke up with Carmen yesterday, I remember—finally, thank fuck—and I played a gig at Gus's, which got mobbed.

After running into *her* on the rainy street.

Stella Juliet Bell.

Her seraphic face is angelic as she sleeps.

She's so damn *young*. So dazzlingly beautiful.

If the pumping thud of my heart, the steel-strong grip of my arms or the ten inches of serious morning wood I'm sporting are any judge, the lion's share of my psyche —and other parts of me—think I'm already in love with her.

She was a virgin.

Fuck.

Did I hurt her?

I could feel that she came many times. I tried to make sure the pain would at least be consumed by pleasure, but I was so overcome by my own lust, it was impossible not to completely lose myself in her. She felt better than anything ever has.

My unicorn girl. Completely untouched.

As if she wasn't already perfect. Not that it would have mattered.

But it does.

She's mine.

And only mine.

Mine.

I came inside her. *With no barriers. Three times.*

There was simply no way I could have disengaged myself from that tight little heaven on earth.

What I realize now is that I don't care if I knock her up. In the back of my mind I think I *want* to.

Which is seriously crazy.

I've never even considered going bareback before.

Ever.

Not even when they beg.

For better or worse, every woman I meet wants my baby. I'm hot, famous, built, 6'3", and I'm steady. I'm rough in all the ways they want me to be, but I also have an ingrained integrity that's like crack to women, fuck knows why. My eyes are honest, they tell me. They trust me. They know I'll take them to the edge of every experience, but also that I'll protect them along the way. I have a moral compass and I'm a natural leader, which they can detect with their baby-o-meters, you can read it in their expressions from a mile away. I'm a guy who stands out from the crowd for all the right reasons, I'm loaded as fuck so I can provide whatever they need on steroids, and odds are I'll give them good-looking little alpha babies with talent and blue eyes and a sweet life on offer. No guarantees, of course, but it's what every woman's basest urges crave. Even if they're not actively *thinking* about those details, their bodies are seeking them out. It's a simple case of Biology 101 rearing its ugly head.

I'm also hung like a porn star, which doesn't hurt.

I'm the kind of guy women want to get impregnated by, and get attached to in profound and life-changing ways, it's just one of those things.

So I've been very careful. I always provide the condoms, to make sure they haven't been tampered with. I don't care if they tell me they're on the pill or have taken care of things. I'd rather double up than be caught by surprise later on.

Not anymore.

With this girl, I'm already *all in*.

I'm a little concerned about my own throw-all-caution-to-the-wind attitude.

I'm not sure why I'm so damn *sure* about her.

It was so instant. So fucking total.

Why?

Because she's the unicorn girl.

Hell.

What if she *isn't?*

What if she turns out to be as crazy as all the others?

She won't.

She's the one.

As if to confirm, my gigantic hard-on, fully-loaded, which is pressed up against the smooth skin of her thigh, throbs hotly, gushing pre-cum like it's seeking her out. *Like it wants to slide back inside all that snug, squeezing ecstasy.*

The scent of her is heady. Lemons. Sunshine. Hothouse flowers and summertime daydreams. She smells like happiness.

She tastes like fucking nectar.

The caveman in me wants to keep her and make her mine in the most profound kind of way.

By putting a baby in her. Is that what I'm trying to do?

I don't know.

Not *actively*, but on some level my body and soul have already chosen her.

I'm not only already willing to bond myself to her for the rest of time, I'm *trying* to.

It's intense.

I watch her as she sleeps, trying not to be over the top about it, but she's in my bed, fully entwined with me, *full of my seed*, so I figure I'm allowed.

I drink in every mind-blowing detail of this seriously stunning girl, fully captivated. She might as well have been made for me, all her features not only ideal but taken to some higher level of what I might have wished for if I'd thought to. Her lush lips are full and soft, lightly parted as she sleeps, her nose is cute and dotted with that little golden C chord of freckles. The long, sweeping arcs of her eyelashes are gold-tipped, just like her colorful hair with all its naturally-bright shades of chestnut and dark red, which lightens to a pale gold at its coiled ends.

She's deeply asleep.

I could wake her again. Feed on my new addiction. *I*

could feast on that luscious little candy-pink pussy all day and all night and never have enough of her.

But she needs rest.

We stayed up most of the night, taking each other over edge after edge with our ravenous need for each other. She's tired. She drove all the way from New Jersey yesterday and the day before, after an emotional week.

Of getting proposed to.

The thought sends a jolt of red-hot possessiveness through my veins. Another gush of pre-cum throbs and spills onto her soft skin.

I'm so fucking hard it's painful.

I decide to let it happen. I couldn't hold it even if I wanted to. The look of her and her scent and the feel of her skin. I grip my rigid length in my fist, being careful not to wake her.

It doesn't take much.

Heat sizzles along my raging shaft as I slide myself against her soft skin. Each smooth touch paints my cock with red-hot ecstasy. I really don't want to be over the top about this but I fucking *need* her. The release billows through me, spilling in hot bursts all over her stomach. I grit my teeth as my orgasm throbs and bursts.

Fuck.

What am I doing?

I've never come as hard as I do with this little almost-stranger. I've never felt so goddamn feral.

Gently, I rub my warm cum over her skin, smoothing

it over her stomach and her breasts, cupping the creamy mounds, coating her nipples with my sticky claim.

Mine. The certainty is unwavering and it fucking worries me. She's already got me so tightly wrapped around her little finger I can't see straight. I've known her for less than a day and I would already kill for her.

One blink of those long, tear-and-rain-wet eyelashes and one starry glance from those gem-green eyes and I was hooked. *Hard.* And it's messing with my state of mind.

What I'm realizing is that all the sadness and loneliness that has plagued me for years is...gone. All that angst because in my heart I knew the woman I was with wasn't *the one*, gone. Because here she is.

Love at first sight is real.

It is possible to *know*, just like that.

Hell.

All I can do is hope like hell she doesn't break my jaded heart.

She sighs then settles, as though she likes what I'm doing, claiming her as my own. It's soothing her.

"That's my girl," I hear myself murmur. I tuck her in carefully, smoothing back a playful curl. I can't help myself: I kiss her lips, softly, so I don't wake her. The fiery craving to slide my tongue *inside* and taste more of her almost overwhelms me. But I want her to feel good, and rested. I want to ease away every shred of difficulty in her life. I'm going to give her everything she needs. And right now what she needs is rest. "Sleep as long as you want, sweet darlin'. I'll be right here. I'll watch over you."

Satisfied that she's as comfortable as she can be, I pull on a pair of sweat pants and go out into the kitchen.

A strange and resolute contentedness settles into me. As crazy as it sounds, *I've found my purpose*. Her. Giving her everything she needs and wants.

It's a cataclysmic shift, like a cloud has moved away from the sun and you can suddenly feel the full effect of its warmth and its light.

My phone is sitting on the counter. I text Gage.

> Looking for a PI. Can you send me your guy's number?

Then I go over to the far corner of the great room, where my vintage Martin D-18 is sitting on its stand. This old dreadnought was one of my first purchases once I started making real money. It dates back to 1937 and was once played by Elvis. The thing's a goddamn work of art.

And it reminds me of the day I bought it. I'd broken up with another past girlfriend, for the same reason I've broken up with every girlfriend.

Because they weren't her.

I know I'm reacting to Stella in a way that's over the top.

Am I grasping for something I've wanted so badly all along but never got? Am I creating something in my mind that isn't actually there?

No. Because I've never actually felt as sure about anything.

I know it's her.

I pick up the guitar and tune it, strumming a few chords.

The song spools through my fingers fully formed. I find some paper and write down the lyrics. About a charmed, rainy night in Nashville. The notes and the words come so easily, I'm sort of amazed by the easy gush of inspiration.

Because I've found her.

I force myself to at least try to chill the fuck out.

I can't, though. The fever burns into the music, inspiring it. Lifting it into one of those rare, out-of-the-blue kind of tunes you can feel in your bones is one of the best things you'll ever write. I know it's a hit already.

My love song to the girl of my dreams.

An hour or so later, it's done.

I hear a soft noise and I look up. She's standing there, wrapped in a short pale-green silk robe that's belted at the waist. Her long, bare legs are lightly tanned. Just the sight of her makes me instantly hard and I don't even know what to do with that. I almost wish I could appreciate her without getting a raging hard-on, but it's impossible. She's too damn sexy. Her colorful hair is a glorious mess. Even from a distance, her stolen-emerald eyes are a bright, vibrant shade of green.

"Mornin', beautiful."

She smiles shyly. "Hi."

As she does this, my chest tightens with an overblown tenderness that digs in and makes my heart beat hotly in my chest.

Holy hell. I am so fucked.

I stand up and sort of instantly regret it because I'm much more than half-cocked. But there's nothing I can do about it so I walk over to her and I smile sort of sheepishly—or maybe wolfishly—because there's nothing subtle about how goddamn *into* her I am.

She laughs at how obvious I am, and it's the cutest fucking thing. What I love the most is that she's *fun.* I'm not used to it.

I stand close to her, looming over her since I'm a good six or seven inches taller than she is. Carefully, I lift her, setting her down so she's sitting on the island. I open her legs and stand between them. I tuck one of her curls carefully behind her ear. We've taken this attraction from zero to sixty without so much as a glance in the rearview mirror. I have half an urge to slow it down, to savor it and roll around in every detail of her, taking my time. "You sleep okay, darlin'?"

"So deeply." She smiles at me and I can't help smiling back. Because she's beaming hundred-proof sunshine into my life. "I can't remember ever sleeping that well."

It's funny, because neither can I. "You all right?" It's a big deal to lose your virginity—and so...thoroughly. I don't want her to regret anything.

Maybe she can read this in me because her expression softens into a gentle smile, like it makes her happy that I would ask this, and care. "I'm very all right. Thank you for enlightening me." Light flags of pink warm her cheeks. "There's only one small problem."

"What problem?" I brace myself. *Whatever it is, I'll change her mind. I'll spend every second of my goddamn wretched life making sure she has everything, that she's not in pain or scared or lonely.*

Stella says it shyly but as she blinks at me there's a playfulness that's blowing my mind. "Now I think I might be sort of...addicted. To you and your enlightenment."

I'm wildly relieved but I say it slowly, more like a comment than a question. "Is that right."

She barely nods.

"Well, that makes two of us."

She glances down and comments softly. "Wow."

I grin, because it's a major situation, no doubt about it. My cock is doing its best to escape the waistband of my sweatpants, leaking pre-cum. "Your fault," I accuse gently.

We're quiet for a few seconds but it's not awkward. More...curious. It's the first time we've seen each other in the light of day. We're taking in new details, locked in the connection of whatever the hell is happening here.

She's even more spectacular this morning than she was last night, if such a thing is possible. The golden hues of morning illuminate her hair, her skin and her eyes like she's lit from within.

I have the urge to get onto my knees and propose to her right now.

Don't be a fucking maniac.

I won't. I'm not going to scare her or overwhelm her.

I'll learn what she likes. I'll give her everything she needs. I'll love her so hard and in all the right ways she'll never want to let me go. I know how to do that. It's what I was put here to do. And now that I've found my little unicorn, I can finally do love justice.

I pull gently on the silk belt that holds her robe together. The fabric falls open, revealing her creamy breasts, her sweet nipples pink and beaded. Her stomach is smooth and so amazingly feminine. I can still see the thin milky film of my caveman claim, dried onto her flaw-less skin. *Mine. This is where my babies are going to grow.*

Hell. Would you listen to yourself?

"Those gray sweatpants should be illegal." Her soft sassiness is getting me even harder.

I'm trying to deal with this overblown and sudden addiction. But it's no use. I'm a goner. I'm so whipped I can't control it. "This kind of perfection should be illegal. It's a crime for you to wear clothes, baby girl."

Her bare pussy is lightly glistening, like candy.

I angle my head just slightly to kiss her, but I don't. I take a few seconds to wait for her, to let her come to me. Because

I'm about to go full caveman again and I want to make sure she's ready and a hundred percent willing. She touches her soft lips to mine and I lick her, almost dizzy with lust. "You're wet for me." My voice sounds growly and deep.

"Your fault." She blinks those crazy eyelashes at me. "I think it's those sweatpants."

I lean down because there's no way in hell I can resist. I slide her hips forward and push her legs open wider, licking a line up her thigh before taking in her scent and sliding my tongue over her wet, luscious pussy. "How do you feel about orgasms before breakfast?" I murmur against her soft, honeyed folds as I slide my tongue into paradise.

She gasps. "I wouldn't know."

I suckle gently on her clit. "Want to find out?"

"*Oh*," she coos, her hands lightly gripping my shoulders.

I eat her out like a starving man feasting on a juicy peach, bringing her to the brink, getting her nice and messy and ready for me, but I don't let her come yet. I want her orgasm to draw my cum deep into her body.

I stand to my full height, positioning myself. I grip my almost-bursting beast of an erection in my fist, rubbing the head against her saturated pussy, opening her. "Let me hear you say it. You want me to fuck you nice and deep and make you come hard, sugar pie?"

Her green eyes are lust-drowsed and awed.

I kiss her lips. "Say it to me, baby girl. I want to hear you say it. Tell me what you want."

Her cheeks get pink but her soft hands are on me. "I want you to fuck me with that big, perfect cock."

Goddamn it, I'm almost coming already, just hearing her say the words. I grip her ass in my hands, lifting her onto me as I slide my gigantic shaft inside her, easing out before driving deeper. *Oh, fuck,* she's tight. "Let me in, baby. You're so fucking gorgeous. You feel too good." Out, then in, trying like hell to be careful with her. Deeper. And deeper, until I'm buried to the hilt.

"*Kade,*" she moans, and I watch her eyes to make sure she's moaning with pleasure more than pain.

My hands knead her sweet ass and I glide the moisture over the tight cove, caressing her there as I fuck her pussy hard and deep, thrusting relentlessly. "You're close, aren't you, sweetheart? You want it so fucking bad. Come on, baby. Come for me. You want me to fill you up with my sticky seed and get you all nice and juicy with it, I know you do."

"*Yes. Yes. Oh my God. Kade.*"

Her pussy clamps strongly around me, pulling on the full length of me with silky, squeezing tugs.

I can't hold on to it. Raging bursts of pleasure explode out of me as my cock bucks inside her, flooding hot ropes of liquid heat deep inside her.

It goes on for a long time and I work it, taking her over another rise, until she's moaning again and her inner muscles flutter tenderly, over and over, in long, lush ripples.

I kiss her sweet mouth for a long time, sliding my tongue over hers with a hungry, almost-perverse need. To taste her. To fuck her. To keep her.

Staying deep inside until the final pulses of my cum throb and spill, I give my seed time to fully flood her. *To saturate and swim.*

I can't fucking analyze it but she already owns me.

When I'm satisfied that she's had enough, I slowly slide myself from her body. The overflow spills from her pussy. Using my fingers, I push some of the spilling liquid back inside.

"I told you I'm on the pill," she says softly, still riding the lingering effects of her rush.

"I know." Doesn't mean it can't happen.

I love the way she looks right now. Her eyes are dreamy and her color is high. Her nipples are rosy from the abrasion of my chest, her skin lightly bruised from my grip, her pink pussy flushed and overflowing with my milky seed.

"I want you just like this, all the time," I tell her. A thread of visceral tenderness passes between us that's heady and more profound than I know what to do with. I don't want to get too heavy but I let myself admit it to her. "I think you might be stuck with me, Stella Bell."

"Yeah?"

"Yeah."

"Maybe I wouldn't mind that." Her smile slays me even more. "Kade?"

"Yeah?"

"What are you doing today?"

I arrange her robe so it frames her unbelievably beautiful breasts. I don't want it closed. I want to look at her while I feed her. "Well, first I'm going to cook you breakfast." I go over to where the paper towel roll is and tear off some. I turn on the faucet and warm the water for a few seconds, wetting the paper towel. I carefully wash some of my cum from her thighs. "Then we're going to go sit in the hot tub for a while and you're going to tell me about your life and your hopes and dreams." I gently clean her, but not too carefully. I take care of the overflow but leave her glistening. She lets me do this, watching me, and I'm basically a puddle of mush for this little goddess. After so much doubt in my life about whether or not I was *capable* of feeling this fucking besotted, it feels more than good. It feels like I've finally found my reason to live. Which is a fairly major shift in the entire trajectory of my life, but there it is. "I'm obsessed with everything about you so I figure it might be a good idea to get to know you a little." I feel the slightest pang of panic at my own question before I ask it. "Why? You didn't have other plans, did you?" I don't say it but what I'm thinking is, *I'll follow you wherever you go.*

"No other plans. That sounds perfect."

"You want to start with some coffee?" I don't know

how she takes her coffee or even if she likes coffee. I don't know what her favorite color is or what songs are on her playlists. It's crazy that I don't know the first thing about the love of my life.

Slow down, tiger. What if her favorite color is black and she only listens to death metal?

I wouldn't care. I'd buy her a black Lambo and expand my genres.

"Coffee sounds fantastic," she says.

"You're a coffee drinker, then."

"My brain doesn't start fully functioning until I have two cups. But two's my limit. And I can't drink it later than around one in the afternoon, otherwise I can't get to sleep at night."

"I don't plan on letting you sleep much tonight anyway," I wink at her, and what I'm finding is that the vibe between us is hot but also playful. Which is refreshing. After all the constant melodrama and the you've-wronged-me-you-bastard accusations that surrounded Carmen like a black cloud of doom, this is wildly different. Stella's aura is golden and infectious. Sexy and fun. I'm in love with that detail as much as the sweet lips, the green eyes, the heavenly haven of her body. The whole package is blowing my mind.

I put the coffee on and put some water on the stove to boil. "I hope you're hungry." I get some of the ingredients out of the fridge and set them on the counter. Jared, the guy who looks after the place for me, keeps the fridge stocked with basics in case I decide to bunk here out of the blue, which happens from time to time. Roxie sometimes uses it too.

"Kade Tucker cooks?" Like she finds this funny.

"It's my third-best skill."

She laughs. "I wouldn't have guessed that."

"I cook whenever I get the chance, which isn't that often, because we're on the road so much. But I think if I wasn't a musician I might have opened a restaurant."

There's a hint of amusement in her beguiled smile. "I love that."

The coffee's ready so I pour two mugs full, adding some cream and half a teaspoon of cane sugar to each one. I hand her a cup.

She takes a sip, then closes her eyes for a second. "Oh, this is so good."

"There's a place around the corner that fresh-roasts their own coffee beans. Best in town."

The pot of water I put on the stove is boiling, so I pour some stone-ground grits into it, stirring before putting the lid on it and taking it off the heat. I put some rashers of bacon onto the broiler pan and put them under the broiler. And I start cracking some eggs into a bowl.

"What are you making?"

"Grits. With a side of bacon and my special omelets."

"What are grits?"

I give her a look. "You've never had grits?"

"No. I don't even know what they are."

"Well, you're in for a treat."

My phone rings from where it's sitting on the counter.

Gage lights up the screen. "It's my cousin. The one who knows the private investigator. You want me to answer it? Or I can call him back later."

I can tell by the way her eyes are shimmery with emotion—it's the way they get when anything touches on the topic of her adoption, and I love that I know this and I can read this—that she does want me to answer it.

So I swipe my finger across the answer button and put him on speaker phone. "Gage."

"I just saw a headline about you," he says. "Sounds like you're enjoying your reboun—"

"You're, uh, on speaker. And I've got a friend here with me. Her name is Stella. Stella, meet my cousin Gage."

"Hi, Gage." She thinks it's funny that he's commenting on my rebound, which could have been awkward. Something like that would have pissed off Carmen to no end. Everything pissed Carmen off to no end.

There's a hint of a surprised pause from Gage. "Hi, Stella." He's probably guessing Stella is the same girl I was photographed leaving the club with last night. Gage calls me a serial monogamist, which he's always found hilarious. He never used to sleep with any woman more than once, never invited any woman to his apartment and was always gone before morning, according to him. Until Luna, that is. For her, he's not only reformed beyond recognition, he also bought half of Key West for her. He couldn't get the rock of an engagement ring on her finger fast enough. "You're going to have a lot of fans in our family, just so you're warned ahead of time," he tells her. "For rescuing him."

Stella blinks her long lashes at me. "I'm not sure I've rescued him."

"She has," I confirm. "Listen, Gage, can you give us the number of your investigator? Stella's searching for someone. She doesn't have a lot of details, so we're going to need some help. You said your guy is the best is in the business."

"He is. He's insanely good. He's in hot demand, but he owes me a couple of favors. I'll get him to give you a call."

"Thanks, man."

"Are we still on for Tuesday night?" Gage asks. "I just talked to Vaughn and he said he might join us."

"I've hardly seen him lately." Then I explain to Stella, so she doesn't feel left out of the conversation, "My brother Vaughn has fallen hopelessly in love with the girl who lives next door to my other brother Travis's new house. Her name is Gigi and she happens to be Travis's fiancée's sister." Vaughn hasn't wasted any time getting as fast and furious as possible with Gigi—which, because it's Vaughn, is pretty damn fast and furious. He's already asked her to move in with him, he's proposed to her and last I heard they weren't going to wait long to get married. After years of being as loose and carefree on every level as a guy can be, we can all admit that Gigi's good for him. She's got a calming effect on him, which is something Vaughn desperately needed. Since he's met Gigi, he's been more steady than I've seen him in years.

"Will Gigi be coming to dinner too?" Stella asks.

"I don't think so," Gage says. "Apparently she has book club at her mother's that night. Vaughn said he doesn't want twenty women fangirling over him all night, so he's going to come out and meet up with us for a few hours. How about this: I'll see if I can get Pete Clancy—he's the PI—to stop in too. He's based in Nashville, so I can see if he can make some time for us. Then you can talk to him in person and take it from there."

Gage is an investment guru who runs his own hedge fund, among other lucrative businesses. He also owns a ton of real estate. So if he asks someone to make time, they always do. Partly because he pays top dollar and also because whatever he touches tends to turn to gold. I know this firsthand because he handles both my accounts and the band's accounts and he's basically quadrupled our money.

"That would be amazing," Stella says.

"Is Luna coming with you?" I ask him.

"Our new designer is here so she wants to stay here in Key West and go through some plans with him for the spa we're opening. I'll fly back on Tuesday night after we have dinner."

"Luna owns a waterfront bar and restaurant," I tell Stella. "They're expanding."

"Wow, that's so exciting."

"You'll have to come check it out when it's done," Gage says to her, like he knows I'm already hooked. Maybe he can detect this because he's just been through it himself. Everyone in my family tends to fall fast and extremely hard when it finally happens. It's all I can do not to fall to my knees and fucking thank whoever's in charge of fate for finally bringing...*mine*. I feel sort of over-whelmed with gratitude. She doesn't even know she's my soulmate yet. But *I* do. And it's a realization that's hitting me like a runaway freight train.

"I'll look forward to meeting you on Tuesday night then, Stella," Gage says.

"Me too, Gage. See you then. And thanks for arranging a meeting with the investigator. I really appre-ciate it."

"My pleasure," says Gage. "Have fun, you two. See you Tuesday."

I press the end button and as soon as I do, Stella's stomach growls.

I sling a dishtowel over my shoulder. "Right. Time for breakfast. My girl needs food."

"That smells so good. I'm starving."

It's so nice to be with a woman who *eats*. It reminds

me again how my life has done a total 180 in the past twenty-four hours. "You're about to get the chef's special, darlin'." I make her another cup of coffee—because now I know she likes two. I flip the rashers of bacon, then chop up some mushrooms and start sautéing them with butter. She watches me with that light smirk playing at the corner of her mouth.

"What?"

She laughs. "I'm just...impressed. He hands out orgasms at the drop of a hat *and* he can cook. I can't believe my luck."

"You and me both, honey pie." Her mischievous streak is getting me hot. "Careful, or I'll have to postpone option two for more of option one."

Her sweet-and-sassy smile lights up my world. "Can I help you do anything?"

"Nope. You can sit right there and drink your coffee and the mimosa I'm about to make for you. And you can start telling me about what makes Stella Bell tick. I want to know everything."

"Everything?" She takes a sip of her coffee, her green eyes spangling. "Where should I start?"

"What's your favorite color? Wait, let me guess." I contemplate her for a second. "Green."

Her eyebrows lift. "It *is* green! No one ever guesses green."

"It has to be. With eyes that color, there's no other choice."

"Everyone I've ever met has always commented on the color of my eyes, so I guess it just felt like a color that was sort of linked to my identity. And I just like it. When I was little, all the other girls wore pink and purple but I always wanted to wear green."

"I bet you were the cutest."

"What's the Magic Man's favorite color? Let me guess." She studies me. "Blue."

"Blue used to be my favorite color. Until last night."

"Why?" Another sweet grin that—*fuck*—gets me even harder. "What is it now?"

I step closer, leaning down as I open her untied robe, and I take her nipple lightly between my lips. "This pink right here."

A light laugh bubbles out of her and she pushes my head away. I return to the stove but cooking with a gigantic hard-on in sweatpants is a new challenge. I'm being careful not to burn the fucking thing.

"Okay, what's your favorite movie?" I ask her.

"Anything rom-com. The fun, romantic ones where they always get their happily ever afters."

"Like what?"

"Sweet Home Alabama, Bridget Jones, Sleepless in Seattle. You know, the classics."

"Sleepless in Seattle. I think I've seen it. Isn't that the one where, at the end, they meet each other at the top of the Empire State Building?"

"Yes, and they almost miss each other." The topic

animates her. "But it was meant to be and they find each other and they both know it's the real thing. I'm a complete sucker for those kinds of love stories. I just think it's so romantic, that they both have this feeling that the love of their life was within reach, but then they came so close to *missing* each other. It must happen all the time."

"What must happen?"

"People *miss* each other. What if it turns out there's only one star-crossed lover for each person in the world, and what if you happen to walk past your person randomly one day and you *miss* them and you don't even know it? And that's it, they're gone and you'll never find them and you'll never even *know* you missed them. It's just so tragic to even think about."

"Good thing I stopped, then." I watch her eyes and I'm just so fucking *happy*. She radiates a whole-souled beauty that's fun and quirky and everything I never knew I needed in my life. I try to tone down my own intensity. "How are we going to get the Empire State Building into *our* love story?"

She likes this idea, I can tell. But she's hesitant, maybe, at my mention of "our" love story, if we have one that will last beyond one night. "I don't know. Maybe we can go there together one day."

"We can go there anytime you want. I have an apartment there."

"You do?"

"It's a loft. In SoHo."

Stella shakes her head slowly. There's a soulful look on her face, like a part of her is pulling back from me.

"What's wrong?"

"Lofts in SoHo. Screaming fans. Platinum records. Grammys. Your life is...unreal." I can almost hear her thoughts: *Your life is so different to my life. Will the two be able to mesh?*

So I answer her. "Yes. Because none of those things are the best part."

She's quiet for a few seconds, like she knows what I'm going to say. "What's the best part?"

"A rainy night in Nashville. And the little unicorn girl who's the prettiest thing I've ever seen."

A soft smile touches her lips. Even though my hands are holding a fork and a spatula, I move closer and I slowly, slowly kiss her lips.

"I think I like you, Kade Tucker," she says softly.

"I think I like you too, Stella Bell."

But then we're distracted by a smoking pan.

"Shit." I go over to the stove and turn the heat down. "The unbelievably cute nymph in my kitchen is distracting the cook."

Her soft laughter is my new favorite sound.

Once the pan is the right temperature, I add some more oil and pour the omelet mixture in, tipping the sautéed mushrooms in and grating some sharp cheddar into the mix. Now that the grits have been off the heat for around twenty minutes, I warm them up again, adding cream and a sprinkling more of the grated cheese. The bacon's ready, so I take it out and start plating up. Popping a bottle of champagne, I pour us two mimosas.

I serve up the grits and the omelets, adding two grinds of sea salt and freshly ground pepper. "Come on, gorgeous. Grub's up." I carry the plates over to the table. Then I lift her down off the island. Taking her empty coffee cup, I hand her a mimosa.

"Champagne for breakfast?"

"Every now and then it's good for the soul, especially when you've got something to celebrate, like we do." I clink my glass against hers. "To *not* missing the one you're supposed to run into."

Her eyes are bright as we both take a sip.

I take her by the hand to the table and pull out a chair for her.

We sit down and start eating. "Oh, this is *amazing*."

"Told you. I'm good."

She laughs. "And humble." Her gaze follows the view of the expansive balcony and the city. "This place is really beautiful. You must love it."

"I came to a party here two or three years ago. It was for sale at the time so I bought the building. I like it but I don't spend a lot of time here."

"Because you tour so much?"

"We've just finished three back-to-back tours. It's good to have a break. Although it's not much of a break since I have a shorter solo tour coming up."

She takes another sip of her mimosa. "I think you came to New Jersey a while back. Some people were talking about it on the radio."

"We did. We played at Meadowlands a few months ago."

"Meadowlands holds eighty thousand people."

I guess it does. "You get used to the numbers after a while."

"I've seen Bruce Springsteen play there twice."

"That must be a requirement of every Jersey girl."

"Of course." She gives me the rock 'n roll salute. "I've seen him eight times."

"Eight? You are a fan."

"I love him. He's old school but still my all-time favorite."

"He's a cool guy."

"You've *met* him?"

Her expression makes me laugh. She's just so fucking adorable. And here's another thing I can do for her. Introduce her. "We recorded with him, for a charity album. We hit it off. I let him stay in my house in Franklin sometimes when he's in Nashville."

"Now you're just showing off."

I laugh again and it's something I notice, because I can't remember ever laughing this much. I love *being* with her. I'm not used to the glittery contentment she inspires. "I'll see if I can arrange a meeting."

"Sure." Like she doesn't believe me. "I'd love to see

your band play sometime. I've heard you guys are amazing in concert."

"I thought you hadn't heard of us." We're sitting close and I lightly bump my shoulder against hers.

"What do you mean? I told you I've heard of you."

"You didn't recognize me, though."

She sits back, her impish little smile measured. My question amuses her. "I'd heard of you, of course I had. I just wasn't expecting *Kade Tucker* to step out of the darkness and guide me out of the pouring rain. I had a lot on my mind and I didn't make the connection at first. I don't usually get rescued by world-famous rock stars."

"And you won't be again. Because I'm keeping you."

Stella narrows her eyes at me, entertained by my vanity, maybe, and now my possessiveness. "Keeping me?"

I smile off-handedly but I don't answer her question, because it might be too much. I don't want her to feel overwhelmed and there's nothing half-assed or uncertain about the way I feel. But it's too soon to lay it all out with the intensity that has already settled into my bones—and other parts of me. *Yes, baby, I'm not letting you out of my sight because I'm addicted and obsessed. You're mine now.* "All right," I say, "We've covered colors, movies, now I want you to start telling me more about what you dream about. What do you want to do most of all?"

She picks up her mimosa and takes a sip. "I want to write a novel."

I love this, and I wasn't expecting it. "What kind of novel?"

"A romance novel." She finishes off her drink, even though it was a quarter full. "I've never said that out loud before."

I'm watching her expression and there's a lot going on there. "Why not?"

"My parents and everyone I know would think it was...I don't know, lame."

"Lame?" I grab the bottle of champagne out of the ice bucket and top up our glasses, not bothering with the orange juice. "How could someone who's talented and beautiful inside and out with the most romantic soul I've ever come across write a lame book? That would be impossible."

She smiles. "Because it's romance, is the answer to that question. Genre fiction. It doesn't matter that it comprises almost half the fiction market or that it keeps most of the big publishers' lights on. It's still not considered 'literature.'"

"Does that matter?"

"To some people, maybe."

"Isn't Jane Austen romance? And aren't those books considered some of the major influencers of twentieth century literature?"

She tilts her head, like I've surprised her, or impressed her. "Yes, they are. Still, romance is considered frivolous, according to the mainstream critics. Cheesy. Formulaic.

Partly, I think, because it's mainly by women, for women."

"Then prove them wrong."

"A lot of people already have. There are plenty of good romance novels. It doesn't seem to change their minds, though."

"Who cares about them? Write it for yourself. And for the romantics like you and me."

"I guess, because my world consists of university professors and literary critics that I...well, it's just not something anyone I know would be able to relate to."

"Then expand your circle to include people who *can* relate to it. Stop trying to please everyone because you never will. Please yourself. When you start being true to yourself, it's a lot easier to achieve the things you want to achieve, and to be comfortable in your own skin. It also tends to lead to more success. Because when you're genuinely *into* whatever it is you're doing, you usually end up at the top of your game. I say go for it, sugar pie."

Her gaze is soft but sure. "That might be the best advice anyone has ever given me."

"Of course it is."

She laughs. "You're cocky as hell, Kade Tucker. But you're also right. And it helps. Thank you."

"There are plenty of people who don't like our music, but that doesn't stop us from writing it or performing it. Fuck the haters. We do it for the people who appreciate it. And most of all, we do it for ourselves."

She nods. "You're right. I need to break free of the shackles of other people's expectations."

"Is it your parents' approval you're worried about?"

She shrugs, but there's a lot of emotion going on behind her expression.

"Even if you spend your life trying your hardest to fulfill every expectation they have of you," I tell her, "you probably won't. So you might as well tune in to your *own* expectations and follow those instead. I know it's not always easy. I get that. Especially when it's your family. That shit digs deep. But you're twenty-one now. And you're in Nashville. You get to make your own decisions."

"I know. You're right. You're absolutely right."

"Just do what you love, darlin'. It's that easy." There's a sadness to her I can't entirely read. Or handle. So I decide to make it my mission to banish it and make sure she gets everything she wants.

"I wish it was that easy."

"It can be, with a little practice. And you've got me now, to help you do that." It's a fairly heavy thing to say, but it's how I feel and there's no point pretending otherwise. I'm good at pep talks. I've been giving them to my three younger siblings—sometimes during some pretty rough times—my entire life. "I'll be right here the whole time." I take her hand, weaving my fingers through hers.

"You might be the nicest person I've ever met, Magic Man."

"I'm only nice to you."

There's the smile I want. "I doubt that's true."

"There's nothing to be scared of. Do what you were born to do. Follow your dreams all the way home. I'm here now. I'll catch you if you fall."

Her eyes are bright, maybe with the brim of tears, but she squares her shoulders, like her decision has clicked into place. "Okay, then. I'm going to write a romance novel."

"Good girl. What's it going to be about?"

"It's about two people who almost miss each other."

A current of quiet, deep-reaching electricity sparks through the space between us. "Yeah?"

"Yeah."

"Tell me more."

"I've got the story mapped out in my mind but I haven't started writing it yet. It's about these two people —she's an artist from New York and he's an architect from Denver. But they're both really successful in what they're doing and their lives are going really well except for one thing."

"What thing?"

"They're sad. They're incomplete. They feel like there's someone out there for them but they just can't find them. No one they meet feels like a good fit at all and they date people but they never really connect and they're both starting to wonder if maybe they'll never find the person they're meant for."

"I think I know that feeling."

"I do too." She bites softly on her lip for a second and stares at me with soulful eyes. I'm so damn besotted with this girl. "And then one day he goes to New York for a conference and he sees this painting in a gallery window and he stops and stares at it for a long time. He *loves* it and something about it just clicks with him. So he goes in and buys it."

"Is it one of her paintings?"

"Yes. But he doesn't know that yet. He just sort of falls in love with it. So he has it shipped back to where he lives in Denver and he puts it in his house. It becomes his favorite thing."

"Then what happens?"

"Well, it turns out that he dropped one of his drawings as he was walking down the street in New York City. Out of his briefcase. It's one of the building designs he's working on. It's a house. He dropped it on the street right in front of the art gallery where he bought the painting and, even though they miss each other by a couple of minutes, she finds the drawing. She picks it up and she's kind of fascinated by it. The design is exactly what she would want, if she was designing a house. She's even thought about some of its exact details before. And so they begin to connect but they don't even know it yet. And then they start to look for each other."

"And they find each other?"

"Yes, but first they miss each other two more times. Both times they're within a few minutes of running into each other and they can sense that, but they don't know why or how to find each other."

"Damn."

"Yeah."

"But they end up together?"

"Yes. Once they *do* find each other they know instantly that they're meant to be together. It ends with them getting married at the top of the Empire State Building."

"No way."

"I know that's kind of derivative of Sleepless in Seattle but I still like it. He's never been up there before but she tells him it's her favorite place because she used to go there with her parents when she was little and it always felt like the top of the world to her. And sometimes she would go there when she was sad and look out and wonder where he was. And she tells him this. So one night he says he wants to go up there together and when they get there all her closest friends and family are there and there's music and he proposes on one knee and they say their vows and dance right there at the top of the world."

"I love this story."

"It's cheesy, maybe."

"Not cheesy, baby. *Romantic.*"

She smiles and now I know what I'm going to do.

"I'll tell you what, little unicorn girl. I want you to stay with me. I'm going to cook for you and make love to you whenever you want me to, which is going to be all the time —for inspiration, and because it would be a crime not to when the chemistry is *this* damn off the charts. I'm going to make sure you get all the time and space you need to write your book. I'll talk through your ideas with you if you want someone to bounce plot lines off of or whatever. And I'll read your pages and tell you what I think, when you're ready. Because I'm a romantic too and know what it feels like to want to fall in love so bad you think you might die from lack of oxygen. I know how it feels to spend half your life heart-broken because you think there's some glitch in your own personal universe because you can't find *the one*, no matter how hard you search. I also know what it feels like to run into someone you can't believe is real, in the most out-of-the-blue kind of way, that you were never expecting. The thing is, Stella Bell, I *get* you. Or I will, in time, because I want to."

Stella's staring at me with this little furrow between her eyebrows, like I'm some kind of apparition she can't believe.

"What do you say, baby?"

"I say I think you'd make a terrible romance hero."

I'm borderline offended by this. "Bullshit. I'd make an awesome hero."

"You're *too* perfect. You're kind. You're hot. You're honest. You're real. You say all the right things. Where's the inherent conflict when the hero is too good to be true?"

"The conflict comes later."

"What do you mean? When?"

I watch her eyes for a long moment. "The conflict comes when anything threatens the love of my life or if she's sad or mad or if something happens to her or she leaves me for some reason. Because I'll love so hard it'll destroy me."

A note of deep gravity touches her expression. "Is that right?" she whispers.

"Yes. That's right." I narrow my eyes just slightly because what I've said is intense and she's feeling it. But not as much as I am. "So what do you say, darlin'?"

"I say...okay. I'll stay for a little while. We'll have to figure the rest of it out. Thank you, Kade."

A little while.

Or forever, if I get my way. Which I fully intend on doing.

I don't push it. Maybe I have my work cut out for me. But I'll convince her, with hot sex, good food and the kind of luxurious care and genuine attention every romantic soul craves. I'll learn what she loves and I'll give her all of it. I'm not letting this little golden angel out of my sight or my bed until she's in love with me. It's too new for her to feel any kind of certainty, but I'll change that. With total dedication and careful, heartfelt persuasion, I'm going to show her that she's mine. From here on in. Which is heavy as fuck and something I'll probably have to pitch just a little less intensely.

"How about that hot tub?" I ask her. "Bring your glass."

I stand up and I pull her deeper into the living room. We get to the far end by the fold out cedar doors, where the L-shaped room opens out to a large entertainment space to the right.

She stares. "You have a bucking bronco?"

I love this. She's so obviously *not* from Nashville. "It's called a mechanical bull, but yes."

"In your *living* room?"

"Yeah, well, it was Vaughn's idea."

Her eyes are vividly, dazzlingly green. "Can I ride it?"

There are thick pads on the floor around it but I don't want her to hurt herself. "I'm not sure if—"

"Please?" The word sounds ten times more persuasive than it ever has, in that sassy-sweet Yankee accent. "I've always wanted to ride one of those."

I don't have it in me to refuse her a goddamn thing. "I'll ride it with you. I don't want you falling off."

She walks over to it. "How do you get on?"

"I'll lift you."

I do, and I climb up behind her, pulling her against me, her back pressed to my front. My cock hasn't deflated since I met her, and it's been an hour or so since I came inside her. My now-gigantic erection stands rigid between us and as soon as it touches her it becomes a beast of pulsing agony. Her robe falls open and I ease the silk over her shoulders, letting it fall to the floor.

"*Kade*," she scolds me, but this is too fucking hot not to go with it. I lift her, pushing the waistband of my sweatpants low so I can nestle my cock against her ass. I use the remote to turn the mechanical bull on, to its lowest speed. Even though the speed starts low, it's still a ride and I grip her closer against me. Her ludicrously sweet body is pliant and accepting. I hold her and reach to touch my fingers to her pussy, where she's slick with honey.

"You're wet for me, my dirty girl. You can't get enough of me. You want me inside your tight pink pussy again, don't you, darlin'?"

She arches against me, answering me with her lithe, supple movement.

She's new at this and I know she must be sore but she's also hot as fuck for me. I'm not the only one who's overcome with this wild, out-of-control attraction. I open her with my fingers and position the head of my cock, forcing my way inside her insanely snug, writhing little body. With each buck of the bull, she arches and I slide deeper, until she's riding me as the bull twirls us slowly. I work her slippery clit as I fuck her in time with the ride. She takes each drive, squeezing me with her impossibly tight pussy, like a wet, gripping, magical fist.

Stella moans and I groan along with her. "You feel so fucking good, baby."

"*Oh, God.*" Her body is tensing, her pleasure rising as her inner muscles quiver and tighten around me.

"That's my girl. You're so beautiful." I can't get over her.

But then, without warning, the mechanical bull changes direction. And I'm distracted.

We lose our balance, toppling off the damn thing.

She squeaks with shocked laughter and as we're falling I shift our weight so she lands on top of me.

The cushioned pads on the floor soften the impact.

"Kade," she gasps. She's laughing. Real laughter. She's lying on top of me, her hair framing her face in a multi-colored halo that catches sunlight from the windows behind her. "Are you okay?"

"Almost." Her laughter is infectious and sweet and I kick off my sweatpants because if I don't *get back inside* I'm going to lose my goddamn mind. I grip her hips, pulling her closer, and she guides me into paradise with her soft hands.

She straddles me, still smiling, but her eyes are full of heat now. Determination.

I finger her nipples, twirling and pulling them into tight little peaks. She's holding my cock in her hands, using the head of my shaft to caress her clit in pressing, rhythmic glides.

"That's it, baby. Ride me. Use me. Fuck me hard, darlin'." She does, lowering herself onto me by star-studded degrees. I'm trying to hold onto this. My chest rises and falls with heavy breaths as she sits onto me, impaling herself inch by inch, using her own wetness to take more of me. And more. "Fuck, yes," I groan. "I'm yours, baby girl."

She's *feeling* it, working it. And so am I, gripping her with brutal fingers as I thrust in tune with her bouncing rhythm. She slides along my rigid length, torturing me with wiggling teases, her pussy squeezing me and pulling me deeper.

A realization has taken hold deep inside my heart and it's as profound as the orgasm that's cresting as she starts coming around me, milking my cock with the lush spasms of her body.

I think I've known it all along but it's only gaining exponential momentum. It's bigger than me, and I *want* it to be. It's who I am now.

I'm madly in love with her.

Hard and fast and irrevocably.

I want her.

I want everything.

I fucking *love* her.

13

Stella

Being back out in the world feels strange.

We've spent several days in Kade's apartment.

It's been the most intense time of my life. I have, in every sense of the word, been enlightened. And I hold his hand like an anchor. Already this night promises to be...a lot. I'm meeting his rock star drummer brother and his billionaire cousin. And the private investigator who's going to start the search for my birth family.

The elevator has a glass wall that looks out over the view as it takes us higher. The doors are about to open and we're going to be seeing people and making our way through crowds. It's a million miles away from the haven we've been wrapped in. Already, I miss the crazy intimacy of having him all to myself.

Kade has been mobbed once already and several security guards are in the elevator with us.

His driver brought us to the restaurant and we had to be ushered through security.

It's hard to get used to.

When people see Kade, they don't just recognize him, they get downright rabid. They swarm around him. They're in awe.

So am I, come to think of it.

In our own little world, he's larger than life, but *for me*. I can handle it. I forget that he's a superstar because he's all mine.

Out here, it's a completely different world.

Women cry when they see him. Hulking men have to block people from grabbing him and trying to touch him. Between the car and the entrance of the building, even though it was only around ten steps, a woman broke through the line. She tried to kiss him and had to be pried off of him.

Which both pissed me off and unsettled me. Who behaves like that?

It's *scary* to get rushed like that, and have people wanting a piece of you so badly. Or *him*, more specifically.

How will we live like this? How will *I* live like this? Can whatever is happening between us last? Or are our lives too different?

In our bubble of privacy, none of this came up. It was easy. It felt like something was taking hold, as though our hearts and souls were entwining along with our bodies.

But in the harsh light of the bigger picture, I suddenly

wonder if our whirlwind connection is just a brief, beautiful distraction from his reality.

And mine.

I don't know what next week or even tomorrow will bring—we haven't really talked about that yet, aside from his vague invitation to stay—but this part of his life would be hard to adjust to.

The elevator doors slide open and we're led out to a top floor foyer, which is full of people waiting in line to get in to the restaurant.

We don't have to wait. As soon as the bouncer sees Kade, we're waved through and the guy shakes Kade's hand and makes a fuss of him, like he's royalty. Which I guess, in Nashville, he is.

Inside the crowded restaurant, everyone's outrageously glamorous. They're funky and hip and gorgeous with a down-to-earth edge. This is the see-and-be-seen glitterati of this town. The rich list. The cool cats and the hotshots. They all know Kade and they yell out to him and slap him on the back as we walk past them and make our way deeper into the room.

Every single person is staring at me.

I'm the new girl, and I'm suddenly very conscious of the fact that Kade broke up with his long-term girlfriend just three days ago. He's on the rebound.

I'm the rebound.

They're clearly all curious about the Magic Man's

newest. There are people murmuring like they hadn't heard the news yet. They're pointing and gossiping.

Weirdly, I don't feel as self-conscious as I might have only a few days ago. I'm wearing a wraparound black dress I bought in New York last time I was there, that's cute and flattering, and my tall boots.

And I feel different.

All that enlightenment has changed me. I lost count of all the orgasms after around Day 2. I can feel the warm, strong clasp of his hand. And more than that. The lingering rush of his gifts. *I know how it feels when he comes hard and spills his gushing cum deep inside me, in seedy bursts that overflow. The growling groans he makes when we come together. The sweat and the surge of his big, driving body.*

Our bond gives me a forcefield, like I'm floating above the scrutiny and the speculation. *He's mine now.*

Yikes.

I don't know what to think about any of it, or what to expect. I'm completely out of my element, but it feels good. It's what I've been craving for a long time. An adventure. A wild, whirlwind love affair. An alpha male beefcake who can—and has—shown me what white-hot lust feels like.

He's definitely that.

I don't dwell on the other half of the equation. The part where he may or may not break my heart because he's beyond my wildest dreams and I don't know if it's realistic to expect all this to be mine.

I try to just glide through it.

We get to a table and a man is waiting there who I immediately guess must be Gage. He has thick dark hair and he's gorgeous, in a cocky, arrogant way. You can tell at first glance that he's exceptionally comfortable in his own skin—and that he has every reason to be. He stands up and even as he shakes Kade's hand his gaze is on me, taking in details of his cousin's new...*lover*. "Stella," he smiles widely. "It's a pleasure."

"Nice to meet you, Gage."

Gage takes my hand and kisses my cheek and I feel Kade's burly arm loop itself around me. "All right, all right," he says, pulling me closer to him, like he can't bear for Gage to touch me.

Gage laughs, watching his cousin like there's something about him he doesn't entirely recognize.

We take our seats, Kade keeps me close to him with his arm slung protectively around me and his warm, solid thigh flush against mine as we slide into the horseshoe-shaped leather booth. His protectiveness is on overdrive.

I don't know what I was expecting but I'm not sure it was this. He's the opposite of standoffish. He doesn't care that everyone in this room is watching him claim me as his own. Which is...nice. It makes me believe all the things he said to me even more, not that I doubted him. But he's practically showing me off.

There's a commotion by the door and the squeal of

girls, who are gathering around someone. Whoever it is pushes through them and as soon as I see him, it's easy to tell who he is, from Kade's descriptions.

Vaughn.

People swarm around him but he's intent on getting to us. His eyes are fixed on me.

I guess the whole family is dying to meet Carmen's replacement. I remember Gage's comment. *You're going to have a lot of fans in our family. For rescuing him.*

As I watch Vaughn make his way toward us, I'm struck by the family resemblance. Vaughn's hair is darker, almost black, and it's shorter than Kade's but long enough to stick up in wild waves. He's tall and built, like Kade, but Kade is slightly burlier. Vaughn has more ink. His black shirt is rolled up at the sleeves and his arms are covered in tattoos.

Vaughn arrives at the table, grinning at Kade, like he's looking for tell-tale signs of something, then at me. "Wow."

Kade gives his brother a warning glance and it's entertaining, watching him try to corral Vaughn's mischief. "Stella, meet my brother Vaughn. Vaughn, this is Stella Bell."

Vaughn's blue eyes—so much like his brother's, rimmed with those thick lashes, but a shade darker, like sapphires to Kade's aquamarines—are dancing. He has an energetic, roguish vibe. Kade had mentioned once that

Vaughn is the wild-child of their band and it's written all over him, that he crosses every line. He's doing it now. "Stella Bell," he repeats, still grinning, as though mesmerized by me. He holds out his hand for me to shake and when I take it, it's calloused, like Kade's. Rough from all the drumming he does, no doubt. "It's incredibly nice to meet you, Stella." He kisses the back of my hand playfully.

"Behave," growls Kade, pulling my hand away and weaving his warm fingers through mine.

"Stella, you are my brand new favorite person," Vaughn says, "because my brother right here has been in a slump of biblical proportions and—"

"Vaughn." Kade cuts him off. "Shut the fuck up. Stella's not interested in that."

I look at Kade's face. He's pissed off and...adorable. It's cute that he'd be concerned about this. I already know about his ex-girlfriend, and how unhappy he was. He told me. "Oh, I'm interested." To tease him. Because he cares about what I think and I love this. His gaze meets mine and his anger completely falls away. His tender smile feels like it's all mine. I'm quietly elated, at his happiness. I can read in his body language as he clasps my hand tightly, that he's happy. *And the reason he's happy is because of me.*

Vaughn laughs and winks at me, like we're in this together. "You should know that he's *really* into you. Kade doesn't disappear off the map for days on end for *anyone*. He's too much of a control freak for that, always checking in to see what kind of trouble the rest of us are getting into because he thinks it's his job to keep us on the straight and narrow. But who could blame him for the radio silence? Kade, she's fucking *beautiful*."

"Yes," says Kade. "She is. Now back off."

Vaughn laughs again, enjoying this. He shakes Gage's hand, taking a seat. The conversation turns to Gigi and her book club, and Luna and the renovations of their restaurant and spa. We order drinks and their banter is fun, and funny.

It's unexpected. Here I am, having dinner with two of the most famous rock stars in the world and their investment guru cousin, who, now that I've met him, I realize I read an article about him a few months ago in Forbes. The article referred to him as a "young, hot Warren Buffet."

All three of them are stunning-looking men, with their blue eyes and their thick hair. Their wide shoulders and their long, lean, muscular builds. Every woman in the room is watching them.

They're also watching me, with a *how did she get so lucky?* wistfulness.

Another world-famous musician I recognize, a guy called Clay McFlynn, whose debut album has taken the charts by storm, takes the stage. With the company and the music and the views, I feel like I've stepped through a portal into another person's life.

Kade notices that I've become quiet as I take everything in. "I'm glad you're here with me, honey. I always felt like this place was too glamorous for me. It's nice to be here with someone who does it justice. With you, I almost feel like I fit in."

His words are exactly the right thing to say, as always. Framing it like *he's* the one who's out of place. And as he gazes into my eyes I'm stunned all over again by how gorgeous he is. His dark, blond-edged eyebrows furrowed in the middle with his concern for me. His eyes that clear, deep, blue-on-blue that kills me just a little more every time I stare into them. That mouth that's given me such insanely intimate pleasure, even thinking about it makes me go wet.

I'm so in love with him.

And out here in the bright light of reality—or something close to it—it's disconcerting. I'm far from home in a strange place and all of this is so incredibly new but at the same time has become so incredibly...everything. *He's become the most important thing in my life.*

In a matter of days.

This has all happened so fast it's hard not to get whiplash sometimes, from the sudden and profound change in the entire direction of...absolutely everything.

I know I can't go back to my old life and carry on with ambitions that were never mine. I'll never be able to settle for anything that's not totally...*outstanding*. And it scares me that Kade Tucker has without a doubt ruined me for anyone else.

Kade, as though he's reading my thoughts again, kisses my lips softly. I sigh a little as he does this because he feels and tastes and smells so damn good, and at the sound he deepens the kiss, touching his tongue to mine, right here at the table.

When I break the kiss and pull back from him, Vaughn and Gage are both casually half-staring and half-trying-not-to-stare.

Vaughn gives me the thumbs up and even though I can feel my face getting hot, I smile.

"Kade, can I send a picture of the two of you to Travis and Roxie?" Vaughn asks him. "They need to see this."

"No. You can mind your own goddamn business unless you want my fist to connect with your ugly face." There's no heat in his comment, though, and Vaughn grins at him.

The brothers obviously have a close relationship. They're relaxed and it's easy to sense that there's a deep affection between them.

The food is served. It's a lot of tapas plates for sharing and everything is delicious.

Kade tops up my glass just as another man approaches the table. Gage introduces us. "Stella. Kade. This is Pete Clancy. He's the private investigator we spoke about. He's the best there is."

Pete Clancy is wearing a dark suit. Everything about him is slightly nondescript. He's hard to describe. You get the feeling that he'd be good at his job of checking things out without anyone realizing he's doing it because he blends so seamlessly into a crowd. "I don't know about that but I can do my best to help you with your search, Stella."

"I appreciate that, thank you."

Pete pulls up a chair. "Before we start," he says, "Kade, I thought you might want to know that a Carmen Mills contacted me two days ago. I did some research and found out as much as I could about her. I didn't take her case but I can tell you that she wanted you tracked. And watched. I wouldn't usually give out this kind of information but since you're Gage's cousin I'm making an exception. She also seemed...unstable. When I refused to take her case she threatened to 'send a hit man after me.'"

"What?" The tension in Kade's question makes me uneasy.

"She wanted a complete and up-to-the-minute report on your whereabouts and also those of...your guest. Which I'm assuming is Stella. She seems to know that the two of you are together."

"Goddamn it." Kade is profoundly pissed off by this news.

"That crazy bitch," says Vaughn.

Kade's grip on my hand tightens. "She must have seen something online about us leaving the club on Saturday night."

"Watch your back, is what I'm saying," says Pete.

"She had a good ten-minute rant to me about how you'd wronged her and you 'deserve whatever you get.'"

"Jesus Christ," Kade mutters. "I knew she had issues but I never expected her to take it to fever pitch."

"Doesn't surprise me at all," offers Vaughn. "She always was a nasty piece of work."

"I'll have to beef up our security." Kade's mind seems to be working on several levels. "And make it round the clock."

Pete nods. "Probably a good idea. At least for a while. I'm sure she'll have hired someone else by now to do the job I turned down. She sounded very determined."

I'm listening to their conversation in a mild state of shock.

Beef up security? Round the clock? Hit man?

What the hell?

Kade loops his muscular arm around my shoulders, keeping me close, as though he's already thinking about threats.

I'm sure they're overreacting.

How crazy can she be?

"I'll let you know if I hear any more about who she's hired."

"Thanks, Pete," Kade says.

Pete turns to me. "Now, Stella, tell me about your search."

So here I go. I'm really doing this. "I'm adopted and I'm looking for my birth parents." It feels weird to say the words. I take the letter the woman from the adoption agency gave me out of my bag and show it to him. "This is all I have. I've also written my birthdate and my place of birth down here, which is Charlotte, North Carolina. I don't know what hospital I was born in, or if I was born in a hospital, but the name and address of the agency are here at the bottom of the page. And my phone number. So this is everything."

"Can I take a photo of this?"

"Of course."

He does, and he reads through it. "There's actually a lot of information here. This shouldn't be too difficult."

"Really?"

"I can start on this tonight and get back to you as soon as I've got any leads. My guess is that I'll be able to get you a phone number by the end of the week, if not sooner."

"Wow."

I'm really going to find them. In a few days, it's possible that I'll be able to make contact with the people who gave me away.

Do I really want to?

Do *they* want me to? What if I call them and they hang up on me? What if they gave me away for a reason: that they didn't want me then and don't want me now.

It's jarring to think that I'm close to finding out one way or the other. The thought of finding them digs deep, even more than usual. I hate that every time I think about this or talk about it, I feel like my soul has taken a hit.

"I'm sorry to cut this short." Pete stands up. "If that's everything, I've got another appointment to get to but it was nice meeting you two. I'll be in touch as soon as I've got a lead, Stella."

"Thank you so much."

"And thanks for the heads-up about Carmen," Kade says.

After Pete leaves, Kade turns to me, reading in my eyes that I'm deeply affected by the scenario of finally unearthing some of the information I've wondered about my entire life.

He strokes the backs of his fingers along my cheekbone. "You're going to be okay, whatever happens. Okay? I'm going to be right here the whole time in whatever way you need me to be, and I'm going to help you through it."

Damn it. My eyes tear up because it's exactly what I needed to hear, even if I didn't know that until I heard him say it. "Kade Tucker, stop being so damn perfect, will you?" I joke, swiping a tear away. I don't *want* to cry over this. "I'm going to go to the restroom for a second." I've probably smudged my mascara by now.

"I'll come with you."

I try to breeze past his concern. "I'm going to the ladies' room. You can't come with me." His eyes are so dark. "I'm fine."

I get up, and smile at him when he won't release my hand right away. He doesn't smile back. His gaze scans the room.

God. Is he looking for her?

Is she stalking us?

Is this dangerous?

But I refuse to be intimidated by some psycho ex.

What kind of person hires a private investigator to keep tabs on a guy who broke up with them?

I don't doubt Kade. I trust him. But maybe he didn't make it clear enough to her that he was ending it.

As I make my way to the back of the restaurant, I can't help checking out the people who stare at me as I walk past them. *Are any of them her? Is she watching us now?*

The ladies' room is full of women checking their look in the wall of mirrors.

I find a space. My mascara isn't smudged. It's the only make-up I'm wearing besides some lip gloss, which is gone, so I search in my bag for it. When I look up I realize someone is standing next to me.

Watching me.

Not just out of the corner of her eye but glaring at me with razor-sharp concentration.

She's blonde, an inch or two shorter than me, and very slim. Her eyes are a pale shade of gray. They're piercing and intense. Everything about her is a strange combination of colorless and at the same time sort of harsh. Her whole demeanor is angry. She's stunning-looking but it's not the first thing you notice. If there was even a shred of kindness behind her expression, she would be drop-dead gorgeous. She has wide, owlish eyes, but her eyelashes are too long and too dark for her small, pale face. They're obviously fake and you can't help wondering why she didn't do better with this detail, because everything else about her is groomed and flawless. She's wearing a lot of make-up. Her cheekbones are defined and the lines of her face are angular and almost too sharp, like she hasn't eaten enough lately and she's slightly emaciated. She could be a model, except that her aggression completely overwhelms her beauty. It's clear that her thoughts are ugly and mean, and they beam themselves out of her eyes. I'm wondering if she's dangerous.

And I know exactly who she is.

Wow, she is just all wrong for him, is what I'm thinking. *No wonder he couldn't love her. Or even like her.*

"Can I help you with something?" I attempt, wishing she would stop staring at me like that. My heart is racing. If looks could kill I'd be a bloody pulp on the floor right now.

"Yes. You can help me, as a matter of fact." Her voice is low but somehow still shrill, and there's an off-color note behind it. Like something about her is slightly unhinged.

Another girl is standing next to her, I notice. Her bestie, possibly, since they're standing close and she's eyeing me up sort of critically. She has long dark hair and she's stunningly beautiful. Like, supermodel beautiful.

But I'm not interested in being judged by these

women. I don't know what they want from me or what they're expecting. Yes, I'm head over heels to the point of not actually being able to even think about being apart from my new...*lover*, but it's too soon to call him my "boyfriend" or anything more. Nothing has been decided. I don't know where we stand. And I hardly want to have a showdown in the ladies' room with his crazy ex.

"You can stay the hell away from my boyfriend, that's what you can *help* me with."

Wow.

It's unbelievable, but I look her in the eye because I hate bullies. I was lucky enough never to have been bullied in school, but that was partly because I tend to stand up to their bullshit. I just have zero tolerance for it. "You're Carmen?"

"Yes." A shadow of vulnerability flickers. "Did he tell you about me?"

I try to say it gently because she's obviously devastated and also a loose cannon. "He mentioned you broke up, yes."

"We didn't *break up*. We had one small argument and we were working through it. We didn't even get a chance to do that before you showed up and now you're ruining everything."

Jesus.

"We were about to get *engaged*," she says. "We were shopping for *rings*."

"I..." Shit. "I don't know if that's going to happen.

But if you're unsure, maybe you should talk to him about it."

"I've been trying to. But he won't answer my calls. Because of you."

"I'm not sure if it's entirely because of me, or maybe he just feels like he made it clear and he's moved on. Now if you'll excuse me, I'm leaving."

"What's your name?"

I don't want to tell her my name. She probably already knows if she's hired a private investigator, and I'm hardly going to give her more ammunition. "I'm leaving now," I say again.

But Carmen and her friend are blocking my way. "How can you just show up like this and steal my boyfriend and think that's okay?"

It's a strange feeling to be face to face with a person who's clearly walking some kind of line. She's either suffering from a serious case of denial, or she has some deeper issues I'm not about to analyze. It doesn't surprise me that someone would go to extreme lengths to keep Kade Tucker, and I get the feeling she would do exactly that, to the point of recklessness. I feel protective of Kade. No wonder he was so unhappy and his family was worried about him. "He made it clear that he wasn't anyone's boyfriend," I say. "I think maybe you should let him go and get on with your life."

"As if I would let Kade Tucker *go* without a fight," she seethes.

I can't say I blame her for being wrecked over losing him. He's about as perfect as a man can be. But I can't help her with that. And I'm done here. "I hope you have a nice night." I try to walk past her but her bony fingers grip my arm. I yank away from her because her touch is *cold*.

"Stay away from him. He's *mine*."

Maybe she's having some kind of breakdown. And this is starting to piss me off. "I don't think *he* thinks he's yours."

"I'm warning you!" That mad, shrill edge to her voice is becoming more pronounced. "He and I have some things we need to work through and you're getting in the way of that. I can't let you do that. Kade is everything to me."

"I'm..." The look in her eyes makes me pause. I say it sort of gently, "I'm not in charge of Kade's decisions."

"Go back to wherever you came from and leave him alone."

I exhale a disbelieving—and slightly terrified—huff. "I'm going back to my table."

"Did you hear what I *said*? Kade and I are meant to be together. He was getting ready to *propose* to me when you showed up! He's practically my fiancé and I'm not letting you steal him! So back the fuck off. I mean it. *Leave*. Now. Tonight."

Wow. I'm trying to stay calm and not provoke her. "I don't think Kade feels the same way. Go and talk to him if you want to. It's up to him to decide who he's with."

"I'm warning you. You'll regret it if you don't take the advice I'm giving you right now."

I've had enough of this. She's freaking me out. I push past her and get to the door, making my way back through the crowded restaurant. It looks different now. More crowded, and darker. When I glance behind me to see if she's following me, I can't see her.

I get to the table where Kade, Vaughn and Gage are standing now, talking to people. Kade sees me and immediately notices the look my face. "Stella. What's wrong? You're white as a sheet. What happened?"

"I just...ran into someone." God. My heart is racing.

"Who?"

I don't even need to say it. "Can we go now?"

"Of course we can." Kade's expression gets very dark. His gaze scans the room and his arm loops around me protectively. "That evil little bitch," he mutters.

Gage and Vaughn have heard the conversation. "Let's go," says Vaughn, and we're starting to head toward the door when the two women approach us.

"Hi, Vaughn." It's Carmen's dark-haired friend, eyeing him up much more brazenly than the situation calls for. She's flirting with him, but he's lost all of his playfulness. His expression is almost as furious as Kade's.

"Amber," he says coldly, and it couldn't be any clearer that he's exceptionally unhappy to see her.

Carmen's tears have smudged her make-up. She frowns when she sees Kade's arm firmly around me. "Kade." She's demure now and has lost most of that psycho-killer edge. "You won't answer my calls. I wanted to talk to you. Why won't you *talk* to me?"

"There's nothing to talk about. Leave us the fuck alone." Absolutely scathingly. Kade is the kindest, most perceptive and empathetic person I've ever met. He's also a big, jungle-cat alpha male, and his brutal aggression gets everyone's attention. A crazy hatred is practically radiating off him in waves.

So he did make it clear to her that things between them were very much over. And he's doing it again now. There's really not even a shadow of a doubt for her to cling to.

Gage signals to some of the security guards and they swarm around us.

Carmen's crying now. "*Please*, Kade. I miss you so much. I know we can work it out. I *love* you."

He doesn't even give her a backward glance as the security ushers us out, blocking Carmen and Amber and preventing them from following us.

"You'll regret this!" Carmen shrieks. "*Both* of you!"

WE DON'T SAY much on the ride back to Kade's place.

Vaughn and Gage had their own rides and, even

though the fun vibe of the evening had been shattered, they were charming and sweet as they said goodnight to us. They insisted that I meet Gigi and Luna as soon as we can make a plan and I told them I would love that.

Which I would.

But I can't think too far ahead.

I'm rattled by the twisted-ex-from-hell confrontation.

Kade seems more rage-filled than rattled, and it has ground all conversation to a screeching halt. It reminds me that we've only known each other for a few days and also that the bond between us feels like it's forged in invisible steel. The combination is confusing me and twisting my emotions into knots. I don't know how to feel.

Kade makes a few phone calls about bodyguards and whatnot in the car and by the time we get back to his house there are already noticeably more of them.

I hate this. I'm glad I'm not famous.

We're being stalked.

We take the elevator back up and just as we're stepping back into his apartment, my phone pings with an incoming message. I've been in touch with my parents only by text and I've talked to Summer once but I should probably call both of them at some point and assure them that I'm still breathing.

As I'm reaching into my bag to get my phone, something falls out.

A small black velvet box.

Kade leans down to pick it up. He's quicker than me.

"What's this?" he asks.

I try to reach for it but he moves it out of reach.

He opens the box. Inside is the diamond ring Theo gave me. "What the fuck is this?" I flinch a little at his question. It feels sort of hard-hitting.

We're both on edge. "It's...the ring. I told you. I got proposed to. By my boyfriend."

"Your *boyfriend?*"

"My *ex* boyfriend, Kade. Obviously."

"You still have the *ring?*" There's a wild flare in his blue eyes I haven't seen before.

"I—"

"I thought you said no."

"I did say no."

"Then why do you still have the ring?"

I don't know why he's getting so riled about this. "He wanted me to keep it for a while. In case I change my mind."

Kade spears me with a blue glare. "Are you *thinking* of changing your mind, Stella?"

"No." His reaction is so over the top.

"But you kept the ring anyway, just in case?"

"I haven't seen him again since then, after that night, to give the ring back."

A hot pause. "Are you *going* to see him again?"

"I mean, eventually, I might—"

"You *might?*"

I almost laugh a little because this is so overblown.

"Kade. The only reason I might see him is to give him *back* the ring. I only kept it because he asked me to. I felt bad about it, that I'd turned him down. He asked me to hold onto it for a while, to make sure I was sure, and I felt like it was the least I could do. After disappointing him like that. I don't know why I have to even explain all this."

Our first argument.

It occurs to me that it's all about *them*. The people that came before who might try to threaten our very-new bond.

But now that we're back in our bubble, those threats feel farther away. Buffered and like they belong in the past, not here and now. I can read that his fury is all about his wild concern that something or someone might come between us.

And there's something shockingly endearing about his reaction.

He *cares*, so much.

And so do I.

Both of us have baggage. His baggage happens to be a fraction more psychotic than my baggage but we're both sort of feverish about guarding and protecting this sudden whirlwind of a relationship.

"Are you having second thoughts about turning him down?" There's so much intensity to him, and also a deep, unmistakable note of panic, like if I did happen to have the slightest bit of indecision over it, it would break his heart.

"No." As if I'd go back to Theo after this. After Kade freaking Tucker. "Not a single one."

He's glaring down at me warily, looming over me with his wide shoulders and his pumped-up muscles, reminding me again of how big he is. *And how beautiful.* He looks wild and worked up. His thick hair frames his face off-handedly, artfully mussed up. "Good. Because I'll fucking kill the fucker."

There's a strange rush that comes from his jealousy. I *like* that he's in knuckle-dragging mode. It's turning me on. And so is the shape of his mouth and its pissed-off glower. "Of course you will." I might be teasing him. Baiting his lust even more.

"I don't want you seeing him again."

My panties go wet and I suddenly feel...*voracious.* For him. All the stress of the night has us both fired up and I can feel that fire pulsing inside me. "I don't want to see him again."

God.

I want to provoke him in a different way, by showing him how much he means to me. I want to feed on his over-the-top beauty and take it inside. *I want to drink it.* I don't actually even recognize myself right now, or how much I need him. All I know is that I'm feeling it. *Hard.* I'm *starving* for what he has to give.

I take his hand, walking backwards as I pull him toward the couch. I'm coy about it but he's watching my eyes. For a second I wonder if he'll pull his hand away, but he doesn't.

"The person I want to see and think about is you." Gently, I push him back so he's sitting. "And there's something I'd like to try...if you'll let me."

More glowering.

"It has to do with you and...what I want to *do* to you. Right now."

The faintest hint that he's starting to relent.

"If you'll let me, that is." I climb onto him, straddling him. He's so much bigger than I am and my smallness makes me feel powerfully feminine. And sexy. I love the way he's looking at me right now, like he wants to eat me alive but also like he absolutely *loves* me.

I take the small box out of his hand and place it on the table next to us. "I told you already. I wasn't in love with him, even before I met you." He's still glaring at me. His eyes flash with his own fire and I can see there his jealousy, his anger, his protectiveness, his raging lust. "And now that I *have* met you, no one could really compare to...well, *this*."

I lean closer. Very softly, I brush my lips against his.

He doesn't kiss me back. He's testing me. I can sense that he's just as ravenous as I am—or ten times more so, and his fury is sort of daunting—but that he's holding it, waiting for me to tell him what he wants to hear.

"Not that I have any basis for comparison, since I'm so new at all this..." I kiss him again, touching my tongue to his lips as I begin to grind against the hard ridge of his gigantic, throbbing erection through the layers of our clothing. "...but I don't think anyone could compare to *this* either."

I untie the wrap of my dress, opening it, easing it off my shoulders until it falls away.

"I haven't thought about him or anything else since the second I walked away. I've been busy, see. *Very* busy. Thinking about someone else. *Feeling* for someone else. Having all my magical firsts with someone else."

I unclasp my bra and let that fall away too and at this point I'm wondering *who is this nympho doing a striptease and what have you done with shy, always-doing-what-she's-told Stella Bell?* But then I forgive myself because this is Kade Tucker we're talking about and also I'm too damn hot for him to worry about it.

"And I've realized something."

I unbutton the top button of his shirt.

"There's another first I'd like to try. I mean, if you don't mind."

His dark curiosity is there, behind his quiet awe and his cool-hot silence.

"It's something I really, *really* want to do. To you. I've never done it before and I just feel like…I *need* it."

I undo another button. And another.

Until his shirt is open.

I feather my fingers through the pelt of hair on his

chest and I lean in to kiss his nipple, taking it lightly between my teeth.

He flinches and—there it is, his surrender—he exhales sharply and grips me with his iron-strong hands, watching me now with a worshipful severity.

I move further down his body, fingering his belt buckle. Undoing it. Unbuttoning his jeans and slowly unzipping him.

"I want to suck on you," I murmur, licking his arrow line of hair. "I want to make you come like this."

Yikes. What am even saying?

I don't care. I do. "I want to taste you."

"You're a dirty little angel." His voice is rasped and I feel a small thrill of triumph that I've broken through. He's going to let me do it, I can tell. He'll give me anything I want. His jealousy has distilled itself into uncut, hundred-proof lust. "How bad do you want it, sugar pie?"

"*Bad.*"

"You want me to fuck that sweet little mouth."

"Yes. *Please.*"

His movement is slow, his gaze lazy and hot as he pushes his jeans lower, taking out his enormous cock like an offering. *Oh my God.* It's hard as steel and dusky, with ridged veins running the length of it, textured and silky. The broad tip leaks with moisture and I lick my lips because he's just so beautiful. So outrageously male and absolutely mouthwatering. I reach for him carefully but some primal craving has taken hold in me and I can't wait a second longer. I want to taste him with a fever I don't even recognize.

My fingers curl around him and I touch my tongue to the slit, licking him. Another surge seeps onto my tongue and I drink it. He tastes milky and salty, and I *love* this. It's a strange, obsessive kind of hunger. I want mouthfuls of him. Easing my lips over the head, I suckle on him like he's sugar-coated. I take more of him. And more. He's so big I can't take all of him but I use my hands to gently squeeze and rub and explore.

"*Oh, f-u-u-uck,*" Kade growls and I can sense that he's totally at my mercy. I can tell that what I'm doing to him is deeply, profoundly pleasurable, to the point that he can barely handle it. His fingers weave through my hair. "*Fuck, I'm going to come. Oh, hell, you feel too good.*"

I love that I can give him this. I love that this big, powerfully-built rock god is entirely slayed by the touch of my tongue and the tender play of my mouth. The carnal need to take him higher becomes everything, until I'm feasting on him, sucking strongly and taking him as deep as I can. It's then that he groans like his heart is breaking. His cock surges, flooding my mouth with pumping bursts of warm, thick cum and I drink him thirstily. It's his magical, seedy essence and I want all of it. It's nourishing me in a way that's completely life-changing.

Kade Tucker is mine. He's inside me and I feel full and perfect and owned.

His breathing is heavy and it takes him a while to recover. I lick and kiss his barely-softened shaft. He pulls me up to him, lifting me and carrying me to bed. He peels off my clothes and wraps his big body around me, staring into my eyes, kissing my face sort of reverently. I feel so safe.

"Unicorn girl," he whispers.

"Magic man," I whisper back.

"I love you."

14

Stella

A LOUD WHIRRING noise wakes us.

Kade's arm is looped around me, heavy and warm.

"Get your lazy ass out of bed, Kade Tucker," someone yells from somewhere inside his apartment. It's a woman's voice. She sounds young.

"Shit," mutters Kade. "My sister's here."

There's more of the whirring sound which I can now identify as a coffee bean grinder and it's not long before the smell of brewing coffee wafts into the room.

"Your tour bus leaves in two hours, your majesty," she yells out. "No one needs that much beauty sleep, not even you."

The loud footsteps of what I'm guessing might be cowboy boots gets closer and there's a banging on the bedroom door. "KJ. Wake up."

"Jesus, Rox," Kade groans. "What the fuck?"

"I'm barging in there if you're not out in five. Coffee's almost ready."

"Then take it to your own apartment and drink it over there. Come back in an hour."

She's quiet for a second, maybe realizing that he has company. "Fine. You've got one hour and not a minute longer." Her footsteps head back out to the kitchen. There's the banging of a kitchen cupboard. Then she walks through the living room and there's the thud of the door that leads out to the deck slamming shut.

"She loves slamming doors."

"Where's your tour bus taking you?" I murmur into the crook of his neck.

"New Orleans. I've got a gig there tonight. Which you're coming to, by the way."

I wriggle loose of his bear hug, or at least attempt to. His burly arm stays secure around me. "New Orleans?"

"Yes. I have a house there. You'll like it."

"But...I can't go to New Orleans."

"Why not?"

"I've never been there."

"That's a reason *to* go to New Orleans, not to *not* go to New Orleans."

We still haven't talked about any kind of plans or how we're going to handle whatever's happening, going forward. "We need to talk about that. I can't just put my life on hold forever—"

"You're not putting your life on hold, darlin.' You're

starting to live it. Exactly the way you want to. Remember?"

But just the mention of real life sort of highlights all the responsibilities I've completely ignored for days on end. "God, I need to go get my car. It's still parked in that parking garage. I hope it hasn't been towed. It said long-term but it's been almost a week and I need to call my sister and let my parents know that I'm—"

"I'll get someone to get your car and park it in my private garage. Which is in the building just around the corner. You can call your sister on the way to New Orleans. And your parents. Tell them you'll be back in Nashville in a week. And you've decided to stay here while you write your book."

He says it so matter-of-factly, like there's nothing to protest or work through. He lays me onto my back. He's kissing my breasts, nuzzling my nipples and sucking one, then the other into his mouth. I try to push him away but there's no dislodging him. "*Kade.* We need to talk about some of this stuff. All we do is have sex and at some point we really need to figure a few things out."

"We just did." He moves lower, kissing a line down my stomach. "Besides, sex with you is too good to think about anything else. Baby, I need my fix so bad."

Before I can squirm away—which is impossible because he's as strong as a damn ox—to try to figure out how I'm going to handle what feels like sort of a major decision, he's pinning my legs wide and his mouth is on me, licking me slowly, tasting me deeply. *"Mine,"* he's murmuring against me as he lazily eats me out. *"Fuck, you are the sweetest thing. You're mine, baby girl. This pussy is mine. Mine. Mine."*

Kade Tucker *loves* going down on me. And he isn't just good at it, he's a freaking genius. His dirty mouth paints me with warm sensation, delving deep as he fucks me with his tongue.

My mind goes blank and I forget what I was about to tell him. I let my fingers weave through the thick silk of his hair, letting him do whatever he wants.

He sucks on my clit, feasting on my pleasure with his sexual-spiritual hunger until I'm shattering in tight, clenching bursts of pleasure as I moan his name.

When the ripples begin to calm, he climbs up my body and uses the wetness to ease his massive cock's entry, sliding his huge thickness deep inside me, forcing me to take all of him. He feels like hot, thick magic. It stretches me, pressing and rubbing every pleasure point I own, driving into me with possessive strokes that give me no choice but to take all of him. I wrap my arms and my legs around him as he whispers sweet words to me. *You're my paradise. I love how you feel. You're the most beautiful girl in the world.*

Until the orgasm becomes the highest and most intense one yet, each time. The pleasure isn't just physical, but whole-souled. My emotions and my cravings have wrapped themselves around this man along with my body.

He's imprinting himself into every part of me so insistently that I don't know how I'm going to survive him. With him or without him. He takes me again to the heights of what I can handle, filling me to the brink with his flooding heat until my body is squeezing and drawing as much of him inside as I can take. Until I'm overflowing with cum and the pleasure overload he insists on.

And when we're both sated, slowly coming down from all that, he says, "Now, what were you saying?"

"I can't remember."

He laughs softly and pulls out. The gush of his cum spills out of me. "Come on. We're taking a shower. Then we're going to New Orleans."

15

Stella

KADE IS HEATING up some homemade biscuits. He pulls them out of the oven and smooths some real butter onto them with a knife. He puts two on a plate and sets it in front of me.

"Where are your keys?" he asks. "One of my assistants can go and get your car."

"Kade Tucker has assistants?" I don't know why I find this funny.

"I think I have three or four of them, I can't keep track. Roxie organizes them."

"I can just go and get it. It's not far—"

"They'll do it."

"Are you sure they won't mind, I can easily—"

"Yes. What do you drive?"

I get my keys out of my bag. "A white 2010 Honda Civic."

His eyebrows furrow in the middle. "2010?" Like this is somehow unbelievable to him. No doubt he drives something brand new and top of the line.

"Well," I say, "we can't all be rock stars. It has a Princeton sticker on the bumper. I have some cash in here somewhere for the parking."

"Put that away, darlin'. I bought you a present, by the way. And now I know the next present I'm getting you. I also thought we could courier that minuscule diamond over there back to New Jersey where it belongs. Since you won't be needing it anymore."

I'm still looking in my bag for the three hundred dollar bills I stashed in a side pocket in case of emergencies. I hope it's enough. I glance over at the table where the small, innocent little velvet box is still sitting. "Sure. But we'd better track it. I wouldn't want it to go missing."

"No, that would be a crying shame."

"I want to include a note." I dig around in my bag to find a piece of paper and a pen. But what to say? I keep it short, scrawling onto the paper: *Hi Theo, I wanted to return this to you. I really appreciate the offer. You're a special person and I'm sorry things didn't work out between us. I hope we can still be friends. xo, Stella*

"*XO?*" Kade's reading the note over my shoulder. "Why the fuck would you be sorry?"

Here we go again. I huff a light laugh. "Seriously?" I once fantasized about meeting an alpha, and I guess this comes with the territory. His jealousy is on overdrive. He's not wearing a shirt, and his big, inked muscles are sort of clenched and pumped up.

So I patiently explain. "I didn't want to write 'love' or 'yours,' because neither of those are true. 'Best' sounds too formal, and so does 'sincerely.' But 'xo' is basically innocuous, almost like a punctuation. I *am* sorry if I caused Theo any sadness, which I did, because he's a friend and I don't like doing that to people. But I'm not sorry he proposed."

Kade's eyes narrow a fraction.

"His proposal was a big part of the reason I needed to get away from Princeton. It's part of the reason I ended up in Nashville, in the pouring rain on the night I ran into you. If it wasn't for Theo, I never would have met you."

He begrudgingly accepts that. "Here." A large wrapped rectangular box is sitting on the marble counter. He pushes it closer to me. "Open it."

"What's this?"

"I guess you'll have to open it to find out."

"I don't want you buying me presents." This whole thing feels very uneven, money-wise. He obviously has more money than God, but still.

"Open it." He pours me another cup of coffee. He always makes sure I get exactly two.

I unwrap the white paper. Inside is a sleek, plastic-wrapped white box. With a very-familiar apple logo on the top of it. "Is this...?"

"It's the newest MacBook Pro."

Wow. These things cost a fortune. "I already have a laptop."

"I thought it might be good for you to have a new one. A fresh start. To write your book."

It's true my old Dell is starting to show its age. I bought it the summer before I started college. But this is way too much. "Kade, I can't accept this."

"No protesting. Surrender to the process. This is the beginning of your new life. We'll get you all set up and I want to see a draft of chapter one by the end of the week."

"I don't want you buying me things, I've told you that."

"I've got more money than I can spend, darlin.' And Gage keeps tripling the damn stuff." He pulls me closer, leaning to kiss my neck in an intimate claim. He unwraps the plastic and opens the box.

I mean, it's a *beautiful* machine. "You're like my therapist, my fantasy man and my enlightenment instructor all rolled into one," I tell him. "And now my sugar daddy too? It's a little much."

"Don't forget knight in shining armor." He takes a bite of a biscuit. Then he laughs.

The door to the patio opens and in walks one of the most beautiful women I've ever seen. Kade's sister. She has long dark hair and the same movie-star blue eyes as Kade and Vaughn. With her boots, jeans and fitted plaid shirt, she's got a real cowgirl vibe. She's petite and cute but you get the feeling from the direct, no-nonsense look on her face that she's someone people would think twice about messing with. She's also clearly another family member who's wildly curious about her brother's guest. "Now that's a sound I haven't heard in a long time," she says, checking me out from head to toe.

"What sound?" Kade asks.

"You. Laughing."

Kade winks at me. "Stella Bell, my sister Roxie. Rox, this is Stella."

Roxie walks over to me, smiling widely. "Can I hug you?"

"Uh, sure."

She gives me a heartfelt hug. "I'm so happy you're here."

"Let's not be melodramatic, honey," Kade says to her, still grinning.

Roxie holds the hug for a few seconds longer. Then she holds me at arms length, with her hands on my shoulders. "Kade, she's perfect. Can we keep her?"

"She's definitely a keeper," he says.

Roxie helps herself to one of the biscuits from the warming tray. "Do you realize you haven't laughed or hardly even smiled *once* in the last few months? This situation is a million times better. And a lot less scary."

She's being subtle, sort of, but I know who Roxie's referring to, of course. "We ran into her last night," I say.

Roxie's eyes get wide. "You *did*? What happened? Did she go ballistic?"

"It was sort of terrifying," I admit.

"Holy fuck," Roxie says. "I've spent all of the past five months worrying that she'd somehow get her hooks even deeper in. She's crazy and unpredictable and I didn't trust her as far as I could throw her."

"Yeah, we don't need to talk about her anymore." Kade is clearly uncomfortable with the topic. "She's ancient history."

"Let's hope so," Roxie adds, "For all our sakes." I immediately get the impression that Roxie's one of those people who says everything that pops into her head. "I just hope she doesn't do something like try to get revenge—"

"Rox," Kade cuts her off. "You coming to New Orleans with us?"

She grins at me. "Stella's going with you?"

"Of course she is. She has a book to write."

"You're a writer?"

"Well, not quite. I'm hoping to figure it out as I go."

"As much as I'd love to be your third wheel, everything's organized, so you don't need me. All you have to do is show up." Roxie pulls her phone out of her back pocket and checks an incoming message. "The bus is here."

Roxie hugs us both again, gushing a few more times about how happy she is to meet me.

A short time later, I find myself on the most state-of-the-art bus I've ever seen. Inside, it looks like a night club, with a big-screen TV, a kitchen, living room and four upstairs bedrooms.

Kade leads me to two leather couches that face each other next to the big windows and I take a seat on one as he answers a phone call.

The bus starts up and we drive through central Nashville and I look out the windows and I'm struck by how at home I feel in this city that's so new to me. Something about it feels like it's already digging in, so easily, like a piece of it already lived there before I even arrived.

We fire up the MacBook and it's not long before everything is set up with my email and office.

I open a brand new document.

Kade's sitting on the opposite facing leather couch picking out a tune on his guitar. I watch him for a while and it strikes me how comfortable it all feels, with him. Some people just have a calming presence about them and he's one of those people. Like he's absorbing angst and emitting it back out as a staunch, manly peacefulness. His relaxed, supportive vibe gives me the confidence to start.

I type in *Chapter One*.

It's daunting.

The little cursor sits there on the blank page pointing at all that nothingness.

The music stops and I look up at him.

"Don't be scared of it," he says, strumming a chord. "Just start writing whatever comes to mind. Don't worry about whether it's good or bad to begin with. Start typing and let whatever you can think of just pour itself onto the pages. Ready?"

I take a deep breath. "I don't know if I can do it."

"Of course you can do it. Just start right there on page one and keep going."

And so I do. I start writing.

It comes surprisingly easily. I realize I've been thinking a lot about how the story is going to unfold. I've read a thousand books and with each one I noticed the things I liked about the characters and the plot lines. The settings and the twists. All of it. I've got everything mapped out in my head.

So I start with my heroine. Her name is Daisy. She's from New York City. I know the landscape of her days. I can see the slant of the light in her one-bedroom apartment she chose for the windows and the view, and the tiny balcony that, if you stand at the southernmost end, you can see the Empire State Building. She bought the apartment with the money from her first exhibition, which got her noticed. Her thoughts land fully formed. Her excitement for her work. Her best friends and her memories of her most recent bad dates. And there, in the middle of everything, is the big hole of loneliness of one specific kind. Not that she *needs* a man. She's self-sufficient. She's the envy of her friends because she's getting serious attention from the critics and the buyers for her talent. She's selling her paintings for real money and one of her pieces was recently written up in the Times.

"We're here, darlin'."

"What?"

The bus has come to a stop.

Wow. I've been writing for six hours straight. "What time is it?"

"Around seven. Come on."

I instantly fall in love with Kade's house in New Orleans. It's grand but also quaint, with original features that have been restored with an artist's flair and modern detailing. Stained glass lamps paint the cozy spaces with romantic, colorful light. The house is rambling, and Kade leads me up to the master bedroom. There's a massive bed that looks like something from a magazine spread. But there are personal touches too. An old bass guitar on a stand. Some photographs on the dresser of Kade as a teenager with his brothers. I walk closer. There's another photo, of a young couple, smiling and looking very much in love. The man has dark hair. I can see Vaughn in him. And Roxie has the same coloring. The woman has light brown hair with sun-bleached streaks of blond. She's dreamily beautiful and I can see Kade in the shape of her eyes. "Is this your parents?"

"Yes. Just before they got married." The heaviness of their memory in him carries weight. "They died in a car accident."

"I'm sorry, Kade."

"It was a long time ago now. Here, I want to show you something. Come with me."

He leads me to the far end of the bedroom where there's a door. He opens it and I follow him up a narrow, curved staircase that leads to another room. It has a double bed, a couch, several chairs and a large wooden desk that sits next to a curving nook of paned, old-glass windows. From up here you can see the garden behind the house and some trees and rooftops.

It's literally the most to-die-for space I could have imagined.

Kade turns on the green glass library lamp that's sitting on the desk. "It could be a good workspace for you while we're here, if you like it."

"I love it," I whisper, sort of stunned by *how much* I love it. I wander through the room, feathering my fingers across the surface of the desk. The chair is one of those modern ergonomically-designed office chairs but it's made of leather, so it fits in with the softer details of this perfect room. I half-sit against the sturdy desk, taking it all in. "I love both your houses but this one's my favorite."

He smiles, his head tilting ever so slightly. His eyes are so soulful and blue I wonder if I'm dreaming him. "I'm glad you like it. I have a few more to show you too."

It's hard to get used to. "Houses. Tour buses. Staff. Number one hits. There must be nothing you haven't achieved."

"There's one thing." He's gotten all intense about it, but he takes his time. One of the things I love most about him is his easy unhurriedness. There's not a rushed or agitated thing about him. He's steady. He's someone you want to lean your life against because you know you won't fall down if he's there supporting you.

"What else could you want that you don't already have?"

"One of the two things I wanted out of life came easily. The music. My brothers and I have been playing together since we were kids. We had some talent, a lot of drive and a look that people were intrigued by. Most of all, we *believed* it would happen. Right from the start, the whole thing gained momentum and took on a life of its own. That part of the equation was sort of effortless. I mean we worked at it and that's basically all we do so I'm not going to say it was easy, but in a lot of ways it *was* easy. Once we made the decision to make ourselves heard, it turned out that a few people wanted to listen."

"A lot of people," I say softly. "Your songs are numbers one, two, four and eight on the billboard charts right now."

"You googled us?"

"I googled you."

A smile plays at the corner of his mouth, like he's pleased by this. "What'd you find out?"

"That you're even more of a superstar than I knew. That you're a 'dreamy beefcake' and 'the sexiest mystery man in music.' Also that you're a one-woman man and you don't usually sleep around. You tend to have long-term relationships, unlike your brothers."

"It said all that?"

"And a lot more."

"Well, that's it right there. That's the other part of the equation. The one that's a lot harder to find."

"What other part of the equation?"

"The other thing I wanted out of life. To fall in love." He's quiet for a few seconds, but then he says, "I felt like I was wasting time and spinning my wheels but going nowhere. I was starting to think it was never going to happen for me."

I get this flutter of wild, tumbling hope somewhere behind my soul but I don't give it oxygen because I couldn't bear it if I'm wrong about what he's going to say next.

"So I decided," he continues, "that I wasn't going to try anymore because it clearly wasn't in the cards for me and it was always just so damn disappointing. Not just disappointing. Heartbreaking. I spent years with a broken heart. So I gave up."

"You did?" I whisper.

"I did. You want to know when I made that decision?"

"When?"

"Exactly five minutes before I ran into you on that dark street in the pouring rain."

"You…did?"

"I did. And right at that moment, as soon as I looked into your green eyes that were breaking my heart even more but at the same time fixing it because there was something so wrong about such a beautiful girl crying and getting rained on, so lost and all alone. But that's when I knew."

He knew.

I can barely whisper the words. "You knew what?"

"I knew that I wasn't giving up after all. Because there you were. And I realize that was, in fact, only a week ago. Which you might think is too soon to be having revelations like this. You might be thinking that we've just spent a week in bed together and it's fireworks every single time but that doesn't necessarily mean it's love, because we don't know each other very well and we don't know all the intricacies of each other's personalities or backstories or families or moods. You might think a week isn't long enough to know if you're in love with someone or not, that it's attraction, and lust, but not more than that yet, because it's too soon. But the thing is, darlin', I don't think it is too soon. Because I knew it from that very first second. I knew it then and I know it now. I've been looking for it for a long time so I know what's been missing and I know when it's not missing anymore. When it's suddenly there and real and it feels better than anything ever has. With you, it felt like I took a direct hit from a million watt lightning bolt. I love the color of your eyes and the way your long eyelashes get blond at the very tips. I love your little dimple and the way it quirks when I've said something you like. I love the scent of you, like springtime. I love that we laugh. I love how you're as beautiful on the inside as you are on the outside. I love that you're a romantic, like me. I fucking love the way you feel. And I realize it's not something you might be able to accept for a while and I get that. It's okay. I can take my time and I'll work on convincing you. There's no rush. But I'm all in, baby. I'm in love with you. Like, *crazy* in love with you. And I don't want you to say anything or do anything but wanted you to know that."

God.

I stare into his blue eyes and I can't believe I've found him. "I'm in love with you too, Kade Tucker."

His eyes get those yummy crinkles at the edges and he steps closer, sliding his warm hand around the nape of my neck. "Yeah?"

"Yeah."

"Well, that's good news."

He kisses me.

And I don't get any more writing done that night.

16

Stella

Our days and nights take on a dreamlike quality. I write with a sort of frenzy that takes on a life of its own. I've never been so totally *immersed* in anything I've done before. Not like this. And my first chapter begins to take shape.

When the pages are ready to show, Kade reads them. His comments are thoughtful and straight to the point. He's perceptive. He's a good first reader and I start to rely on his insights.

He cooks for me and insists I eat well to keep my energy up. I tell him he could definitely have a second career as a chef but he says he's too busy keeping me satisfied.

When I'm not writing, we're making love. Sometimes I'm writing *while* we're still connected. It often feels like one long, constant act because we can't bear to separate ourselves. He'll sit with me in the writing room and play his acoustic bass guitar, or the old rhythm guitar that's the one from his room, which has a deep, resonant sound. He'll quietly work out new songs or he'll play me the older ones, which I love. His music becomes a sort of playlist that inspires me as I dig deeper and write more pages, and more.

Kade plays three shows at different New Orleans venues on three consecutive nights, and I go with him. At the New Year's Eve show, Kade sets up a place for me backstage where I can watch him. Word is out that Kade Tucker has a new love interest and people want to know. They want gossip and they want photographs. Which is sort of terrifying. We do our best to maintain as much privacy as we can.

I try not to think about his ex or the private investigator or any of the rest of it. He has more than enough security to keep us safe. But it's *there*, in the darkness beyond the faces of the crowd. The feeling of being watched, like a silent threat that sometimes worries me.

When he's on stage, Kade sings to me, that's how it feels and that's what he tells me. He told me he's never played better. I don't know if that's true but his music has become like the man himself: a part of me. He's my first reader and I'm his favorite fan.

Occasionally as I watch him or as he feeds me or as we lay in each other's arms with our bodies still deeply, blissfully connected and still rippling with the intensity of our lovemaking, I can't help myself. I wonder if this is too good to be true.

Can two people really fall this *deeply,* this *quickly?*

Yes. I think that's possible.

I *know* it's possible.

Our relationship has clicked into place so easily. It's both fun and hot, thrilling and at the same time comforting. We've had only one argument so far—if it was even that—over the ring Theo gave me. Kade had it couriered back to Princeton and we haven't discussed it again.

Kade Tucker is gorgeous and sexy and alpha as all hell, but my favorite thing about him is that he's *kind.* He's profoundly *good.* It's this quality (along with the sex on a stick masculinity and that giant magic wand he insists on pleasuring me with all day, every day as a close second) that I love most of all.

But I can't help wondering sometimes...*can it continue to be this easy and this perfectly in tune, with no bumps in the road or doubts or intrusions?*

I don't know.

Probably not.

Maybe it can.

My concerns pass when Kade looks into my eyes or thrusts even harder or writes me a new song.

I decide not to question it. I decide to let it be as beautiful as it is.

What I realize is that Kade has given me, along with all that comes with being his lover, the gift of myself. He's helped me tune into the things I want most of all but have never really given the time to breathe. With him, I feel like the best, technicolored version of myself. It's an outrageously addictive feeling.

Kade is cooking me breakfast when Summer calls me on FaceTime. I've talked to her regularly but this is the first time she's called for a video chat. "Let me see him. I don't even believe you're dating Kade freaking Tucker."

"I'd show him to you but all he's wearing is a very skimpy apron."

"I don't want anything important getting burned," he says.

Summer whispers a squeal, "Is that *him*?"

I hold the phone up so she can see his face. "Kade, I'd like you to meet my sister Summer. Summer, Kade Tucker."

He puts his spatula down to hold the phone. "Hey, Summer."

Summer is momentarily speechless. But then she recovers enough to gasp, "Oh my God, it *is* you. I thought she was making you up." She laughs. "I am the *hugest* fan."

"You'll have to come to one of our shows sometime," he tells her.

"I would love that so much."

Just then, another call comes through.

Pete Clancy.

Holy shit. He might have news. "Mooch, can we call you back? Another call is coming through."

"Sure you can. Bye, Kade. It was nice to meet you."

"You too, darlin'."

Kade hands me back my phone.

Summer is swooning. "Ahh, that *accent*—"

"I'll call you back, Mooch. Love you." I press the *End and Accept* button. "Hello?"

"Stella, it's Pete Clancy."

"Hi, Pete. I'm putting you on speaker. Kade's here too."

"Hi, Kade."

"Hey, Pete. How's the research going?"

"Very well. Are you sitting down, Stella? I've got a lot of information here for you. I've taken a few liberties but they're all positive so I hope you'll forgive me in advance."

Liberties? "Of course." Am I *sitting down?* That sounds ominous. I am sitting down, on a stool at the marble island. "What did you find out?"

"I'm just going to lay it all out but go ahead and stop me if you have questions."

"All right." *Am I ready for this?*

"I used the information and was able to narrow it down fairly easily to a woman named Madeline Jeanne Archer. She lives in Mt. Juliet and has most of her life, aside from a year in California when she was a child when her family moved to Sacramento for her father's job. She married briefly about a year and a half after you were born and had a son, whose name is Samuel. She divorced her husband two years after her son was born. She never remarried and she doesn't have any other children. I took the liberty of contacting her to ask her if she did indeed give up a baby for adoption at the time of your birth and she confirmed she had, in North Carolina. When I spoke to her, she was very emotional."

"*She was?*"

"Yes. She was extremely happy to hear from me. She said she was never given any information about where you had been placed or who had adopted you, or even the name of the adoption agency, so she had no way to search for you. She told me her parents had made the decision to put her baby up for adoption because she was only seventeen at the time and they didn't approve of her marrying your birth father. She was sent away and was told not to have any contact with him again. They prevented him from following her by keeping that information from him, about her whereabouts."

"Oh." Wow.

"She said they were in love, but their families were of different social classes, which was important to her parents at that time."

Wow.

"Stella?"

"Yes?"

"She asked if she could meet you. She very much

wants to. She asked me to tell you she was sorry. She felt like she was doing the best thing for you at the time and she was given no choice. She gave me her phone number and her email address and she'd like you to get in touch when you feel ready. She hopes she'll get to meet you."

I realize then that my face is wet. Silent tears are absolutely streaming down my face. Kade smooths my hair back and uses his fingers to wipe away some of the tears. "Yes. Of course I would. I...I mean, I'll call her. Or I'll email her. I..."

"There's no rush," Pete says. "Take your time to process everything. I realize it's a lot to take on board. I'm going to text you the info and you can contact her when you're ready to. She said she has so much to tell you. She wanted me to tell you that she loves you. And that she's thought about you every single day, praying that you're safe and happy."

Wow.

Wow.

Wow.

"Stella?"

"Yes. Okay. I will. I will. Pete?"

"Yes?"

"Thank you so much."

"My pleasure. I'm glad I could find her for you."

17

Stella

THE NEXT DAY, I email my birth mother.

I tell her I'm happy to have found her. I tell her that I've had a good life and that I understand why she couldn't keep me. I tell her I'd like to meet her and that I'll be in Nashville next week, and possibly longer than that.

Kade and I still haven't made any official plans together yet, but it's hard to imagine leaving him. I know he feels the same way. Within two short weeks, my life has somehow weaved itself around his in a way that feels almost disconcertingly...stable. *Permanent. Everlasting.* I can't bring myself to analyze any of it yet. Instead, I try to work on my book.

Two hours later, my heart almost jumps out of my chest when I receive a reply.

"Kade," I gasp. "She wrote back."

He's walking into the room with two glasses of sweet iced tea. He sets them on the table next to where I'm sitting on the couch with my laptop. He's wearing a pair of worn jeans that are frayed at the cuffs and he's shirtless and barefoot. He sits down next to me and pulls me onto his lap. He's so *in* this with me, it's making me reliant on his devout interest and his empathetic support. I'm not entirely sure how to feel about that. Having always relied only on myself when it comes to all the emotions that go along with being adopted, it's very addictive to have him so incredibly *invested*. "Read it to me."

So I do.

My Dearest Stella,

I can't begin to thank you enough for reaching out to contact me. It's such a comfort to me to know that you are happy in your life.

When I received the phone call yesterday I knew immediately that it was about you. It's so brave of you to search for me. I've thought of you every day and I'm so sorry that we were separated. At the time, I thought I was doing the right thing for you so that you would have a better life. I didn't give you up because I didn't love you. I will always love you.

I dated your birth father for two years in high school. When my parents found out I was pregnant I was sent to my aunt's house in North Carolina. The decision was made by my parents to give you up for adoption and I had no means to care for you without their support. When you were born, I went to a hospital in Charlotte. You were so beautiful and so tiny and the short time I was able to spend time with you was so very special to me. I had no contact with your father during the pregnancy because my parents wouldn't allow it but I was able to let him know that he had a daughter. After that, I didn't speak to him for a long time. He called me out of the blue around four years ago. It was nice to talk to him. He told me that he had moved to Houston soon after you were born. He was married and ran his own small tax accountancy firm. He did not have any other children at that time. I haven't talked to him again since then. He's a good man and I know he cares for you.

You have a brother named Samuel. He's 19 and he's wonderful. He's a student and a talented musician. He didn't know about you. But last night after the phone call with Mr. Clancy, I told him about you. If you're willing, he would also like to meet you.

I work as a book editor. When I'm not working or spending time with Sam, I like to read, write, walk and spend time with my close friends. I have a sister who's two years older who also lives in Nashville and maybe one day you could meet her too if you'd like. She and I have always been very close.

I know I can't go back and change things. I've thought about you every single day and I have always prayed that you are safe and would have a good life.

This letter will be a lot to take in. I'm so grateful that you made the effort to reach out to me. If you'd like to, I'd very much like to keep this communication open. I'd love to learn more about you and your life and I'd love to get to know you.

Your loving birth mother,

Madeline

P.S. Please take your time to decide, but if you would like to call me, I'd love to talk to you. And I would love so much to meet you, Stella. My phone number is 615-490-1122.

After reading Madeline's letter, I cry my heart out and it's a very cathartic experience. Kade closes my laptop and puts it aside. He holds me for a long time, his arms secure around me, smoothing my hair, kissing my head, crooning sweet words to me, until the hitching of my breath evens out and my tears, finally, dry up. Like that particular well is now no longer needed.

"It's good to let it all out, honey."

"There's such a sense of relief to know that she didn't give me away because she didn't want me. She gave me up because she loved me." That simple revelation fortifies me and grounds me in a way that's very hard to explain. All the insecurities that undermined my belief in myself that have somehow lurked like sticky shadows behind my entire life, have shifted. Like a cloud has moved away from the sun, revealing the world and its possibilities in an entirely new light.

"I can imagine you never stop loving a baby that was a part of you for nine months," Kade says. "It must have been excruciating to wonder all those years about where you were and whether or not you were okay."

"I've never thought about it that way. That maybe they missed me."

"Of course they would have."

"I used to wonder if they ended up getting married and having lots of other children together and then lived happily ever after without me. It's strange to think that they never even saw each other again."

"Sounds like her parents were hell-bent on keeping them apart."

"I wonder why." It's a question I'll ask her. It's amazing: *I can ask her questions.* I have so many. "It's nice to finally know at least a part of the story."

Kade's brawny arms are wrapped around me. We're sitting on the squashy leather couch in the writing room with the sun streaming in through the old-glass windows.

He's gorgeous, all lion-like masculinity and sculpted, inked muscles. The sun paints his hair with edges of deep gold. The stubble of his beard is dark but with diamond-touched glints of blond and red. It makes me wonder what color hair our children would have. Maybe one would have brown hair, one blond and one red. With eyes of blue and green.

I'm so grateful to have him here with me. Because he *cares*. He's done so much already to transform the things that hurt me into memories and yearnings that are so much easier to bear. He catches my tears with his fingers and licks one of them, like he did that very first night, as though he's saying, *This pain is mine now. It's ours. It's inside me too. I'll help you carry that weight until it can't hurt you anymore.*

Somehow, by fiercely believing in me and supporting me and also by enlightening me with the kind of pleasure that's intensely emotional, Kade has freed me. His enthusiasm, his patience, his advice, his steady presence and his magical body have opened my soul.

"Kade?"

"Right here, baby girl."

"Thank you. For helping me with this. And for being here for me."

His voice is deep and husked when he says, "It's all I want to do. It feels like that's what I was put on this earth to do. To be yours."

"I love you."

His blue eyes take on all kinds of depth. "I love you too, my sweet little unicorn darlin'. You're the one."

I hold his face and I kiss his mouth. Our kisses turn slippery and greedy.

All I'm wearing is a light cotton nightie with nothing underneath. Kade lifts me and lays me back on the couch and I *need* him. Something in me has broken open and I need him to fill me and anchor me. I fumble with the button of his jeans and he frees himself and—*oh my God, I'll never get used to how huge and hot and perfect he is*—I slide my fist along his growing length, swirling the moisture at the tip. He pushes his thick cock inside me, feeding himself into me inch by star-studded inch. I grip his shoulders as he drives deeper, using his own moisture to wet my pussy, pulling out then pushing deeper as my willing body goes wet and begins to accept his gigantic, rigid length. He stares into my eyes as he thrusts. Everything about him is so full of total devotion. He drives harder, and deeper, working a hot, sweet rhythm with his big, relentless body that takes me to the highest peak and tips me over its brimming edge. The silky spasms of my body squeeze his deep, ridged length, pulling lusciously until he groans and comes in flooding throbs, filling me with his lustrous heat.

"*Fuck, I love you so much, baby*," he groans as he comes.

He's a life-changing, magical gift and he's mine.

Please, please be mine.

18

Stella

And so my relationship with Kade Tucker gains momentum. It wraps itself around me and becomes one with my life in a way I don't know how to slow down. I don't *want* to slow it down, of course I don't. I want to lean into it. I'm in love with him. And he's in love with me. There's nothing to doubt or question.

But two and half weeks is a very short amount of time to meet the person who feels like he is and always will be the love of your life, to lose your virginity to him, to spend the entirely of that two weeks in his bed clocking up your tally of orgasms like nobody's business, and to go on tour with said love of your life who also happens to be a world famous rock star with tour buses, insane fans, a crazy ex and a handful of over the top houses.

It's a lot.

And I'm tired tonight.

We arrive in Austin, where he'll play two shows. Kade's condo is a four million dollar "crash pad" in the heart of the downtown area that looks like an extremely upmarket converted barn on the penthouse floor of one of Austin's high rises.

"I don't know if I could ever get used to all this," I say, as he sets our bags down.

"Get used to all what?"

"This." I gesture to the view and the furniture and the bar, with its rack of gleaming glasses hanging overhead and the lights of the city twinkling below us like a million stars. I feel unsettled, because I've made arrangements to meet with my birth mother and her son—*my brother*—when we get back to Nashville. The whole scenario is exciting but also nerve-wracking. My stomach keeps doing funny little curls. "What am I going to wear?" I open my small suitcase that was supposed to last me a weekend or, at a stretch, a week. "My black dress again, maybe." I definitely didn't pack for my brand new lifestyle.

Kade takes out his phone and makes a call. His eyes are on me and they're full of smug mischief. "Rox, hey. Yeah, I need you to set up a shopping spree in Austin's best department store...what?" He laughs. "No, it's for Stella. Tomorrow, yes. She needs an entirely new wardrobe...yes...okay, text me the details in the morning and let me know where we need to go and when. We've got four or five hours to kill in the early afternoon. Good. Thanks, Rox." He ends the call.

I'm glaring at him. "No. You're not—"

"Oh yeah. I'm taking you shopping."

"Kade. I told you—"

"Gage just texted me and told me another one of our investments quadrupled overnight. I've got money burning holes in my pockets. And there's nothing I'd rather spend it on."

"I don't want you spending more money on me." I'm in a mood. I don't know why I'm feeling so surly tonight. It just feels uneven. "Maybe I want to take *you* shopping. Did you ever think of that?"

There's an alert amusement in him, at my tone. He walks over to me, tipping my chin with his fingers until I'm gazing into his blue eyes, sort of petulantly. "What's wrong with my girl? She's stressed out because something life-changing is about to happen and she's feeling it. Luckily for her, she's got me. I'm going to hold her hand and everything is going to be fine because she's not alone and whatever happens I'm going to be there for her."

"You know what your problem is?"

He grins down at me. "What's my problem?"

"There's no trope for you. You're a hot, low-angst rock star billionaire. It's too easy."

He smiles, but there's an edge to it. "I'm just a star-crossed lover who knows what he wants. Besides, angst is overrated. I've been mired in it my whole life, for a lot of reasons. There'll be more than enough angst along the way as we fight for our happily ever after. Always is. It's called life. And I'm not a billionaire. I might be if I hadn't given a lot of my money away."

"To who?"

"I have a foundation that gives to different charities that are doing a good job. Building schools in other countries. Fighting child cancer. Providing college funds for kids who can't afford it. That kind of thing."

Well, hell. He's not only a hot, low-angst rock star, he's a good person. Which I already knew. And I'm being grouchy for no reason. "I'd like to do that too one day. I mean, not on the kind of scale you are, obviously. But it's really nice of you."

He shrugs. "Seems a shame to hoard all that money when it can help so many other people." He walks over to the bar. "You want a drink, honey?"

"Just water. Thanks. My stomach feels funny. I think I'm just nervous about all this meeting-my-birth-mother-after-a-lifetime-of-wondering-who-she-is stuff."

"Understandable." He opens a bottle of chilled water and pours it into a glass. "You sure you want me to come with you when you meet her?" We'd made arrangements to meet at a restaurant downtown that has a private balcony that overlooks the river. "I can wait outside if it would be easier. I can understand if it's something you want to do by yourself."

"Of course I want you there," I tell him. "If you want to be there."

"I'd walk through fire if it would ease your mind, baby girl. I'm here for you. You know that."

I *do* know that. He's become my (dirty talking) rock and my (very orgasmic) best friend. I'm still adjusting to the magnitude of all that.

Maybe I'm crazy for giving him every piece of myself, and so quickly. So irrevocably.

Maybe I'm setting myself up for a fall with this beautiful, dreamy man with houses and tattoos and a kindness that has dug into me with a ferocity I can't bring myself to question. There's hardly any conflict, no enemies-to-lovers gauntlet, no fake boyfriend ruse. Just the kind of fall that feels epic and, if he decides to walk away, like I would never, ever recover. It's scary to even think about. Everything about him is too damn good. I just wish I didn't have this feeling that something *is* going to try to come between us. That it can't be this perfect without bumps in the road.

Kade reads me easily, like always. He walks over to me and he carefully scoops me into his arms. I think about protesting but he's so strong. So warm. He carries me into the bedroom and he sets me down on the enormous bed. "My baby's got the blues tonight. I can't have that. I'll give you a few minutes to get ready for me. Then I'm going to give you the best massage you've ever had and ease all your troubles away."

God, I really do feel tired. And that sounds too good to refuse.

Just then, my phone buzzes in my bag. I fish around for it and pull it out.

Theo.

The engagement ring I sent back must have arrived.

"It's Theo," I say, because I feel like maybe I should answer it. He's called me every day since I left Princeton and I haven't returned any of his calls. I've known Theo for several years, first as an acquaintance then as a friend, and I dated him for six months, so I do actually want to make sure he's okay about everything. And I don't need to feel bad about that. I also don't need Kade's permission. "I'm going to answer it." But then, in the interest of peacefulness, I add, "All right?"

Already I can detect the pissed-off edge. And a subdued hyper-awareness. "Go right ahead."

"You don't need to stand there and listen if you don't want to."

"I'm good." Leaning one burly shoulder against the wall, not budging an inch.

I wouldn't mind Kade *not* listening in and overanalyzing every detail of my conversation but I know there's no way in hell he'll leave me to it. Now or at any other time. So I answer the call anyway. "Hi, Theo."

"Hey, Stella. Where are you? Why haven't you been answering my calls? Is everything okay?"

"Yeah, it's good. I've just been really busy. I'm in Austin."

"You're in *Texas*?" Like he can't understand why anyone would want to go to Texas.

"Yes."

"What are you doing in Texas?"

"I'm, uh——" Where to start? "I'm traveling. I've never been here before so I decided to come check it out." Not entirely the whole truth and nothing but the truth—which Kade is, of course, acutely aware of. He's watching me, one hand shoved loosely into the pocket of his well-worn jeans. His black shirt is rolled up at the sleeves, exposing his tatted, hair-dusted, muscular forearms. He's wearing a thick leather belt with its sexy cowboyish belt buckle. He looks gruff and crazily...*hot*. He could be standing there posing for a Western-themed photo shoot. I sometimes forget how gorgeous he is. I've almost gotten used to it. But right now, despite the scowl, he's nothing less than dazzling.

"How is it?" Theo asks.

"It's good. How are you, Theo?"

"I'm fine. I got the ring."

"I'm glad it got there safely."

"So I guess you haven't changed your mind yet."

This is sort of awkward. Especially while being eagle-eyed by a possessive alpha rock star. "No."

"I really wish we could get together again and talk things through, Stella. Everything feels so abrupt. I really care for you. I was hoping you might give me another chance."

"I care for you too, Theo. As a friend. But not more than that. I'm sorry. I've...met someone else."

"What?" Theo goes quiet for a few seconds. "When?"

"After we broke up. In Nashville."

More stunned silence. I don't want to hurt Theo even more than I already have but I also don't want him to think there's any chance of us getting back together. And Kade is...well, Kade. If I don't make it crystal clear to Theo that I've very thoroughly moved on, it's probably unfair to both of them. "Wow, that's really...fast," Theo says.

"Yeah. It just sort of happened. I wasn't expecting it. But he's really good for me, Theo. I know you'll find someone perfect for you too."

"I thought *you* were perfect for me."

This is harder than I thought it was going to be. "You'll find someone even better."

"I was thinking maybe I could come see you, Stella. I wasn't expecting Texas but, hey, why not? I'm just...well, not ready to admit defeat yet. I could come down to Austin and we could talk everything through and—"

"No." That would definitely not end well. "Theo, it wouldn't make a difference. It's over. I'm sorry. I'm with someone else now."

"Really?"

"Yes. Really."

"Is it serious? I mean, you only just met him. Who is he?"

"No one you know, Theo." Actually, that's probably not true. There was a time or two on the way to the movies in Theo's car when the radio was tuned to radio stations that would have played Kade's band's songs. Maybe we even listened to one. Anyway, it doesn't matter.

"Stella, are you sure you're not just, you know, sowing some wild oats or whatever this is? This isn't like you at all."

It's true this isn't like the old me at all. But I've changed. This is the new me. The *real* me, the one that was always waiting for my moment to break free. "Theo, I have to go now. But you take care, okay? I'm glad we could talk."

"If you ever change your mind..."

"You'll be the first to know. Goodnight, Theo."

"You're still the prettiest—"

I end the call and set my phone down on the bedside table.

I look up at Kade, who's still watching me. "I guess you're mad at me now?"

"I'm not *mad* at you. Although if he'd said one more word about how pretty you are I might have had to take the phone and set a few things fucking straight."

"You heard that?"

"I heard everything. I don't mind fighting for you, baby. I'll do whatever the fuck it takes."

"You don't have to *fight* for me, Kade. I choose you, okay? You know that. I told him what he needed to hear and now it's done. I can't control or change anything that happened before I met you. Just like you can't."

"I know, darlin'."

I could slice through the tension in the room with a knife. "There's nothing else I can say about it. And I don't have to justify breaking up with my ex—again—as gently as I could."

"I'm going to give you a few minutes to get ready for me. Then I'm going to come in and show you *why* you chose me. And who you belong to."

"I already know both those things."

"Even so, phase ten of the enlightenment process is a fairly intense one."

He's almost making a joke. "There's a phase ten?"

"Oh yeah."

Soon after I get into bed he comes in. He sets some things on the bedside table but I'm too comfortable now to open my eyes. I don't bother wearing anything to bed anymore because he peels it off instantly. And I like being skin to skin with him. He's warm. "Are you still mad?" I whisper. "You're not going to take it out on me, are you?"

"Sure am." He eases me onto my stomach. He warms some lotion on his hands then smooths it onto my back. "No one can make my girl feel as good as I can," he murmurs. "You're *mine.*"

He starts massaging me with his strong hands,

working the muscles in long, careful strokes. I moan as he finds a knot of tension and works the deep tissue.

"Oh, that feels so good."

Kade's thorough fingers work the tension from my body, until I'm so blissed out I can hardly move. Then he glides lower, over my ass, roving intimately. He massages my thighs, dipping between them to rub my pussy. Of course I'm wet for him. Because he's made of magic. He lifts my hips, opening my legs. He leans over me and licks me from behind, eating into my pussy until I'm messy from his greedy mouth and simmering with desire for him.

"*Mine*," he growls.

Then his tongue finds the secret cove of my ass and he plays it. I squirm because it feels so intimate but he holds me with his unbreakable grip, insistent. His tongue licks and prods as his fingers tease my clit in playful, pinching pulls. A warm current of pleasure builds, between the place where his fingers glide and his insatiable, exploring tongue.

God.

The lick of his tongue is replaced by his slick fingers as he lifts my hips higher and mounts me, the thick girth of him pushing between the saturated, delicate folds of my pussy. With one smooth, forceful thrust, he drives all the way to the hilt and I moan because he's possessing me so fully, so outrageously *completely*. The slick friction of his big, ridged cock as he fucks me feels too good. The pleasure of him is the only thing I know. I hear a low buzzing noise and Kade touches something to my clit. A smooth, vibrating hum takes over my entire being. His fingers rub the slippery pucker of my ass as he fucks me deep and hard and the vibrator warms the pleasure into something otherworldly. I come so hard I lose myself. I shatter into a million stars of pure, raw bliss.

He does it again. And again. Until the pleasure touches on something spiritual. And wildly emotional. I'm floating. I'm coming. I'm his vessel. All I can do is receive him and all the crazy pleasure of him and his thick cock and his warm, pumping cum that floods and spills. He thrusts into my highest orgasm, working the ebb of my pleasure all the way to the end.

When he finally pulls out, I'm boneless and spent. Beatifically used. I whimper softly as he wraps himself around me and kisses me, whispering low, husky words as a deep, soothing sleep overtakes me.

"That's my girl. I'm here now. I'm yours and you're mine. I'm going to take such good care of you. I love you."

19

Stella

WE ARRIVE at the place where I'm going to meet my birth mother and my brother for the first time. We're in Kade's McLaren 720S Coupe (he pointed out), which is basically like riding in a spaceship. We pull into the parking lot and he parks near the door.

I can't bring myself to get out of the car.

"Just remember that you're the most dazzling girl in the world," Kade tells me. "They'll fall in love with you the minute they meet you. Just like I did."

"You're doing that thing again."

"What thing?"

"That thing where you say exactly what I need to hear exactly when I need to hear it and you're going to make me cry if you keep doing that because you're..." I don't know how to say it except to be honest with him. "...everything."

He leans close to my ear. "I really want to fuck you."

I gasp a little. "Kade."

"I want to eat your pink pussy and raw dog you like nobody's business."

"*Kade.*"

He laughs at my expression. "Is it working?"

"Is what working?"

"Relax. Think about all the things I'm going to do to you later and how good it's going to feel. Now cowgirl up and let's do this. This is what you've been wondering about your whole life and it's going to be better than you ever expected. Let's go."

He's right. I can do it. We get out of the car and I take a deep breath and stare up at the building we're about to enter. I'm holding Kade's hand for dear life. He gently tugs on my hand. "Come on, sweetheart. You've got this."

I'm wearing a cute white dress with three-quarter sleeves and a short flouncy skirt, and suede ankle boots. Kade took me for a ride in the Lamborghini he keeps in Austin, then on a shopping spree, where a team of personal shoppers basically brought me the entire store to try on. Kade sat by the windows scrolling on his phone as they trotted me out in outfit after outfit. *Don't ask me,* he told them. *To me she'd be gorgeous in a paper bag. Give her every-thing she wants.* Four hours later, he'd bought half the women's department for me, despite all my protests. So I ended up with an insanely killer wardrobe that's ten times the size of the one I left behind.

"Whatever happens," I tell him, "I want to say thank you for being here for me. I'm so happy I met you and I've had the best two weeks of my life." I don't know why I'm confessing all this right now, like I'm about to jump off the side of a ship and I don't know if I'll be able to swim.

He laughs softly and leans in to brush his lips against mine. "You're going to be fine. She's as nervous as you are."

We go inside and we're led up the stairs and shown into the private room Kade reserved, with its tables and its outdoor heaters and its view of the river. Only one table is occupied. The one that's closest to the railing.

Two people are sitting there and they both stand up when they see us come in.

A woman and a tall, good-looking young man.

God, my heart is going a mile a minute.

As I get closer, I can see that the woman...looks like me. And so does her son. I mean, it's not surprising, but I wasn't expecting them to look this...*familiar.* She's in her late-30s but she looks younger than that. She looks like one of those people you might see riding a bike along a vineyard path in France. I don't know why I say that, but she looks slim and fit and sort of glamorous in a low-key, natural kind of way. The happiness in her very-green eyes is edged with a sorrowful depth. Her hair is exactly the same color as mine, a little shorter and differently styled. I might be two or three inches taller than she is.

Her hand flutters up to cover her mouth and there are welling tears in her eyes.

I stand in front of her and she drinks in the sight of me. No one has ever looked at me the way she's looking at me right now. Like she is infinitely, desperately happy to see me. "Stella," she whispers.

She hugs me. It's a hug that I feel all the way down to my bones. I hug her back and we stand like that, hugging each other, crying silent tears and feeling this connection for what it is: a bond that was broken but never really went away.

After what might be several minutes, we pull back and she holds my face in her hands and smiles through her tears. "I can see him in you. Oh my gosh, it's so good to finally *see* you."

"It's good to see you too." We both laugh and use the tissues we've both brought to wipe away the tears.

"Stella, this is your brother Sam."

Sam smiles sort of cheekily at me and I love him already. I feel *this* connection too. Instantly. He could be my twin if he wasn't six inches taller and a few years younger. "Hey, sis. Wow, you look like me."

"Hi, Sam," is all I can manage because this gambit of emotions is crazily intense. I'm laughing, crying and my soul feels like it has doubled in size. Most of all, there's an outrageous sense of *relief*. I've found them. I don't have to wonder or search anymore. I no longer have to feel like a piece of myself is missing. Because here they are.

Sam leans down to give me a gusto-filled hug. "I'm not surprised my sister is dating a rock star, but Kade Tucker? I like it. Judging by her genes, it's a good match. You're a lucky man," Sam grins.

"Don't I know it." Kade holds out his hand to shake but Sam hugs him too and then Madeline hugs him and even if she's a little bit starstruck by him, it's me she wants to stare at and talk to. It's my hand she wants to hold.

So we sit and we order drinks and we spend the entire afternoon talking. Madeline and I have a million cautious, careful questions for each other. And over the course of the afternoon, she answers all of them.

My adoption caused a wound in her family that never really healed, she tells me. It created a rift between Madeline and her mother that only grew wider as time went on. Madeline never forgave her parents for the decisions they made for her when she was seventeen years old, even though she knew they thought they were doing the right thing for her. Madeline's mother and father both died of lung cancer and had been smokers, a habit they couldn't kick even when they got sick. "All our lives were touched, and haunted even, by the idea that you might not be safe, or loved, or have the life we all hoped you would."

It's heavy information.

"None of us were ever the same," she tells me. "We all carried you with us every single day. It was the not knowing that was the hardest. It unraveled each of us in our own way."

"I wish it hadn't," I say. "I wish I could have told you I was okay."

"Me too," she whispers. "We all made so many mistakes. We all wished we could rewind time and fix them."

I carefully ask her about my birth father.

"His name is Jack Vane. I met him when I was fourteen. God, I just fell for him so hard. We dated for two years. He was handsome and fun, but also quiet. He was perceptive and kind, but he also had a...I don't know, a coolness. An edge. There was something sort of separate about him and even though his family didn't have a lot of money, he had an exotic aura to him, like royalty in exile." She laughs lightly. "I don't know why I say that. He was a special person. My parents could never see that, though. Or they didn't allow themselves to. His parents were working class, with five children. Mine were country club members—not that Jack or I could see why any of that mattered—and we lived, I guess you could say, on opposite sides of the tracks. My mother was concerned about what people thought. She felt a lot of social pressure and she didn't want anyone to know I was pregnant. She wanted me to have it 'taken care of' but it was the one thing I was able to stand up for. I absolutely refused. I wanted you to have a life, even if I couldn't be a part of it. So she made arrangements for me to go to her sister's in North Carolina because she lived alone and no one knew me there. I could have the baby and give it up for adoption and then return home and finish high school and no one would ever know. I would move on and find someone else eventually and I wouldn't have to live with my mistake, that's how my mother saw it. She didn't think Jack was good enough for me. They thought he would drag me down. They refused to tell him where I was, even though he camped out on their doorstep for several days, demanding answers. He loved me. We loved each other. It should have been his decision too. And mine."

"Yes. It should have." I hold her hand as she wipes her tears.

She contemplates me with green eyes that are so much like my own. "I wish so much that we'd fought harder, Stella. I wish I'd been stronger. I'm so sorry."

"You were so young," I say, understanding how hard that would have been. To try to stand up for themselves. I can't even tell my parents I want to take a semester off, even though I'm twenty-one and fully independent. I know for a fact that if I'd been in a similar situation when I was seventeen, I would have felt powerless to defy or overrule my parents' decisions. "It wasn't your fault. It wasn't anyone's fault. And I've had an amazing life."

"Promise me you'll always trust yourself. And fight for the things you want most. My parents made those decisions for me. And I let them do it. It's my greatest regret."

"I will," I promise her, and I feel the resolve forge into place. *I will.*

"Your father proved them wrong, though." She smiles sadly. "That's why he called me all those years later. To tell me he ran his own tax accountancy firm. It's small but successful. He'd gone all the way through law school and he's doing well for himself. I think he wanted to prove that, if only to himself. He said he was married but he'd made the decision that he didn't want more children. He didn't feel like he deserved them."

It makes me sad, that he would have felt that way.

"I called him," she says.

"You did?"

She squeezes my hand. "I googled his office and I called him after we emailed each other. I wanted him to know that you'd made contact. I told him I was meeting you here today. I invited him. He said he might try to come. But he wasn't sure."

Wow.

"He was very happy to hear that I'd found you," Madeline says.

"He was?"

"Yes."

We're both crying again. "H-how is he?"

"He said he's okay. Business is good. He's divorced now."

"Oh."

"He asked a lot of questions about you and I told him

everything I knew. We both cried. We both said we wish we could rewind time. But we can't. And now that I've met you, Stella, I wouldn't want to. Look how beautiful you are. Look how wonderful your life has turned out to be. I wouldn't want to change anything for you."

It's true that I can—maybe now more than ever before—fully appreciate everything my life has been, and in a different, deeper way. I'm grateful. For every single thing.

We talk until the sun gets lower in the sky and the conversation turns to lighter topics. Her house and her life and her job as a book editor. When I tell her I'm writing a romance novel—and I don't even gloss over that part, I just tell her everything—she's excited. She edits nonfiction but when she reads for pleasure, she reads romance. It's her favorite genre.

As we talk, it's strangely and instantly comfortable. I tell her everything she wants to know, without holding back. It feels uncannily like I'm talking to *myself*. What we're finding is that we're very similar people.

We talk about Sam and his studies at Vanderbilt, where he's studying music.

Turns out he plays the double bass and the bass guitar. "No kidding," Kade grins.

So the two of them talk music and Kade asks him for his number, saying maybe they can get together sometime and play together.

Sam looks like someone just offered to fly him to the

moon. "My number's easy to remember. 615-565-6565." We both key it into our phones and exchange numbers and we make plans to see each other again.

Just then someone else arrives. A man. The hostess is showing him to our table.

He's tall and dark-haired. He's good-looking. In his late thirties.

Madeline gasps lightly but even before that, as he gets closer, I know who he is. Because the shape of his eyes is exactly the same as the shape of mine.

He looks at me, then Madeline, and for a few seconds all we can do is gaze at each other, taking in the similarities and the family resemblances, which are crazily obvious. "Sorry I'm late," he says. "I'm Jack."

"I'm Stella."

Jack hugs me and there it is again, that desperate *relief.* In me, but even more in him. "I'm sorry I'm twenty-one *years* late." It never really occurred to me that they would have missed me as much as they clearly have. But I can feel it now. "Are you okay?" he asks me. It's a layered question with caverns of deep emotion behind it. Jack, my birth father, immediately strikes me as a complex character who's had a difficult life. I realize part of that difficulty may have had something to do with me. Maybe I can try now to ease some of it—and maybe I already have.

Jack is introduced to Sam and Kade. We sit and talk for a while. Jack and Madeline are fascinated by me and also by each other. It's been a long time and there's too much to say to say it all tonight. But we don't have to.

We have time.

It gets late and we hug some more and cry some more. We make plans to keep in touch and we say goodnight.

And just like that I become a fully formed human being. There are no more shadows, no more dark, empty questions to haunt my thoughts and my dreams.

I make a decision. To forgive them, if there's anything to forgive. To live fully and whole-heartedly, like maybe they never quite managed to do. Because of me, or because of decisions they made that they could never undo.

I decide to stop second-guessing who I am and what I want.

I'm in love with Kade Tucker. I'm going to write a kick-ass romance novel. And I'm going to live exactly the way I want to live.

I decide in that moment to become a hundred percent *me*.

20

Stella

Kᴀᴅᴇ's ɢᴇᴛᴛɪɴɢ ready to go to his last gig of his solo tour, which is at a newly-opened nightclub at home here in Nashville. Here I am, describing Nashville as *home.*

It's starting to feel that way.

I've been writing all afternoon and I'm deep in the scene where my two main characters finally meet. Kade likes me to come to his shows, though, so I save my document, email it to myself, back it up on the cloud and onto a flash drive, and close my laptop.

"How do you feel about meeting my parents?" I ask him. "My *other* parents," I clarify. "My actual parents. The ones who raised me."

"Yeah?" He smiles. "Are we ready for that?"

"Are *you* ready for that?" I nudge him with my elbow.

"I was always ready for that."

So I FaceTime my parents. After weeks of giving

vague answers and non-committal replies, it's time. My family's expectations have lifted me up in my life, but they've also acted as a weight that has held me back or made me doubt my own path. That's gone now.

They're both there, in the kitchen, listening to my father's favorite jazz playlist. "Hi Mom. Hi Dad."

"Stella," my mother starts. "We were wondering when we might hear from you." Her tone is slightly miffed, which doesn't bother me like it would have a month ago. "How's your little adventure going? Have you found your-self yet?"

I ignore the light gibe. "I want to introduce you to someone. A friend of mine. We're seeing each other. His name is Kade."

"Very nice to meet you, Professor Bell. Mrs. Bell." Kade's so easy in his own skin I can't help smiling. And loving him even more. For his steadiness. And his abso-lutely alpha charm.

My father studies him through the screen. "Kade *Tucker*?"

"Yes, sir."

"I saw you play with Dusty Cunningham at the Underground in New York City last year. That was one hell of a show, son."

"You saw that?" Kade says. "Oh, that was a good one. One of my top five favorite shows of all time. Very few feel as perfect as that one did."

"It was phenomenal," my father replies. "I'm a fan, Mr. Tucker."

My father's a *fan*? Now, *that*, I was not quite expecting. Kade mentioned he played jazz sometimes, but I never knew he performed it.

"Please. Call me Kade, sir."

And just like that, Kade Tucker not only slots himself into another major facet of my life, but makes it easier for *me* to navigate.

I tell my parents I'm staying in Nashville, I've applied to defer a semester, I'm writing a novel and I've moved in with Kade. Maybe it's the time apart or the resolve in my voice, but they accept all of it with some surprise but also with grace. "I love you guys so much," I tell them, "and I appreciate everything you've done for me more than you'll ever know," and both my parents get choked up by this.

"We love you too, honey."

I don't tell them the part about me meeting my birth parents but I will. It's something I'd like to do in person.

We end the call and I'm happy with the way that went but I also feel strangely exhausted.

My stomach does a funny lurch. I go into the bathroom, wondering if I'm going to be sick. The room spins and my skin has gone clammy. But after a minute or two, the feeling passes.

What the hell was that?

I go over to the sink and splash my face with some cold water.

My reflection in the mirror looks...good. I look different than I did a month ago. My hair is shiny. My eyes are bright and my cheeks are flushed. It's a weird thing to admit to myself, but I don't ever remember looking as *beautiful* as I do right now. My enlightenment feels downright complete and it shows.

Another wave of nausea rolls through my stomach.

Ugh.

Did I eat something? Maybe something didn't agree with me.

I wait until the wave passes, which it does. I dry my face and go back out to the bedroom. I can hear Kade packing up his guitar in the living room so I go out to find him.

"Hey, beautiful. You ready?"

"Kade, would you mind if I stayed here tonight? I'm not feeling that well."

He stops what he's doing, his gaze stern and worried. "What's wrong?"

"I'm just a little tired."

"Do you want me to stay home with you? Do you need a doctor?"

"No, it's nothing like that. I think I might just need to have an early night."

"I'll cancel my gig. It's not—"

"*No.* Definitely don't do that. You go. I'll be fine. Really."

"I don't want to leave you if you're not feeling well."

"I'll curl up in your big bed and go to sleep and I'll be right here waiting for you when you get back."

He pulls me between his knees from where he's half-sitting against the couch. "You sure?"

"Absolutely sure." It's true that we haven't been apart at all, since the day we met.

"I don't want to leave you."

I smile because he's a sweetheart. "It's only for a few hours. You go. I wouldn't want you to disappoint your fans."

"You're more important than my fans."

"I'm fine. I want you to go."

I finally talk him into it, and after a few scorching kisses, Kade leaves.

It feels strange to be without him.

I go into the kitchen to get a glass of water, thinking maybe it'll settle my stomach. I open the fridge and grab some bottled water, standing there for a few seconds to inspect the contents of the fridge because I suddenly feel hungry. My nausea is completely gone and now I'm craving food.

Something sweet.

Chocolate.

And ice cream.

I search his freezer but it's empty, aside from a bottle

of vodka. Ugh. The thought makes my stomach lurch again, but once I close the freezer, my craving is even stronger.

I search his cupboards.

There are a lot of canned foods, coffee beans, packages of grits.

But no chocolate.

I could ask one of his security guards outside the front door of the apartment to go get me some. There's a convenience store right down at the corner that's only a few minutes away.

But then, they might call Kade and tell him. They report every single thing that happens. I don't want them to interrupt him. I have this feeling the slightest hint that I need something will have him canceling his show and rushing back to make sure I'm okay. Which I am.

Except that I feel like I could murder a pint of Ben and Jerry's. Holy hell, I literally *need* Salted Caramel Brownie ice cream right now.

There's a back entrance. There's a staircase at the far end of the patio that leads down to a side door. I know the code. And I don't think it's guarded.

It's probably a four minute walk to the corner store.

I shouldn't. We're being stalked, after all. Hence the brigade of body guards. It's an unnecessary risk, even though no one would be expecting it and I'm sure it would be fine.

The craving for ice cream hits me again, followed closely by another wave of nausea.

Why am I nauseous? And why would I be craving chocolate *this* badly?

A manic wave of realization hits me.

Holy shit.

When is my period due?

I get my bag from Kade's bedroom and I take out my birth control pills. There's one pink one left and then it's white sugar pills.

But what day is it? I remember the date I got my last period because I had a paper due on the—

Oh my God.

Did I take them every day?

I don't think I did.

I think I missed some.

When I met Kade and we got so swept away and spent 24/7 of that first week in bed...*having very unprotected sex*, I think I must have forgotten to take a few of my pills.

How could I be so stupid? What the hell was I thinking?

You were thinking about getting thoroughly fucked by a dreamy beefcake musician and counting down the minutes to your next orgasm.

Shit shit shit.

I think I forgot to take four. Maybe even five.

I sit down on the bed and have a mini panic attack.

Is it too late for the morning after pill?

I google it.

120 hours or five days after you have sex.

It's too late.

I do the math in my head, thinking about my last period and counting backwards.

I'm five days late.

Holy fuck.

Maybe it's just the intensity of the last few weeks that has my cycle messed up.

It's possible that I'm just a few days late because my periods don't always run like clockwork.

Pretty close, though.

I'll go find a CVS or something and I'll take a pregnancy test and it'll be negative and everything will be fine.

But I don't really want to ask the burly bouncers outside the door to do that run for me. *Excuse me, could you go pick up a pregnancy test and two pints of Ben & Jerry's please? Thanks so much.*

I'll go myself.

Kade will be gone for another few hours and his evil ex has probably moved on by now. It's been more than two weeks since our encounter at Speakeasy. Surely she's forgotten about her twisted vendetta against me. She's an heiress and influencer, or something. She must have better things to do.

I decide to do it.

So I put on my coat and pull on a pair of black ankle boots. I grab my phone and check my bag to make sure my money card is still there. I haven't spent any money since I met Kade. He pays for everything.

Which isn't really ideal, but I've kind of gotten swept away in the haven he provides.

No kidding. That's why you're in this mess.

I let myself out onto the patio and find the locked gate that leads down the back staircase. When I get down to street level, there are no guards.

It actually feels sort of liberating to not be trailed and watched. All the crazy scrutiny is a million miles from what I'm used to and it's nice to just go unnoticed for once.

I walk the two blocks to the corner and go into the store, where they have an entire glass freezer dedicated to Vermont's finest. I grab two pints. Then I find the pharmacy aisle. To see if they have a pregnancy test. Turns out they do. So I grab one and the tiny photo on the box of a pregnant woman hits me hard.

What if I'm pregnant with Kade Tucker's baby?

Maybe that's something you should have thought more carefully about when you were—

It doesn't matter. There's no point churning about what I should or shouldn't have been doing. It's done now.

I made a mistake.

Just like Madeline did.

God. I'm not ready.

But I also know, after everything that's happened and because of who I am and where I came from, that if something has taken hold inside me, it's with me for life.

I've already made my choice.

You wanted conflict, Stella? Here's some conflict for you.

Like he said, life will offer up its own angst, and plenty of it.

Can you sense the choices people will make when you first look into their eyes? Can you see the decisions they'll make are in sync with your own?

I don't know.

As if everything he's done so far isn't enough, *here's* where the hero Kade Tucker steps into his own. Because I already know the choice he'd make too.

I remember asking him what he was doing when he pushed his cum back inside me with his fingers.

Keeping me inside you.

I'm scared. More than scared. Terrified.

I'm also...completely sure about what I'll do.

I'm keeping it.

Somewhere on the other side of my fear, I'm already in love with it.

Making my way back outside, I head back down the street toward Kade's, walking quickly.

A black car pulls up next to me.

I look over at it, thinking it's pulling over to park, but two men jump out. I'm entirely not expecting it. One of them grabs my bag and the other pushes me into the back seat of the car.

Before I can even scream or struggle, the car door slams shut and it pulls away from the curb.

21

KADE

I GET TO THE GIG, but my heart's not in this tonight.

It's the first time we've been apart and I'm out of my fucking head. Someone may as well have scooped my soul out of my goddamn body and left it back at the house, wrapped around my beautiful girl. I can't feel anything except her absence. There's an invisible cord wrapped tightly around my heart, pulling me back to her. It's painful. Even more painful is the *other* invisible string, wrapped even more tightly around my goddamn dick, which—and this sounds fucking ridiculous—is lonely as fuck.

Is she okay? Is she missing me? Does she need me?

My problem isn't that I'm *this* whipped. My problem is that I don't care about anything else. Nothing. I don't give a fuck about the fans or the end-of-tour hoopla. The screaming, crying people are faceless. Their energy doesn't touch me at all. The club feels confined and empty of her and entirely not where I want to be.

Even the music doesn't flow. The chords sound hollow. The lyrics don't jive because *she can't hear them.*

I'm going mad because she has become my entire reason to live.

I need to get a grip.

I can't breathe.

I feel manic. Restless as fuck.

All I want to do is get back to her and be near her. *Get inside her. Protect her. Love her with everything I've got.*

I'm in love and I'm addicted and there's just no point doing any of this without her.

I decide to do one more song, then I'll cut this short tonight.

The place is packed, as always. People are everywhere, trying to get close.

Fuck off, I feel like yelling. *Leave me alone. You're not her. I'm hers. She's mine.*

She's the only thing I can feel.

Is she thinking about me? Is she craving me as much as I'm going fucking insane because she's not here?

What I realize is that I don't have Stella's phone number. I can't even call her to check on her.

Why the fuck didn't I think of that? We've never been apart so I've never *needed* to call her. But I fucking need to now.

I finish the last song of my first set. The screams are

deafening but I don't even acknowledge them. I leave the stage and go back to the tiny dressing room. I chug some Jack straight out of a bottle to try to take the smallest edge off.

Something's not right, I can feel it.

I'm leaving.

There's a knock on the door.

I open it, and it's one of the bartenders. He hands me a small white envelope. "This was delivered for you, Mr. Tucker."

I grab the envelope and rip it open.

It's a letter, written in small, neat handwriting.

Dear Kade,

I'm so glad we got to spend this time together. I'll always treasure what we shared. But it's still so new and everything has happened so fast. I'm not sure the rock star lifestyle is for me and I'm feeling very overwhelmed. I'm so sorry about that.

And I'm sorry to leave without saying goodbye, but I need to go home for a while and reconnect with my life and my family. Lately I've been feeling that I'm way out of my depth and I need some time to think everything through.

Please don't follow me. Please give me some time. I'll contact you when my head is clearer and we can talk about everything then. Please just let

*me figure things out for myself. I'll get in touch
with you soon.*

   Thank you for everything, Kade.
   Love,
   Stella

I stand there staring at the letter for a few seconds, my heart hammering in my chest.

What the fuck?

This can't be real.

This isn't her.

This isn't my Stella.

My eyes trace the small, neat letters. The S of her name. I remember thinking it as I read the other letter she wrote—to the guy who proposed to her—even though I was pissed off at the time, I still noticed that her handwriting was unique, with its whimsical loops. It had struck me at the time that it was the handwriting of a romantic. It made me fall for her even more, despite the cloud of jealousy I'd been mired in.

This isn't the handwriting of a romantic.

A cold wash of something that hits somewhere between terror and a focused, resolute rage ices through my veins.

Stella wouldn't write this letter. Stella *didn't* write this letter.

And there's only one person who would be twisted enough to pretend to be her.

I storm toward the door, seriously wondering if my sanity is about to shatter. But I hold onto it. I need it in place.

I find an exit, completely oblivious to everyone around me. I get out onto the street and I start fucking *running* toward my house, which is only six or seven blocks from the club. People stare at me but I don't give a fuck about anything except finding her.

I get to the door of my apartment and I'm fishing the key card out of my wallet when I notice someone's here. Standing behind me.

I'm in such a state it takes me a few seconds to recognize her.

It's her. It's fucking Carmen.

I have never felt so feral or so furious in my life as I do right now, but my mind is working on several levels. There's a calmness behind my fury that's all about finding Stella. If I lose my cool I'll lose my mind.

I stare at Carmen.

Would she really be evil enough to do this?

Yes, is the answer to that question. Evil or desperate, in this case they're one and the same.

Of course she's trying to steal my joy. She always has.

And if she does have something to do with it, which I'd bet my life on, then I need her close. I need to know what she knows.

First, I need to see if Stella is here. It's possible this

was a fucked-up misunderstanding or a communication breakdown.

"Can we talk?" She's wearing jeans and a nondescript shirt under a long white coat, and cowboy boots. Her make-up is more subtle than usual, without those spidery eyelashes. It's what she knows I used to like: less of a fake, try-hard, staged look and more of something real. "Kade?" Her voice is soft, without that hysterical edge she'll no doubt eventually work her way up to. I know, in a single glance, that she's pulled out all the stops tonight. She's trying to be what I always wanted her to be.

I say nothing, but I allow her to follow me inside, and into the elevator. She picks up on the vibe that if she gets too close to me, I'll react badly. And she's right. She keeps her distance.

It would be easy if my nemesis was a man. I could beat him to a fucking bloody pulp until I got the information and the bloodthirsty revenge I needed, if this is what I think it is.

With her, I could crush her skull with my fist. I could throttle her scrawny little neck so very easily. My fingers twitch with the violent urge to do exactly that.

"Kade, I want to tell you that I'm so sorry. I'm sorry if I was pushy or needy or scared. Please forgive me. I can do so much better. I can love you just the way you need, I promise I can. You're *everything* to me, Kade. You're my whole life. I just want to be with you and love you. I can't live without you, baby. I love you so much. I want so much for us to be together again. Can I please show you how much I love you? Will you please give me another chance?"

The elevator slides open and I walk into my apartment. I can hear voices, outside on the balcony. Roxie. Travis. Ruby. They're back from their trip. They're laughing.

I can't hear Stella.

I walk to the open doors of the balcony in ground-eating strides, looking for her.

She's not here.

"Kade," says Travis, looking up. "You're back early." He stands up and starts walking over to me.

"Is Stella here?" I say, not to him directly. To Roxie. To anyone. My voice sounds cold. In the husk of it I can hear my own anguish.

She's not here.

"Isn't she with you?" Roxie seems surprised. My tone has upset her. She's even more surprised when Carmen walks up beside me. "Carmen."

I rush back into the apartment, looking for clues.

To the bedroom.

All her things are still here.

Her clothes.

Her laptop.

She would never leave her laptop behind if she was going home.

Another wave of cold terror pulses through my veins.

She's in danger.

I can feel it.

Blind with my own dread, I'm back in the kitchen. On the counter are her car keys, where Jared left them after moving her car to my garage.

Her car is still here.

Carmen's eyes are wide. She wasn't expecting me to react this way.

I hold up the letter that's crumpled in my fist. "I know you wrote this." Slowly, willing myself not to ease my hands around her neck, I grab the front of Carmen's coat with my fist. In her eyes, I can read her guilt. "You're going to tell me where the fuck she is. And if even one hair on her head is out of place, I'm going to fucking kill you with my bare hands. Tell. Me. Where. She. Is."

Carmen's eyes fill with tears.

"*WHERE IS SHE?*" I yell in her face. My voice doesn't even sound like me. It sounds like someone capable of doing terrible things. The kind of things that'll get a person locked up for life.

Roxie hears it. So does Travis.

So does Carmen.

"Hey." Travis is worried as fuck. He eases my fist loose, smoothing Carmen's coat back into place, putting his hand on my chest as though to calm me. "What the fuck's going on?"

I shrug him off.

Carmen is crying hard now. "She's completely safe,

Kade. Of course she is. I wouldn't do that. She's at Amber's. Having a spa weekend."

"A what?" *Amber's?* I vaguely remember that Amber is one of Carmen's friends.

"I just wanted some *time* with you, Kade. To talk things through. Everything was so abrupt and you've been with her the whole time and—"

"You fucking *kidnapped* her?"

"No. Of course not. Amber invited her and it just means you and me can have some time to—"

I grab a fistful of my hair. I can't believe this. "Where the fuck is Amber's? *Tell me where it is.*"

"It's in Forest Hills," she sobs. "I'm sorry. I just so much wanted to—"

"I know where it is," says Travis. "I went to a party there with Vaughn once. My car's right out front."

I'm already in the elevator.

"Why didn't you ever love *me* like that, Kade?" Carmen whines.

"Because you're capable of doing things like this. And because you're not the one and you never fucking could have been." To Roxie, I growl, "Don't let her leave. And if anything happens to me, make sure she gets locked the fuck up."

22

Stella

I grab for the door handle of the car and frantically claw at it.

It's locked.

A light hand places itself on my arm and I flinch and recoil but it's a young woman sitting next to me.

I know her. Do I know her? Why does she look familiar?

"Please don't panic," she says, and her voice isn't menacing or malicious. It's friendly, and calm. "I'm taking you to my house and it's really nice and this is not a big deal. We just need to get you out of the way for a couple of days. So, please, just calm down. You're not in any danger."

What? "Who are you?"

"I'm Amber. I'm a friend of Carmen's."

Amber. I remember her. From the bathroom. She's the friend who looks like a supermodel.

"We met a few weeks ago at Speakeasy."

"Why are you doing this? Let me out."

"I will, I promise. After Carmen talks to Kade. Please don't panic. We'll go to my house, you can sit in the hot tub, I've got champagne and Netflix and you can chill out until Carmen gives me the okay."

"What are you talking about? This is *kidnapping*, not a fucking *sleepove*r. Let me out."

"I'm so sorry, but I can't. I mean, I would *never* have agreed to do this, but I owe her one and she's desperate."

She's conversational in a way that doesn't fit this situation at all. "Amber. This is a *felony* you're committing right now. You could go to jail for this. Now let me out of the car. Please. Be reasonable. This isn't worth it."

"The thing is, she was there for me when I was at my lowest and now that she's at *her* lowest I feel like I need to help her if I can. I get how she feels because the same thing happened to me."

"What?" I can't believe this.

"I was totally in love with Vaughn and I thought maybe he was in love with me too because he didn't usually, you know, give his time to the same woman for more than one night. But with me...I don't know, at the time I thought we shared something special. I thought maybe I could mean something to him because I would literally have done *anything* for him. I was *so* in love with him. I still am. Like, *crazy* in love. I mean, you've seen him. He's gorgeous, he's fun, he's just a beautiful person. I wanted so much to be with him. But then he met someone else and he wouldn't even talk to me after that. He became completely cold and indifferent. I was heartbroken, and that's putting it mildly. I felt like he was my one and only. But he didn't feel the same way at all and it was just so devastating, and in a way I'm not sure I'll ever get over entirely. Hopefully I will, but how could anyone ever beat that? Do you know what I mean? And Carmen, she was there for me. She helped me through it. I'm not sure I would have even made it through all that if she hadn't helped me. So I need to try to do the same thing for her. I have to at least try to help her. You understand, right?"

This is crazy. "No, Amber. You can't just kidnap a person and think that's okay. Please. Just let me go. This isn't the way to help her. Kade will be worried. I need to go back to him. I need to call him. Please."

"I didn't *want* to do it. I mean, she's talking about *hurting* herself, Stella." She says my name so comfortably and it's eerie. Like she knows me. I guess it makes sense, if they've been plotting this. They would have thought it through carefully. They would have been watching, and waiting. "I wouldn't be able to live with myself if that happened. All she wants is to talk to him. Alone. And he's never alone. He's always with you. So she was prepared to go to extreme measures. I'm sorry about that. It wasn't my idea."

Amber actually seems like she could be a nice person, under different circumstances. It doesn't change the fact that she's *abducting* me right now. "You can let me go and she can still talk to him. I wouldn't get in the way of that. This isn't necessary at all. Kade will be going out of his mind with worry if he comes home and finds me gone. Please."

"Carmen will let him know. She's going to tell him that..." She hesitates. "I probably shouldn't say. But it's all taken care of. He won't worry."

"What? *Tell me.* Amber, what's she going to say to him? It hardly matters if you tell me."

"She's going to tell him that you left. That you went home because you couldn't handle the lifestyle."

What? "He'll never believe that. Amber, please. This is insane."

"I know what you're thinking, that we're unhinged and desperate to the extreme. But these are *dream men* we're talking about. They're hot, rich, beautiful. They're rock stars in every sense of the word. That kind of thing just doesn't come along every day of the week. You don't let them go without a fight. They can make all your dreams come true."

"But...not if you're *forcing* them to. It doesn't work that way."

"*I* know that. I let Vaughn go when I could see that he didn't want me anymore. But Carmen is stubborn like that. Besides, it's different. She's been *dating* him, living with him, touring with him, for almost six months. She thought he was going to propose that day that he left and then he's been holed up with you ever since. So the breakup was a real shock to her. And then the rebound—you—so soon after. She's gone a little crazy over the whole thing. She's not herself."

"Amber. *Please.* You have to be reasonable. Please. Just stop the car and let me out."

"I'm sorry. I can't. I promise I'll take good care of you. Your room has a balcony and a T.V. and—"

"Amber. *Please.*"

"It's only for a day or two. She's convinced she can win him back."

"She can't."

Amber smiles gently. "I don't think she can either. But she does. We'll see."

Despite my pleading and trying to reason with Amber, she doesn't budge.

I can see through the tinted windows of the car that we're driving through an iron gate. There's a tall stone wall that encloses whatever this place is. "Where are we going?" I feel more angry than panicked now. Amber doesn't seem malicious, just resolved. In her mind, she's being a good friend. The best kind of friend. I don't think she has bad intentions toward me.

"This is my house. My parents are away in the Bahamas at the moment, so there's no one else here."

"You live in a *fortress*?"

"My father is a hedge fund manager, among other things. He needs a lot of security." Along the top of the stone wall, there's a line of barbed wire.

Shit. This is not good.

"Can I at least have my bag back?" I'm sort of on the verge of tears but I hold them. I let them turn into something else. I need to stay focused.

I need to get out of here.

"I can't give you your phone, Stella. I think we both know that. I'll hang onto it. I'll keep it safe. Please believe me when I say I have your best interests at heart. You're safe here. As soon as Carmen has a chance to talk to Kade, I'll have my driver take you back. It might only be a day or so. Maybe even tomorrow morning. Until then, we can hang out—"

"I don't want to *hang out*. I want to go back to Kade's."

"We're here." The car pulls to a stop in front of a huge stone house. "And Stella?"

"What?"

"Don't try to run or scream, okay? It won't help. We're two miles from the nearest neighbor or road and the only people here are my security, who are being paid a lot of money to do exactly what I tell them to do. It's best for everyone if you just accept that this is happening and go with it."

"I'm going to say the same thing to you when you're being delivered your jail sentence," I tell her.

She smiles, like she's above the law. Maybe she is.

As we get out of the car and I'm led into her mansion, I don't scream. I don't run. Mainly because the two hulking guards are watching me. I take in every detail, looking for exits or phones or something that might help me.

"It's late," she says. "Do you want me to show you your room?"

"Okay." Adrenaline is pumping through my veins. I'm a *hostage*. And I'm worried about Kade. Is he home yet? How will he react?

I'm not worried that Carmen will win him back. I know—I *hope*—that's unlikely to happen.

I can admit there's a tiny shadow of doubt at the back of my mind. *You haven't known him that long. Maybe you're wrong. Maybe a part of him still feels attached to her.*

I force it out of my head.

I believe everything he ever said to me.

My bigger worry is that he'll hurt her. That he'll do something that'll get him put behind bars. Or that he'll hurt himself somehow, trying to find me.

I have to get out of here.

Amber shows me to a palatial bedroom with every luxury known to humankind.

"There's a mini-fridge with some food and wine if you're hungry," she says. "There's a jacuzzi bath, an entertainment system, and a small balcony. From which no one will hear you if you yell, by the way. The guards will be outside your locked door. And we're on the third floor so I wouldn't advise trying to jump. The walls are too high to climb anyway. Use the intercom if you need anything. My room is number 7."

"Are you sure you can't just take me back, Amber? Please?"

Her eyes, despite everything, are empathetic. "Hopefully tomorrow. Everything will be fine, Stella. Please just cooperate. I'm sorry, but I had no other choice."

"Of course you had another choice. You could have refused."

"I've already explained why I didn't. Goodnight, Stella."

So I go into my room and the door is closed and locked.

I'm too amped up to try to sleep or to eat.

I need to get out of this room.

I go over to the French doors that lead out to the small balcony, and open them. Around twenty feet from the window, I can see the stone wall and its line of raised barbed wire that runs along the top of it.

Who needs *barbed wire* around their house?

Maybe Amber's father is some kind of mafia boss or shady businessman. It wouldn't surprise me.

I also notice there's a tree next to the balcony. A big one, with thick branches.

One of the branches is within reach. And it stretches out to one of the pillars of the stone wall.

Don't even think about it.

If only I could contact Kade. I want him to be okay. I *need* him to be okay.

I know for a fact that he'll be going out of his mind. Carmen is telling him, maybe even right this minute, that I've left him. That I couldn't handle the "lifestyle" of his fame.

Please figure out that she's lying.

Please don't do anything stupid. Like hurt her. Or kill her.

He wouldn't do that.

Would he?

More likely is that he'll do something crazy, trying to find out where I am.

I don't want anything to happen to him.

I need him to be okay.

Before I can overthink it, I pull myself onto the tree branch, straddling it. I glance down and see that three stories up looks like a *long* way down. My heart's racing but I try to stay focused. I inch my way along the tree branch, getting closer to the wall.

As I make my way along it, the branch gets thinner, bowing slightly under my weight. By the time I reach the wall, I have to strain to curl my fingers over the smooth stone of the top of the wall, hoping like hell my hand isn't going to trigger some high-tech alarm system.

I brace myself.

But nothing happens. No sound. No lights.

So I keep going.

I try to pull myself up.

But it's too smooth. I can't get a grip.

I'm starting to panic now. This is dangerous. I could break a leg if I fall from this height.

What about my baby?

This isn't safe.

I don't know how I can already love the tiny seed of a human growing inside—and I'm not even sure if it's there yet, but some part of me can feel that it is—but I do. *I love it.* I think about whether it will be a boy or a girl and what we might name it. I wonder if it'll look like me or like Kade. Or Madeline. Or Sam. Or Jack.

Shit shit shit.

But I'm this far along now and turning back is just as dangerous as going forward.

So I reach higher, to the string of barbed wire, feeling for a space between the barbs that's smooth enough to grab. With one hand.

Please.

Then two.

It's good.

It's tightly wound. It will hold my weight. I can get a secure enough grip to pull myself up.

I do it.

I climb up and get one foot onto the wall. I'm close enough to one of the pillars to use it to hoist myself up.

I can do this.

I can climb over this wall.

As I'm pulling myself up, one of the barbs claws my jeans, ripping a hole and scraping a cut into my leg. *Damn, it's sharp.*

I ignore the pain, focusing instead on my balance. With careful concentration, I lift one leg over the barbed wire, making sure my foot is securely placed. Peering down the other side of the wall, I can see it's less of a drop. Maybe fifteen feet. There's grass and a few rocks. There's a field with trees beyond it. We're on the other side of the wall from the entrance. I'm sure there will be a road somewhere. She said two miles, which isn't far. She won't discover I'm gone until the morning and by then I'll be long gone.

I step my other foot over.

I'm over.

Just then the sound of a night bird close by startles me and I lose my balance.

Shit.

I'm falling.

As I do, I try to jump instead of fall, toward a patch of grass. But as I do this my arm scrapes hard against the barbed wire, painfully slicing a deep gash along my inner arm.

The fall feels strangely timeless. I'm aware of each second that passes.

I'm even more aware of the hard ground as I hit it. There's a sharp pain on one side of my head.

For a peaceful moment, I look up at the sky. I can see

a star in the black expanse of clear sky near the half moon and I make a wish. Or what feels like a wish, because all I want to do is say it to him.

I love you.

Then the world goes black.

23

Stella

Ow.

Ow.

My head.

I reach to touch the side of my forehead where the pain is searing and it feels hot and sticky. I pull my hand away and my fingers are slick with blood. My wrist hurts and I can see that there's blood there too.

A lot of blood.

Jesus.

I got kidnapped and climbed over a wall.

I'm lying in a field. I blacked out and I'm bleeding.

I'm bleeding a lot.

The delicate skin of my inner wrist is cut. Deeply. It's exactly the kind of cut you'd make if you—

If you wanted to kill yourself.

Which I really, really don't.

I take off the jacket I'm wearing and I wrap it around my wrist, doing my best to tie it as tightly as I can.

I need to find help.

Should I go back to that house?

Am I dying?

I don't feel like I'm dying. I feel light-headed and dizzy and I have a terrible headache. But I'm outside the wall.

And I don't want to risk getting locked up again.

I need to find Kade.

I need to make sure he's okay.

I try to stand up. It takes me a minute to find my balance—my equilibrium feels off—but I finally do.

I start walking across the field.

The woods aren't too thick and the night is clear so I can see enough to make my way through. I listen for the sound of cars or a road but I can't hear anything.

I keep walking for what might be a half hour. Or an hour. Or two. It's hard to tell.

The woods start to clear out into an open expanse of field.

My headache feels like it's going to bust my skull open and the jacket tied around my wrist is now dark with blood. I touch my head and the bleeding there seems to have slowed but the side of my face is sticky.

I just need to keep walking.

I hear something.

My heart skips a beat because I'm alone in the wilderness. The scene is like something straight out of a horror movie and I no doubt look the part. But I stop walking and listen to the sound.

It's a car. In the distance.

I'm getting close to a road.

I keep walking and practically faint with relief when the stretch of road becomes visible.

God, my head is spinning. But I have to keep going.

I get to the road and I look both ways, and there, maybe around a hundred or more feet to my right, is the neon sign of a gas station.

It takes me a long time to get there.

It's open, but there are no cars.

It must be very late.

Where are pay phones when you need them? In the movies, there's always a pay phone outside the gas stations where the people in trouble can call whoever they need to and they know their phone numbers. They have quarters in their pocket or they make a collect call.

There's no pay phone.

And I don't know his number.

I go into the gas station. The bright fluorescent lights hurt my eyes.

As I approach the counter, the guy sitting behind it stands up. He's young, maybe a few years older than me. His eyes get wide.

The look on his face shocks me.

Do I look that bad?

"Excuse me," I manage to say. "Can I use your phone? I don't have mine. I need to call someone."

"Uh...s-sure. Shit. Are you okay? You're bleeding."

I feel strange. Like I'm viewing this scene from somewhere outside my own body. "Do you have a phone?"

He pulls one out of his back pocket. "Here. Use mine." He keys in the passcode and hands it to me.

"Thank you." I take the phone and stare at it for a few seconds. I so desperately, desperately want to call Kade. But I don't know his number. I don't want to call my parents. They're too far away and it would only worry them. The obvious choice is 911. But then I remember something.

My number's easy to remember. It's 615-565-6565.

Sam.

Sam has Kade's number.

God, my fingers are slippery. *Why is there so much blood?*

I key in the number and hold the phone up to my ear.

He answers on the third ring. "Hello?"

He sounds like he just woke up and I'm sorry about that but I say, "Sam? It's Stella."

I half expect him to say *Who?* or *Why are you calling me?*

But he doesn't. He says, "Stella. What's wrong? Are you okay?" Maybe he can hear in my voice that I'm not.

"No."

There's a brief, electric pause. "Stella, where are you?"

"I'm at a gas station. I need help. I need you to call

Kade and tell him to come get me." I glance up at the guy, who's watching me with concern. "Where are we?"

The guy tells me the address and I tell it to Sam and the place is really starting to spin. The guy takes the phone and he's helping me to a chair by a table. "She needs an ambulance," the guy is saying to Sam. "Yeah, definitely. She just wandered in here. We're a few miles west of town. Yeah, okay. I'm going to hang up and call 911."

Time passes and I weave in and out of consciousness.

The guy who's with me—his name is Billy, he tells me—holds my head and gives me sips of water. He lays his coat over me and tells me I'm going to be fine. They're on their way, he says. He can hear the sirens.

I don't want sirens, I tell him. I just want Kade. I want to tell him I love him.

I'm crying because I want to *live.* I want us to stay in our writing room and have our baby. I don't want him to worry. I want to give him everything he needs. I want to take care of him.

"You going to do all that," Billy assures me. "Here they are."

The sliding doors of the gas station open and the wild relief slays me. *There he is.*

God, I'd forgotten how big and how freaking glorious he is.

He sees me and he looks more than shocked. He looks worried and sad and furious, all at the same time. He comes over to me and he kneels beside where I'm leaning against Billy on a hard, plastic bench.

"Stella." Kade sort of gasps my name and he sounds edgy as fuck. And wild with a quiet storm of emotions.

I don't want him to be sad. Or mad. I try to tell him this but I can't quite figure out how to form the words. I'm too dizzy.

Someone else is with him who looks a lot like him and I guess it must be his other brother. Travis. But then the room spins again and I need to close my eyes or I'm going to be sick.

With infinite care, Kade lifts me and he carries me to the door, where an ambulance is pulling up.

He climbs inside the ambulance with me and there are people around me but I cling to Kade's hand with everything I have.

Someone pokes a needle into my arm and there's a cool wash of numbing comfort.

Wait, I want to say.

I want to tell him I love him.

I have so much to tell him.

24

KADE

I INSIST on driving and Travis can see that I'm in no mood to be argued with. I don't fucking care if I get arrested and even though he drives like a maniac himself, he's clutching the side handle of his Mustang by the time we get to Forest Hills. As we're driving, we don't say much. But my mind is buzzing.

I've lived my whole life half broken and half devastated. It started with our parents' downward spiral, which affected all of us but sometimes I think it affected me most of all, because I was aware of it. I was the oldest and I could see that they were both doomed. The crying and the fighting. Their love that was so strong but so damaged by his addiction and her refusal to see it or even really acknowledge that he needed help. That they both needed help.

Later, after my parents died and I was finally able to

get some distance from all that, I knew I could fix the thing in me that was broken if I could only find someone to *prove* that I could do it better, with everything I had. And now I have. My unicorn girl, who walked into my life and lit the whole thing up like a shining sun, finally giving it meaning and infusing it with a blazing kind of love that has become everything about me.

"I don't know if I can live without her." At first I don't even realize that I've said it out loud. "I don't want to live without her."

Travis stares at me. "Kade. You won't have to." He's shocked by the way I'm acting. It's not normal. I'm usually the calm one. The one who holds everyone else's lives together. "You just met her."

"I don't fucking care about that! I need her."

"I'm sure she's fine, Kade." His attempt to reassure me has no effect on me whatsoever. "Everything will be fine."

"Whatever happens to me, I want you to take care of them, Travis. Vaughn and Roxie. The two of them are more fragile than us. You'll have to make sure Vaughn's okay, and Roxie—"

"Kade. What are you talking about? You're going to do that yourself. You're not going anywhere. Come on. Don't say shit like that." There's a lot of tragedy in the backstory of our family, and Gage's, so what I'm saying digs deep and it should. I can relate to all of it now. All that long-ago sorrow is rising up.

"Something's wrong," I tell him. "I can feel it."

"Slow down. This is it, up here on the right."

We pull up to the gate of the house and I punch on the intercom buzzer.

"Hello?" It's a girl's voice, slurred from sleep.

"Amber, it's Kade Tucker and I'm coming in. Let me the fuck in or I'm calling the cops and having you put away for a very long time. Open the fucking gate and open your goddamn door."

There's a pause. "It wasn't my idea, Kade."

"I don't give a fuck whose idea it was. Let me in." Fuck, my voice sounds cold. I'm a different person now. My heart has been stolen from me and I'm an empty shell of rage and revenge. The gate starts opening and I gun the accelerator up the long driveway then screech to a stop in front of the door.

Amber is there and she holds the door open for me. "Up the stairs. Third floor. It's the last door on the left. I've told the guards to let you in."

I run up the stairs, taking them in threes.

"It wasn't my fault," she yells after me.

The guards are expecting me and they cooperate, probably picking up on the fact that they'll go to prison if they don't, and possibly might anyway—and that I'm fully prepared to kill any fucker who gets in my way.

I storm into the room.

It's empty.

There's not even a sign that she's been here.

But the doors to the balcony are open.

There's a tree.

A wall.

A very high wall with barbed wire running along the top of it.

She wouldn't, would she?

My phone rings in my pocket.

It's a number I don't recognize. But then...I do recognize it. *My number's easy to remember. 615-565-6565.* Maybe he knows something. "Sam?"

"Kade? Stella just called me. She needs you. She didn't have your number. She's hurt. It's bad, Kade. She needs help."

25

Stella

I open my eyes.

This takes some effort. They close again and I drift for a while. I try to wiggle my fingers. One of my arms feels heavy.

I try again to open my eyes.

The light is bright.

I blink a few times.

I'm in a bed.

I'm in a hospital room.

"Good morning." A woman dressed in scrubs is adjusting a tube that's attached to my arm. "You're awake."

"Where is he?" My voice is rasped from sleep and lack of use.

"He's right here," she says, gesturing to the other side of my bed. "He refuses to leave."

Kade is asleep, sprawled in a reclining chair. His hair is a mess and there's some blood on his jeans. The sleeves of his shirt are rolled up and I can see there's a small bandage on the inside of his arm. "Is he okay?"

"He's fine. Stubborn as a mule, but fine. He's a universal donor."

"A what?"

"You lost a lot of blood and he gave you some of his. You're A positive. So it was a match. We were a bit low so he insisted, even though it was more than we'd usually take from one donor."

The sound of voices wakes him. Kade's eyes open.

He sees that I'm awake and he climbs out of his chair. He comes to me, leaning over me with so much love in his eyes, it brings tears to mine. "Hey, little unicorn girl."

"You're here."

"You scared me." He smooths a strand of my hair. "You just can't do that to me, baby." Gently, he kisses me. "I need you too much."

The nurse tsks. "Easy now, cowboy. You both need rest."

Neither of us answers her. We're too busy staring into each other's eyes.

It doesn't surprise me that he's literally given me his lifeblood. I can feel him coursing through my veins and in the beat of my heart.

"Now," the nurse says, consulting her clipboard. "I have the results of some of your tests here that I'd like to discuss with you, Stella. If you don't mind giving us some privacy, Mr. Tucker, you can wait outside."

"I told you to call me Kade, Nurse Jenkins."

She titters like a teenager. "And I told you to call me Marla. You're a devil, that's what you are, Kade Tucker." Like the two of them are best friends. It's easy to see she's charmed by the big, blue-eyed rock star in her charge. She taps her pen on her clipboard, feigning impatience, waiting for him to leave. "Out you go."

"Kade can stay," I tell her.

The nurse eyes me, then Kade. "I think you might prefer to hear these test results in private."

"It's okay," I assure her. Because I know what she's going to say. "He's the father."

Kade stares down at me sharply. There's shock in his expression, and a deep, layered concern as his gaze drops to the I.V. in one of my arms and the bandage on the other. But then I can see in his expression a subdued happiness. And a cautious, whole-souled hope. "What are you trying to tell me, darlin'?"

"I can confirm," says the nurse, enjoying his reaction. "Stella, you lost a lot of blood but thanks to Mr. O over here, all your vital signs have returned to normal. You've suffered a minor concussion. The wound on your wrist was a nasty one but it's been taped and is healing nicely. And you're pregnant."

When she confirms it—loudly like that—I would never have expected to feel so much...*relief.*

Kade sits on the side of my bed and holds my face in his warm hands and leans his forehead against mine, staring into my eyes. "You're going to have my *baby*? Stella. My girl. My beautiful girl."

We're immersed in this bubble of gravity, love and the magnitude of this news.

And how it feels remarkably like it's meant to be.

I'm only twenty-one. My life was on a completely different trajectory only a month ago, and one that never quite felt like a perfect fit.

This one fits. It absolutely, completely fits.

The nurse tells us she'll give us some time to adjust to our new status as parents-to-be and she leaves us to it. We barely notice.

"I didn't mean for it to happen," I tell him. "That first week we met, I forgot to take a few of my pills."

"I think I can take some of that blame too. At least half. Maybe more than half."

"You're happy?" *I hope he's happy.* I don't know why *I'm* so happy.

"Of course I'm happy, baby girl. I'm over the moon."

"All that pushing yourself back inside," I whisper.

There's a dazzling, cocky glint in his blue eyes. "I was trying to knock you up."

This makes me smile, despite everything, because...well, maybe he was. Thinking back on it now, it sort of seems like he might have been. He definitely didn't hold back. "You were very thorough about it."

"I was, wasn't I?"

"You really were."

His tone becomes more serious. "You're my *life*, Stella. When I lost you, I thought—" His words catch in his throat, like he's overcome with emotion.

"I'm okay, Kade. We're together now."

"I'm never letting you out of my sight again."

"I guess you're stuck with me."

"Stella, marry me. Please marry me. Fuck, I love you so much, baby."

I'm so happy it hurts. "I guess I'll have to now."

"I guess you will." His smile is tender and staunch and alpha as all hell. He's my dream man, my star-crossed lover and my hero, all rolled into one sexy, beautiful package. I can't believe I get to spend the rest of my life with him. "We're going to have the best life together, sweetheart. We're going to do everything we always wanted. With our babies and your books and we'll travel the world and we'll never be apart."

I kiss his perfect lips. "I love you, Kade Tucker."

"Is that a yes?" With a thread of hopefulness, like he's still not entirely sure I'll say yes to him.

"Yes, Kade." I smile and kiss him again. "Yes."

Stella

I GOT DISCHARGED from the hospital four days later, and Kade took me home to his other Tennessee house, in Franklin, just outside of Nashville. It sits on seven acres and is without a doubt the most beautiful home I've ever seen. It's newly built, with all the mod cons. It has six colossal bedrooms, each with its own bathroom, a chef's kitchen, three living areas, a game room, a recording studio, a library and a gigantic stone and glass conservatory with vaulted wooden ceilings. There's an outdoor entertainment area too, complete with a pool, fountain, TV area and a hot tub. Gated rolling lawns are dotted with trees, sculptures and statues, and there's a pretty lake with a dock, as well as a guest house that's at least three times the size of my rental apartment back in Princeton.

"I want to live here forever," I told him.

He laughed. "That can be arranged. You haven't seen

the New York loft yet, but we'll do whatever makes you happy. That's the only thing I care about."

The property is right next to estates owned by Travis and Vaughn, so we see a lot of them. I've gotten to know Travis's fiancée Ruby and her sister Gigi, who's engaged to Vaughn. Sometimes Gigi and I spend our afternoons by the pool, as I write and Gigi studies for her degree in social work. She's got a calming presence and she's fun. We've become close.

My relationship with Madeline has become a sort of gift in my life. She's patient and kind and so relieved just to know me that it has grounded me in a way that's hard to explain. When I talk to her on the phone or we meet up for lunch or we email each other, which we do often, I sometimes feel as though I'm talking to *myself*. It's uncanny how similar we are as people.

I'm in touch with Jack less often but he's written me several emails. He said he wants to tell me the whole story, starting at the beginning. So far it almost feels like the first few chapters of a novel, starting from his very first memories and his early childhood. He's explaining to me the details of his family life and his upbringing and said he wanted to do it in order, so I can begin to understand what happened, and why. So far he's only up to his eighth birthday and I've asked him to keep going. Every sentence is fascinating to me. He's a born storyteller and his writing style is giving me ideas. He promised me he's working on the next chapter and that he'll send it as soon as it's ready.

Madeline and Jack have also struck up a renewed friendship. I don't have any visions of them rekindling their old relationship and I'm not sure if either of them wants to, but for now, it's nice just to know they're in touch.

I told my parents that I'd done the search and I'd found my birth parents. They were supportive and they both told me they would have wanted to do the same thing if they were in my shoes, but that they knew it was my own journey and my own decision. My mother even said she'd love to meet them one day, and to thank them for me —one of the two best things that has ever happened to her. Hearing my mother say that to me was both touching and therapeutic. I don't have to feel like anything's missing anymore. I don't have to feel like a square peg in a round hole, or feel guilty for wondering about who I am. And I'm excited by the thought of introducing my two families, if they ever want me to, when the time is right.

I know who I am in every sense of the word now and it's an incredibly powerful feeling.

Sam has visited us several times and he and Kade play music together. Kade was impressed by how good he is and has even asked him to collaborate on a song on his next solo album. When Summer visited us for a week during her last break, Summer and Sam got along like a house on fire. Summer said that if he's *my* brother then he's also *her* brother and they joke and tease each other like actual siblings, which for some reason makes me as happy as anything ever has.

Kade gave Billy—the guy who worked at the gas station and who might have saved my life—three hundred thousand dollars, a brand new Shelby GT350, two back-stage passes to the band's next show and his phone number, in case Billy ever needed anything. Billy wrote a gushing thank you note telling us he quit his job at the gas station and has applied to medical school, which has been his lifelong dream but one he could never afford. Kade offered to pay for it.

Kade's lawyers prosecuted Carmen to the full extent of the law. She was fined $25,000 and sentenced to two years in a minimum security prison. At my insistence, the sentence was downgraded to two years of community service and two years of weekly court-ordered therapy. She's also not allowed to contact us or come within two miles of us. If she breaches any of those terms she'll be sent directly to prison with no possibility of parole.

I didn't want her to go to prison. She was devastated to have lost him and in some ways I could understand that. Either way, I thought prison sounded excessively harsh so I wouldn't budge on at least giving her a chance to redeem herself.

Kade finally relented, but he made sure she understood that next time he wouldn't be so forgiving (in slightly more colorful language).

Amber and the two bodyguards got a lesser sentence of a $5,000 fine each and sixty days of community service. My bag was returned to me and, through her lawyer, Amber sent me a long, heartfelt apology, telling me she was sorry I was hurt because of something she'd done. I wrote back to her and told her I forgave her. I don't have room in my life for holding grudges. It's too full of the good stuff.

Kade Tucker is a dream in every sense of the word. Every day I wonder how I got so lucky.

He dotes on me and cooks for me. He plays music to me and he tells stories to the baby growing inside me, which he's convinced is a girl. We've decided not to find out. I've never met anyone who's so excited about becoming a father as Kade is and I know he's going to be amazing.

My own parents were, of course, surprised by the news that I'm expecting a baby and that I'm engaged. I don't know if it's because my father's a huge fan of Kade's music, or if it's just because I'm deeply and resolutely happy and content in a way that's new, or if it's because I spent time in the hospital and they're thankful that I'm okay, but my parents were surprisingly accepting of our news, and even sort of wildly excited about it. I told my dad I still might continue with my PhD one day but not right now and he was understanding, considering everything else that's been going on.

I even told my parents about the book I'm writing and they were intrigued, especially my mother. Turns out she reads romance. She only has literary fiction and the New Yorker and the New York Times Book Review on display on the bookshelves and coffee tables where she entertains the economics department—but her Kindle is loaded with "the good stuff," she told me, which made me laugh. In this way, the two of us have connected on a whole new level.

I haven't heard from Theo since our last phone call but my father did mention that he's dating his new teaching assistant, who happens to be writing her thesis on Tolstoy. Sounds like a perfect match.

My cuts healed and my concussion, I'm convinced, has spurred a creative rush that has basically consumed me since the second I got out of the hospital. For several weeks, Kade had to pry the laptop from my hands to make sure I wasn't overworking or wearing myself out. But the book is going well. The words literally pour out of me and I'm sometimes struggling to type fast enough to keep up with my thoughts.

The first draft is finished. I'm still working on the edits. Kade has been helpful and insightful all the way through. He asks all the right questions and the book is much better for his input. He keeps telling me he thinks it would make a great movie. He said he has a friend who's a producer that he's going to get in touch with, but I told him to wait until it's ready.

I'm now sixteen weeks pregnant and starting to really show.

"I'm taking you to New York," Kade says. "We're leaving tonight."

"Why tonight?" I almost protest. I love this house and the thought of traveling all the way to New York feels like a lot of effort.

"I have something special planned for us for the weekend. It's a surprise. We're taking the bus, just the two of us." Kade hates flying so anytime we go somewhere we always take the tour bus, which is like a luxury apartment on wheels. "I'll make sure you and my baby are taken care of and well-rested every step of the way. But first there's something I need to do."

"What's that?"

We're sitting out by the pool in the outdoor living area. It's still hard to get used to the opulence of my new life with Kade. I don't need any of it, as long as I can be with him. I still sometimes have to pinch myself that he's real.

I'm sitting on a lounger with my laptop. It's spring and the air is warm in Nashville. The property is dotted with flowering trees and the fountain over the pond in the distance casts a glittering rainbow.

"Click 'Save,'" Kade says.

"It saves automatically."

He takes my laptop and closes it, setting it aside. He takes something out of his pocket.

In the sun, his eyes are a clear, tropical blue.

He gets down on one knee.

"Stella Juliet Bell, you're the love of my life, my unicorn girl, my muse, my dream lover, the reason I want to keep breathing, the mother of my baby and the best friend I've ever had. I love you more than I could ever put into bass lines or words. I want to give you everything I have and spend every minute of every day—and every night—trying my hardest to make you the happiest woman in the world. Because you light up my life. Baby girl, will you marry me?"

I'm crying and kissing him because my heart is overflowing with love for this beautiful hero who stepped out of my wildest fantasies and showed me how to be the very best version of myself. "I already told you yes, Kade Tucker. A thousand times yes."

He smiles, sliding a ring onto my finger. It's two delicate rose gold bands held together by a chain of glinting diamonds. "Good. Because a dress designer and his team are arriving soon. Roxie said he's the hottest designer in New York right now and she's coming too to help you get fitted. I don't want to wait any longer. I want you to be my wife."

The designer, whose name is Christian, arrives five minutes later, along with Roxie, Gigi and a team of no less than ten of Christian's staff, with drawings and fabrics, photographs and patterns. They're all buzzing with ideas and Roxie and Gi help me decide on a silk bodice (that will accommodate my growing baby bump), a long, light-weight skirt with feather detailing and a veil embroidered with tiny musical notes.

As soon as the design has been decided, Kade tells me the bus is waiting and we're leaving for New York.

We sleep on the bus and the driver drives through the night. Kade makes slow, hot love to me and holds me in his arms all night long.

"How would you feel about getting married this weekend?" he asks me.

"Well, I think we'd need to organize—"

"If all that was taken care of, how would you feel about it? Would you feel ready?"

"Yes. Of course." Just as he asks the question, I feel the tiniest flutter inside me. "*Kade*. I just felt something." I place his hand on my growing tummy. "I think she likes that idea."

We get to New York City in the late morning and Kade takes me to his SoHo loft—and now I'm having a hard time deciding if this is my new favorite of his houses or if it's tied for first with the Franklin house, with the New Orleans house a close third.

The loft takes up the entire top floor of a corner building. It has huge open spaces, the kind of natural light New Yorkers kill for, wooden beams, exposed brick, four large bedrooms, a state of the art kitchen, and even a roof garden.

From the roof garden, you can see the Empire State Building. It reminds me of our conversation about it, how I happen to think it's the most romantic location in the world for some reason. Maybe we can figure out how to fit it into our own love story while we're here in New York. I think about suggesting it to him, but his phone rings and the moment passes.

In the morning, Kade cooks me breakfast. "Roxie's arriving soon and she's going to take you out for a few hours," he tells me.

"Roxie's in New York?"

Just then the buzzer of the door rings. Roxie arrives and the two of them are full of a smug mischief I can't quite read. "What's going on?"

"I'm taking you to a spa for the day," Roxie says. "We'll see Kade tonight."

I'm a little confused by their knowing glances. I go along with it because I think I can guess what they're up to but they won't tell me anything.

Before we leave, Kade holds my face gently with his warm hands and kisses me. The kiss is so full of feeling I can't help asking him, "What's up? Is there something I need to know? Are we—"

"I love you," he says.

"I love you too."

"Come on," Roxie laughs, pulling me by the hand. "You'll see each other in a few hours."

She takes me to a spa where we get massaged, waxed, plucked and groomed to within an inch of our lives, then we get our hair and make-up done. "Rox, can you please tell me why we're getting glammed up to the nines?"

"I'm sworn to secrecy," is all she'll say.

When we're finished, the make-up artist holds up a piece of black silk. She turns me around in the chair and she blindfolds me. "What——?"

"Just go with it, Stella," Roxie says. "Trust me, you're going to love this."

Blindfolded, I'm ushered into a waiting car by Roxie. We drive for a few blocks, then I'm helped out of the car and we enter an elevator, which takes a long time to get to the top of whatever building it is.

The elevator pings and Roxie guides me out, where some people gather around me.

"Can I take the blindfold off now?" I ask her.

"Not quite."

I'm helped out of my clothes and into a dress, which by now I can guess what it might be—because I can feel that they're pinning a veil to my hair, arranging it and the fall of the feathery fabric.

"Roxie," I gasp. "Am I about to get married?"

"Only if you say 'I do'," she laughs.

"But where are we? Where's Kade?"

"He's here. I'm going to take off your blindfold in just

a few minutes." Once the people who are in charge of dressing me are satisfied, Roxie leads me through a door. I can feel that the air is cooler, like we're outside.

"Stella?" Roxie asks me.

"Yes?"

"Are you ready to become my sister?"

"Oh, Roxie. I can't wait."

Roxie gives me a huge hug. Then she takes off my blindfold and places a large bouquet of white roses in my hand. "These flowers are from Jack," she says. "He couldn't be here today but he got in touch with Kade and the two of them arranged it, so something from this day could be from him. He wanted you to know that he's thinking of you today."

The flowers are beautiful. Roxie's grinning at me. She's wearing a jade green silk jumpsuit and she looks gorgeous.

I look around me. It's dusk and the space is lit by a purple sky and hanging decorative lights. There are white flowers everywhere. And a small crowd of familiar faces.

We're at the top of the Empire State Building. On the observation deck.

He remembered.

Kade is standing by a flower-decorated altar. He's wearing a beautifully-tailored tux with black suede detailing. It's not a regular tux, it's the tux of a rock star.

My rock star.

I love him so much.

He's smiling at me and he's so gorgeous I can't believe my eyes.

There's a minister standing next to him, as well as Vaughn, Travis, Gage and Sam. They're all wearing tuxes. On the other side of the minister stands Summer, Gigi, Ruby and Piper. They're all wearing that same deep green as Roxie but each of them has a uniquely-designed dress with some of the same feather detailing as my own dress. *He even remembered my favorite color.*

My parents are in the crowd and so is Madeline. Some of my friends from college are here. My mother's sister. And...*Bruce Springsteen?* He's holding a guitar and standing by a microphone and he winks at me. *Wow.*

My father walks over to me and kisses my cheek. "I'm so proud of the person you are, Stella. Are you ready for me to walk you down the aisle?"

I hold back the tears but it's hard not to feel over-whelmingly happy. I take his arm. "I love you, Dad."

"Love you too, honey."

A band starts playing and my father walks me down the aisle as Bruce Springsteen sings our wedding song.

Is this a dream?

But then we're at the altar my father kisses my cheek. He shakes Kade's hand then he places my hand in Kade's.

And I gaze up into Kade's face like I did that very first night we met in the pouring rain. "You're the most beautiful thing I've ever seen, darlin'," he whispers. "Do you like your surprise?"

"I love it so much. I love you so much."

We say our vows right there at the top of the Empire State Building, surrounded by our family and friends. The minister pronounces us man and wife and Kade kisses me for a long time.

We dance our first dance to She's The One, my favorite Bruce Springsteen song—sung by the man himself. Then he joins the party and Ruby sings a song, then Travis. And then Kade. It goes like this:

> I used to look for her in the faces of the
>   crowd
> In every stranger's smile
> Every country road, every city mile
> I searched in every golden sunrise and
>   every purple dusk
> Always hoping she'd turn up
> Once, my unicorn girl was made of
>   dreams
> I'd fall to my knees
> I'd beg her, lover, please
> Show up for me
>
> One starstruck night
> Lost and found, there she was
> Laughter in the pouring rain

Fixing all my forgotten pain
With emerald eyes that shine
She's mine
The loneliness gone
With her in my arms, I'm where I belong
My star-crossed lover
My unicorn girl

We dance until late and it's the most magical night of my life. Because I'm Stella Juliet Bell Tucker and I get to keep him.

KADE TAKES me to Key West for our honeymoon and we spend a week at Gage and Luna's new spa and resort. It's fabulous.

Kade's newest tattoo is my name, in my own handwriting, which for some reason he loves, inked right over his heart. With a unicorn next to it.

And five months after our wedding I give birth to a baby girl. We name her Adeline Pearl Bell Tucker. She has white-blond hair, like Kade did when he was very young, and bright green eyes exactly the same color as mine.

Kade is absolutely smitten. He won't allow her to cry herself to sleep or fuss at all and I sometimes tell him he'll spoil her too much but he says that's impossible. He says spoiling the two of us is the only thing he cares about and that's all he's ever going to do.

We spend most of our time at the house in Franklin but we also regularly visit New York, where we can see my parents, and New Orleans, where Summer and Sam came to visit us and Kade and Sam had their first gig together. Sam just put out his first record. Partly because he's credited with co-writing a song on Kade's newest album but also because he has a beautiful voice and he layers his sound with harmonies on his double bass, which I'm convinced he's a genius at, he's already had a million downloads.

I finished my book and sent it out to my dream literary agent—who offered to represent me on the very same day I sent the email. One week after that, there was a bidding war between publishers and the book sold for *a million dollars*. I couldn't believe that. I'm well-aware it could have something to do with my brand new last name, but they genuinely seemed very excited about the story too. The book's sex scenes were described as "smokin' hot" and "authentic"—maybe because...well, I've done my research. And I know how lust at first sight with the true love of your life actually feels. I gave the money to Kade's foundation, which I'm now one of the directors of. Two weeks after that, my book got picked up by Netflix and is going to be made into a movie. I know Kade played a hand in that part because he called his friend who's a producer, but he insists the rest was all me.

I'm not entirely sure either way, but what I do know is that Kade was right: when you start being true to yourself, it's a lot easier to achieve the things you want to achieve, and best of all, to be comfortable in your own skin.

They're already asking for the next book.

I often think about the kismet behind our own story and all the details that had to line up perfectly to make our chance encounter happen. The adoption agency letter that made my decision. Theo's proposal that spurred my need to leave. The Airbnb host not answering their doorbell. All of it. And how every piece of my soul is so overwhelmingly thankful that *I didn't miss him.*

I never did end up leaving a review for the Airbnb host. I wasn't charged for it and there were no messages. I was almost tempted to write a thank you note. *Thank you for not answering your door that night. Because of you, I ran into the love of my life right there on the street outside your door.* In the end, it felt best to leave it, and to just appreciate that Kade's stars and my own, for whatever reason, were perfectly aligned on that rainy night in Nashville.

When Addie is seven months old, I find out I'm pregnant again.

We name our second daughter Savannah Grace, after both our mothers. It was only then that I realized that Adeline's name is so similar to Madeline's. Maybe it was a subconscious tribute to her, after not knowing where she was for so long, and finally finding her.

Savannah's hair is a pale, coppery red—we have no

idea where that came from, although Madeline once mentioned her mother's hair tinted red in the sunlight—with ringlet curls, and her eyes are a bright blue-green. Like Jack's. Their color changes with her moods. She's full of mischief and has a definite twinkle in her eye. Kade is so tightly wound around her little finger it makes me laugh sometimes. It seems she's inherited Kade's musical talent because she became obsessed with her miniature guitar before she even learned how to talk and started picking out little tunes, which charmed her father to no end. They play together all the time and he's teaching her, but she has her own flair which he's nurturing and encouraging.

My mother and Madeline have struck up a unique friendship and I love this. All those old questions are gone now and I'm thankful. I used to feel like I stood out from the crowd for all the wrong reasons, that I'd been abandoned, or unwanted. Now I feel like I was given a lucky score, of two families, who now feel like one. Sam and Madeline even spent last Christmas with us.

Jack's story that he wrote for me is finished. It's a sad one and it explains so much. I asked him if Madeline could read it and he said he wouldn't mind. Last I heard, she'd gotten in touch with him after she finished it, they talked for a long time and he invited her to visit him in Houston.

Carmen not only fulfilled her community service but became a major benefactor of several of the homeless shelters she worked at. Through the lawyers, she wrote me a letter thanking me for not sending her to jail, apologizing for everything, and telling me that her community service completely changed her outlook on life. For her sake, I hope that's true. Apparently she's dating another Nashville musician and the two of them recently got engaged.

Two years after Savannah, we have a son named Kade Jacob Jr. The name is a good fit because he's the spitting image of his father, with the same blue, soulful eyes. We call him KJ, which was Kade's childhood nickname. He spends all his time with his pencils and his pad of paper. Even though he can't quite write the alphabet yet, he fills up his papers with scribbled lines like he sees in books. He tells us convoluted stories of pirates, dinosaurs and spaceships, or some combination of all three. He adores being read to. And banging on Vaughn's drums like there's no tomorrow. He's my little shadow and he follows me wherever I go.

Now, it's late and I'm in bed with KJ at my breast. He'll be two in a few months, but it's his favorite bedtime ritual and he's so cuddly and sweet I can't bear to give it up, especially since there were complications with KJ's birth that might mean I can't have more children.

Kade comes in after putting the girls to bed and lifts our sleeping son. "I want mommy," KJ whispers in his sleep, but he doesn't wake and Kade carries him to bed.

Kade returns, and he closes our bedroom door and

climbs into bed with me. "I want mommy," he says, nuzzling my breasts. "I love my wife." He draws my nipple into his mouth, fastening around the taut bud.

I push at his head. I don't know why he loves doing this, but there's no dislodging him. He's holding me down, suckling on me, pulling tenderly with his mouth. The sensation is indescribable.

"I love you," he's murmuring. "Your face, your hair, your eyes. I *love* you. All of you. Your body. Your heart. Everything, everything."

He kisses a line down my stomach and I'm self-conscious now about my stretch marks and the scar from the surgery I had to have with KJ. None of my pregnancies were easy ones, and each birth left me with new battle scars. Like Kade always said, life will give you as much angst as you can handle. The morning sickness, the emergency surgery, the early arrival of Savannah at only thirty-four weeks and her month-long stint in the hospital.

Kade absorbed all the angst, beaming it back out as the purest kind of support I ever could have asked for. He's so *there* for me, so in love with me, so much my shoulder to lean on.

He kisses each scar, despite my attempts to push him away.

"*Mine*," he growls. "You're more beautiful to me now than you've ever been, darlin'. You're the most perfect creature who ever walked this earth. My love. My life."

So instead of pushing him away, I just let him love

me, as he insists on doing. Every imperfection and every flaw. He never seems to see any of them. He never has.

He peels off my panties and I can feel the hot, silky bulk of him as he slides his big cock against the skin of my thigh, seeking, finding, using his own moisture to wet me as he sinks his thickness deep inside me.

Fully possessing me, he gazes down into my eyes. "Have I told you how much I love you yet today?"

In fact he has. Many times. Like he does every day. "You're my star-crossed soul mate, Kade Tucker. My Nashville dream."

He kisses me as he thrusts deep and fills me with his magic. "And you're my unicorn girl. You're the one. You were always the one."

Thank you so much for reading **Nashville Dreams**. If you enjoyed Kade and Stella's story, please consider leaving a quick review or rating on Amazon.

Below I'm including the first chapter of **Arrogant Player**, which is Gage and Luna's story. Gage is a player who thinks he's incapable of love—until he meets his one and only. Luna is the very last thing he was expecting and I had so much fun taking him down a notch. His character arc is one of the most dramatic I've written and he ends up being one of my most romantic and favorite heroes.

I'm also including a sneak peek at **Nashville Lights** — Roxie's book!

xoxo,
Julie

Please come join my Facebook reader group, Julie Capulet's Romantics, where I share cover reveals, insider info and we discuss all things romance!

Sign up for my newsletter to receive my free bonus content and get access to sneak peeks and exclusive giveaways!

Visit my website @ www.juliecapulet.com

Luna LaRoux has poured her heart and soul into her waterfront bar and restaurant, which has the best sunsets in Key West. The only problem is, Luna's best friend and business partner Josie is having money problems, and with twins on the way, Josie has no choice but to sell her half of the business. Actually, it's 51%.

Gage McCabe is spending the weekend in Key West when he happens to overhear an interesting conversation. Between a very pregnant majority shareholder and her stunningly beautiful—and deliciously desperate—business partner.

Gage can't resist. The bar is obviously a thriving business, and his new partner will just have to get used to *him* calling the shots … if she doesn't kill him first. It's this detail that frustrates him the most: she seems entirely immune to his charms. Unheard of. Gage is so sure of his own allure, he bets Luna his share that she'll surrender to him within a month—or the bar is hers.

Perfect. All Luna has to do is resist his drop-dead gorgeous looks, his smug charisma and his impressive …

endowments, then she'll be rid of him for good. Easy, right?

Arrogant Player is a sexy standalone enemies-to-lovers romance starring a reformed alpha playboy and the one woman he can't control … or stay away from.

McCabe Brothers

Chapter One

Plink. I drop one of the nails I'm holding and it splashes into the turquoise water below. I lean further over the railing of the deck of my Key West seaside bar—so far, in fact, that at any minute I might lose my balance and tumble head first into the water. I cling to the rough wood, and feel a giant splinter slide deep into the pad of my thumb. "Shit." I ignore the pain as I hold the nail in place and bang it with my hammer.

"Now *that's* a view I could get used to."

I glance behind me.

It's Kyle, our busboy. He's a competitive weight lifter. He has veiny, pumped-up muscles that look manufactured and steroid-enhanced. "When are you going to go out with me, Luna?"

"I don't date employees, I've already told you that." Around seven hundred times. It wouldn't be appropriate. Besides, he's not my type. Sure, muscles are great but not to the point of resembling an oily, spray-tanned Incredible Hulk.

"Need help?" he says.

"If it's the kind of help that means you get on with your job, then yes, that would be fabulous." I smile at him to take the edge off.

"Come on. How about one little after-work drink tonight?"

When hell freezes over, is what I'm thinking. I don't date pumped-up gym bunnies. Or prowling suits on their conference business trips. Or drunk, over-eager tourists. And *definitely* not home-town jocks. I'm…between types at the moment. For reasons I don't dwell on, especially on a beautiful day like this one.

The sunlight glints off the water in shimmery flecks, glazing everything with its magic, or at least that's how it so often feels to me here in Key West. This little island has become my haven, as though the surrounding barrier of blue water is providing a necessary forcefield. Out there, beyond the Seven Mile Bridge, somewhere among the amber waves of grain and just before you get to the purple mountain majesties, lies my past and all my regrets. Here, I can breathe. The sugar sand and lush humidity comfort me in ways I didn't even know it was possible to be comforted. "See you inside, Kyle," I say lightly, pretending to threaten him with my hammer.

"Aw." He wanders off and I resume my work, leaning a little further over the railing, holding on for dear life and desperately hoping I don't catapult myself overboard. I bang another nail into place.

"As if that's going to help," I hear another voice behind me say. I recognize the voice instantly as my best friend, the one and only Josie Farrell. My family moved into the house next to Josie's in Cedar Rapids, Iowa when we were both nine years old. I'd just arrived from New York City still in my city clothes. Josie saw me sitting on my front step, completely lost, like I'd spent so much of my childhood. Over the course of an idyllic summer, she showed me how to hand-squeeze lemonade. How to whistle with a blade of grass. How to find the best hiding places in the barn loft during our long hazy afternoons of playing hide and seek with her older brothers. How to get good height on the rope swing before you let yourself go, to get to the deepest, coolest water of the swimming hole. We've been inseparable ever since.

Her family became my family. My family is what you'd call...what's the word for it? Broken. Dysfunctional. Blended. Or some unhappy combination of all three. My parents divorced very un-amicably (i.e. they basically loathe each other) when I was six years old. My father ran off with his knocked-up (by him) secretary, who definitely didn't want a step-daughter in tow, especially one who was the spawn of her new husband's evil ex-wife. My mother is what you might generously refer to as a social climber. I think somewhere deep down inside her gold-digging heart she genuinely loved my father. The fact that their marriage imploded made her, in a way, give up on love altogether. So she went for money instead. Luckily for her, she was—and still is—beautiful enough to get away with it. Before the ink on her divorce papers was even dry, she moved us out of the only home I'd ever known and in with husband number two, a Manhattan real estate developer. I somehow found myself mired in the world of the super-rich. A limo driver drove me to my private school each morning. We had chefs and house-keepers, an indoor pool and gym, even a helicopter pad on the roof. My mother thought she'd died and gone to heaven. Me, not so much.

I discovered I'm not cut out to be super-rich. Maybe that sounds strange since so many people seem to crave it or aspire to it, but I just don't happen to be one of them. I spent three years living someone else's warped fantasy, which to me felt more like a gilded prison. Like being forced to wear a diamond-studded suit that didn't fit.

I prefer the simple things in life. A good friend to laugh with. A late-summer field of wheat to walk through. A beach at sunset. A cold beer after a hard day's work.

People sometimes call me a hippie or a free spirit. I'm not sure if I'm either of those things. I am what I am, and it's…unique, so I'm told.

In Iowa, with its rolling hills and big blue skies, I finally felt free. I could get dirty and ride a bike and play flashlight tag in the dark. I could see the stars.

And Josie was there for all of it. Her family was everything mine wasn't. Big and loud and fun and close-knit. I found out what it feels like to laugh and to feel loved. It didn't matter that it wasn't my own family loving me. Josie's family felt more like mine than my own family ever has. So when my mother's second marriage fizzled out a few years later and she decided to move to Los Angeles for husband number three, I stayed with Josie.

The next two years ended up being a time of my life when I could have used a mother, as it turned out.

No one ever tells you the hard stuff can be harder than you ever imagined. No one tells you that some of that hard stuff is going to cut you down until you know for a fact you'll never be quite the same. Or that you're going to need more courage than you ever knew you had.

Somehow, I survived those two years.

The day after we graduated from high school, we jumped into Josie's beat-up old van and headed for Flor-ida. We couldn't get out of there fast enough. For her, it was her one chance to get out of the town she'd been born in and had never left. For me, it was a form of recovery. I needed to get out of that town like a drowning man in shark-infested waters needs a lifeboat.

We decided on Key West for no other reason except that we liked the sound of it.

And after three days of travel, as we drove through the tiny, sun-charmed, character-laden town, I knew I'd found the place I wanted to stay. Forever is a long time, but for me, something about the lazy heat that oozes out of this place answered a craving in my soul that was hard to explain. I still can't see myself ever leaving.

We got jobs as waitresses. We found a run-down one-room apartment, swam in the ocean and saved all our money. Turns out waitresses can earn good tips in Key West.

Three years later, when Josie's father died and left her a small inheritance (her mother had died years earlier, before I met her), we pooled all the savings we had, I sold an emerald bracelet Stepfather Number One had given me for my eighth birthday, and we somehow managed to scrape together enough money to put a down payment on a business that had just come up for sale. Our bar, where we'd worked all along.

It's a business that could do with a few upgrades. Okay, more than a few. It costs a lot of money to run—more than we ever anticipated, and exactly as much as it earns, barely—but I like a challenge. We jumped in at the deep end and we're trying like hell to learn how to swim. That was exactly ten months ago. "We're going to have to get this deck repaired by someone who actually knows what they're doing, Luna."

"I know. We will. But we can't afford to right now," I say cheerfully. I climb back over the railing. I'm wearing a cut-off pair of jean shorts and a fitted pink t-shirt with our bar's logo on the front. *Sea Breeze.* Which is now very dirty from my handywoman failure. The railing doesn't look any sturdier than it did five minutes ago. "Maybe a coat of paint will help."

Josie gives me a look. "Paint doesn't hold things together, Loon." It's the nickname she gave me a long time ago.

Josie has brown hair that's pulled back into a messy bun. Her dark eyes glint with that familiar twinkle and a slightly-exasperated expression. Her cheeks are pink with health and the kind of glow that could only mean one thing. Josie found out around six months ago that she got pregnant after a one night stand with a guy she never heard from again. The discovery was a shock, of course, and the past few months haven't been easy for her, to put it mildly. We cried together, because the whole scenario reminded us too much of the reason we left Iowa in the first place.

But once Josie got used to the idea, we decided there was no reason the two of us couldn't raise that baby right here in Key West. I promised I'd help her every step of the way. Of course I will. Besides, it won't be a bad thing for that little baby to grow up watching sunsets and playing in the sand, we figured.

"How'd your appointment go?" I ask her.

Her eyes fill with tears.

"Josie." Fearing the worst, I pull her into a hug. "What's wrong?"

"It's *twins*, Luna."

"Twins?" I pull back and hold her shoulders gently as I take in this information.

"Twin boys."

"Wow. Josie. That's…"

"Scary as fuck. I know. I don't know how to raise a baby by myself, let alone *two*. Luna, what am I going to do?"

I hug her again as she breaks down. She's done a lot of worrying over the past few months and I don't blame her. We have a budget health insurance plan that won't cover all her costs. Our bar gets plenty of customers but the rougher edges of the much-needed maintenance are really starting to show. Who am I kidding, they were always showing. It would be very easy to take this business to the next level—*if* we had a pile of cash to throw at it, which we don't. We tried to borrow more but the bank said we don't have enough equity. In fact the loan officer we spoke to was amazed we got the loan we did in the first place.

But we'll figure it out, like we always do. That's the thing about life, you *have* to figure it out. There's no other choice. "You're going to have those babies right here and we're going to take care of them together. On the beach, like we always talked about."

"That fantasy included true love and filthy rich men, Luna. Not destitute single mothers."

I don't remember the men being filthy rich in our fantasies, not mine at least, but I don't bother saying this. As for the destitute single mothers comment, I let that slide. When you're seventeen and on the road to Key West, running from your past and finally excited about what your life might become, your fantasies star hot hunks with surfboards and a sensitive side. When you're twenty-three, alone, pregnant with twins and working all hours of the day and night to keep your struggling business afloat, I guess things tend to change. Anyway, I try to look on the bright side. "Everything will work out, Josie. You'll see."

"Would you get *real* here, please, Luna? I'm knocked up with twins by a man whose last name I don't even know who's now long gone. And I spent my inheritance on a failing business that needs a complete overhaul." I guess the pregnancy hormones are really starting to kick in. Then again, when she puts it like that, it does sound sort of dire. "Did you happen to see the latest online review, Loon? It went something like this: 'The food was hearty and the cocktails were strong as hell—and thank God for that because I needed four so I could concentrate less on my concerns that the dilapidated deck was about to collapse and hurl me into the sea, which, four cocktails in, would probably have drowned me.'"

I saw the review. Someone posted it last night. "That's our only one star review," I say defensively. It's the reason I got my hammer out this morning to see if I could try to spruce things up a little. But all I've got to show for my efforts is a big-ass splinter, blood dripping from my thumb and dirt all over my clothes. And what was I even thinking, trying to improve the look of the place with a hammer and a few nails?

But I'm a salt-of-the-earth type of girl. I don't sweat the small stuff. Not that being pregnant is small, but still. We've handled bumps in the road before. Including the bumpiest one of all, which I make a point of shoving back into its hidden corner of my most difficult memories.

"We'll figure it out, Josie. We'll get through this. Everything's going to be fine."

"*Fine?* How will it be fine, Luna? And how will we get through this? You don't *get through* parenthood. It's with you forever." The comment digs deep, for both of us. Tears pool in Josie's eyes. "I'm sorry, Loon. I shouldn't have said that." She hugs me. "Now I know how you felt," she sobs. I ignore her murmur. There are certain things from my past I definitely don't want to revisit right now. Or ever.

"Come on." I put my arm around her shoulders and lead her inside, where it's cool. One of our bartenders, Rico, just arrived and is starting to set up for the lunch crowd. I give him a little wave, grab some napkins and hand them to Josie. I help her up the back staircase that takes us up to our two-bedroom apartment. "It's not all bad. At least we *have* a business. An awesome one. It's what we always wanted. In time, it'll be just perfect."

I lead her over to the couch, which is in front of the windows and bathed in sunlight.

I love our apartment, even if it is "retro," as Josie generously describes it.

It's rustic and on the small side, but the views are to die for. From up here, when the sun sinks over the water, you feel like you're flying on wings made of gold. Like, despite the underbelly of desperation that sometimes infuses your days, from up here the melting horizon is so full of promise that nothing can touch you.

But now, in the blue light of mid-morning, things *have* touched us. Again. Very real things that are going to cry a lot and require healthcare and food and round-the-clock care and supervision.

"I'm going to call Owen," Josie says. Owen is her brother who lives down the street from their family home in Iowa, which is now owned by Josie's oldest brother Marlon. Her other brother Drew lives one street over. I can already see that it's this detail—one of the reasons we hit the road all those years ago in the first place—that's calling to her now. Five years ago, we couldn't imagine staying put like that. We were different from the people we knew. We had a wanderlust that no one understood except us. And I, in particular, had a lot to work through. I needed to leave, is what it boiled down to.

I bring her a glass of water and a box of tissues and set them down on the coffee table. "I'll go help get ready for the lunch crowd. You just relax and I'll bring you up some food."

"Thanks, Luna."

"We'll figure it out, okay?"

"Sure." She smiles at me weakly and it makes me sad that she's so beautiful and that the man who slept with her and left her in the dust with his babies on the way will never even *know*. We looked for him for months. He was blond and handsome and had a cool, surfie vibe—Josie's absolute weakness. *I didn't mean to have unprotected sex with him,* she sobbed after she peed on the stick and those two unmistakable blue lines showed up. *He told me he wasn't looking for anything serious. And neither was I! We just got carried away.*

It happens.

They will have made some beautiful babies.

But even though we wandered the streets and the hotels and the bars and asked around for a tall, sandy-blond Californian named Noah, he was already gone.

The only thing our online searches revealed is that there are a lot of people named Noah in California.

And I don't like the defeated edge to her voice today.

I leave her to her phone call and walk past my tiny yoga studio where I do my practice every morning at sunrise. I go into my bathroom where I start stripping off my dirty clothes. I take a quick shower and pull on a sleeveless yellow sundress. I run a towel through my hair, which is dark and cut into an angled pixie bob. It has a wave to it that has a mind of its own. Even if I try to straighten it, within around five minutes it's starting to curl again, especially in the Florida heat, so I comb it into place and leave it at that. Then I head back downstairs to help Rico and the kitchen and waitstaff.

I don't care that our bar isn't the fanciest in town. It has *character.* It's funky and fun. Original and old school. It was a case of buying the worst business in the best location, because it was all we could (barely) afford. All the tables and chairs on the deck are colorful and festive, an effect that's enhanced by the shimmering blue water behind. We have a small beach and a dock where our customers can tie up their boats or park their jet skis. Our menu is basic American fare done well.

Maybe we could get another investor. Someone who has an interest in contributing money from afar, so Josie and I can continue to run our business without too much interference. We were only just getting going when Josie found out she was expecting. Her enthusiasm hasn't been quite the same ever since, with the morning sickness and the fear, but she'll come round again, once she has her babies and settles into a routine. We'll figure out how to grow the business *and* raise her little boys.

Everything will be fine.

Roxie

Nate Boone. My brother's best friend and the country boy I had a serious crush on all those years ago when we were both just kids. A lot has happened since then but a part of me never really moved on. Who am I kidding, *all* of me never moved on.

And now I'm heading back to Sugar Mountain to see my bestie—Nate's little sister—and to catch up with the extended Boone family, who have always felt like my own.

What I find is that Nate Boone is *alll* grown up, hotter than the Tennessee sun and not quite as forbidden as he used to be …

Nate

Roxie Tucker. No one knows about our history and our connection because I walked away and never looked back. I had to. She was a hundred percent off-limits.

I haven't seen her in years, until she shows up out of the blue, so beautiful it hurts. And I now know why I could never even think about getting real with anyone else. Because they're not her.

I shouldn't, of course. She's like family. And my life is complicated.

But she's too perfect and the pull is too strong. She's my dream and the one I could never let go of. I lost her once and I have no intention of losing her again. She's mine. She's heaven on earth and I'm a hundred percent addicted.

Now that I've had a taste of forever, this time, I'll risk whatever it takes to keep her …

Nashville Lights is a steamy standalone small town brother's best friend romance, starring a sweet & sassy band manager and the love of her life.

Music City Lovers

Chapter One

ROXIE

"Have fun, Rox, and stay out of trouble." My oldest brother Kade's familiar drawl sounds as tired as I feel.

My phone is perched on its holder on the dashboard and I can see on the video call that Kade is back at his house downtown. He has a few houses in Nashville and he keeps a spare apartment for me at the one that's just off Broadway. I know he's got a gig tonight at the Lucky Seven. Not a solo gig, but he's agreed to be a guest for a couple of friends who are performing.

We've had a grueling few months of touring. My three brothers are the Tucker Brothers Band, and currently have songs at number one, two, four, seven, eight and ten on the Billboard charts. As manager of the band, I'm as exhausted as they are. We hit thirty-eight cities and did forty-eight sold-out shows over ninety-nine days. It was by far the biggest tour the band has done and it's taken their fame into overdrive.

"I will, KJ. You have fun too. And please get some rest." I can't help adding, "Finally." He knows I'm not referring to the tour with that last comment. I'm talking about the recent breakup with his hellish girlfriend Carmen. None of us could stand her, mainly because she made Kade's life miserable for the entire five months they were together. He told us he broke up with her but there was something cagey about the way he'd said it. I'm starting to wonder if he's actually done the deed yet. I'm pretty sure it's a sure thing, I just don't know if he's telling us what we want to hear until he cowboys up and lets her down gently. She was never going to go without a nightmarish meltdown. "I hope you're okay."

"Don't you worry about me, darlin'. You just make sure you're getting some good R & R at the Boones' place. Don't let them wrangle you into doing any farm work."

"Nope, I'm going to be sitting on that wraparound porch enjoying the view of Sugar Lake with my feet up and my phone on silent mode."

"Good girl."

"I'll talk to you in a few days."

"Say hi to the Boones for me."

"I will. Later, KJ."

I end the call and crank the radio up. Miles of open highway stretch out before me as I cruise along in my faithful old pickup truck with the windows down. My brothers tried to insist I let one of their drivers take me or at least take one of the new cars they bought me that are sitting in the huge garage underneath the band's Nashville warehouse. But if I'm going back to the farm, there's no way I'm doing it with a chauffeur or in a fancy sports car. The Boones would laugh me straight back down the dusty dirt road.

After months of being cooped up in crowded tour buses and arena green rooms, the warm summer breeze feels like heaven on my skin.

I drive past cornfields, barns, and the occasional rundown gas station. For once, my phone isn't buzzing with concert schedules, press releases, or my brothers' bickering in the family group chat. I finally have a moment to breathe.

Don't get me wrong, I love being the manager of my brothers' band. And I'm good at it, they keep telling me. With forty-eight sold out shows and six of the new album's tracks currently in the Billboard Top Ten, I'm hardly going to argue with them. The band is riding a high and we're making more money than we know what to do with. But I'm twenty-three years old and bone tired.

Three solid months of packed stadiums, screaming fans and non-stop life on the road takes its toll. I might not be the one singing or playing my heart out every night, but it's just as demanding keeping everything behind the scenes running smoothly. Corralling the rabid crowds, making sure security is air-tight, staying in touch with the label and organizing all the publicity is just the tip of the iceberg.

It's also a lot of work keeping Kade, Travis and most of all Vaughn steady and focused on what they need to focus on. Kade has been dealing with his awful relationship. Travis is head over heels with our new opening act, Ruby Hayes—who's insanely talented and who I'm also managing. And Vaughn is just…Vaughn. As wild as always, and even more so now that he also thinks he's in love. With Ruby's sister, no less. Which of course Travis isn't happy about at all.

I can always trust Vaughn to stir things up.

It's safe to say that for the first time in my life, I'm ready for a real break. Three blissful days in the country to clear my head and catch up with my best friend is just what the doctor ordered.

As if on cue, my phone rings.

Dakota flashes up on the screen and I hit the accept button. "Hey, Dee."

"How long until you get here?"

"I'm only around fifteen minutes away."

"I can't wait to see you, Rox! I have the biggest surprise."

"What surprise?"

"You'll have to wait and see." Dakota almost lost her mind when I called her a week or so ago and asked her if she wanted a visitor for the weekend. "It's been way too long since you came out to Sugar Mountain, Rox. I have a lot to fill you in on. Hurry up and get here already. I just made iced tea and put a bottle of white wine in the fridge. And of course Betty-Ann and Tobias are in the kitchen making your favorite fried chicken with cornbread and all the fixings."

"You have no idea how heavenly that sounds. I haven't had a home-cooked meal in I don't know how long. I'm in need of some serious R&R that involves having none of my brothers within a fifty mile radius."

"You get my brothers instead," she says. "But we can avoid them as much as possible."

"You and your brothers—and of course Betty-Ann, Louise and Earl—are the reason I'm staying in Tennessee and not spending a week on a sun lounger in Cabo. I can't wait to see all of you."

"Well, if I'd known Cabo was an option, I'd have packed my bags," Dakota laughs. "The farm won't be anywhere near as luxurious."

She thinks I'm exaggerating when I say there's nowhere I'd rather be, but it's true. Sugar Mountain Farm has always felt like my second home. It's not really a mountain. It's more of a series of sloping hills and picturesque farmland—and the closest thing to a real home that I've got.

The Nashville warehouse and the various apartments my brothers have bought for me don't really count. I have plenty of money to buy my own houses, but they keep buying buildings or compounds with lots of living spaces. Which they insist I live in. To keep an eye on me, they say.

My brothers are my home, in a sense, especially since we spend so much time together. And also because our parents died young and they've always felt responsible for me. But on the back end of a tour as intense as this one was, we all need some space.

I've spent every summer from the moment I was born, right up until I left to work with my brothers, visiting my Aunt Louise and Uncle Earl. Uncle Earl is my father's brother, even though it's safe to say the two men couldn't have more different personalities. Earl is a cheerful teddy bear of a man. My father was much more complicated, and those dark complications ended up cutting both his and my mother's lives short—something I don't want to revisit in my thoughts right now. I'm too happy.

So I let my memories drift back to Aunt Lou and Uncle Earl. They never had children of their own, but Aunt Lou's second cousin and lifelong best friend Betty-Ann, her husband Gus, and their five children live right next door. Sugar Mountain Farm is theirs. And it was their house that was literally bursting at the seams with love and laughter and all the best things about family and home.

The smells of apple pie and fresh-baked bread.

The sounds of laughter and good-hearted bickering.

Pots clanging with the promise of our next home-cooked meal.

They welcomed my brothers and me with open arms right into the middle of all that, from before my memories even begin. They became our family in the truest sense of the word.

The two houses sit side by side, with a joined drive-way. Aunt Lou and Uncle Earl's farm and house are smaller, the house always neater because they didn't have five children running wild. Aunt Lou always made up beds for the four of us, but we hardly ever spent a night in them. We were having too much fun having sleepovers with the Boones, camping in tents, building blanket forts to sleep in and generally living our best lives.

So it's the Boones' house I remember most fondly. Half the memories of my life are in that house—and all the best ones.

I know every inch of this road. And with each land-mark—the old red barn where I learned to dance, the Country Store where we used to go for triple-scoop ice cream cones that would drip over our fingers in the summer heat, and the familiar road signs that mean I'm getting closer—I feel another layer of the tour-hardened manager I've become peel back, and I'm ten again, bursting with the fizzy excitement of summer.

It's the one place I can guarantee will make me feel like myself again. The blinding stage lights are suddenly a million miles away, and I'm surrounded by nothing but cornfields and the warm Tennessee sun.

"What are your brothers up to this weekend?" Dakota asks. "Don't they all fall to pieces when you're not there?"

"Pretty much."

Most of the time, I'm cursing the fact that three grown men rely on me as much as they do, but I know I'd miss the buzz of excitement that surrounds them if I wasn't doing this job. Not to mention the fact I don't trust anyone else to have their best interests at heart, especially now that they've gone stratospheric.

I sort of stumbled into being their manager by default. They weren't getting along with their former manager and, since I've taken care of the three of them my whole life anyway, I stepped up and started organizing their schedules and making their phone calls. One thing led to another and when Vaughn fired their former manager out of the blue after an argument, it made sense for me to take on the role. I've been doing it ever since, learning on the job and mostly loving every minute of it.

All three of my brothers are insufferable at times but, even so, I couldn't love them more if I tried.

"You know I saw Kade when he came to see Nate, not too long ago," Dakota says, "but I haven't seen Travis or Vaughn in ages. They haven't been back here since before they became superstars."

"Well, they're no longer the ragtag Tucker boys you grew up with, that's for sure." I'm not sure she'd be able to reconcile those ragamuffin kids she remembers with the rockstars who now have the world at their feet—and every possible temptation thrown at them on a daily basis.

"Anyway," I say, "I'm only going to be gone for a few days. Even the Tucker brothers can survive that. And besides, Travis and Vaughn are so loved-up with their new girlfriends, they won't even notice I'm gone. One thing about my brothers, once they fall, they fall *hard*."

"I think my brothers will be the same. I'm not sure why I say that since none of them are in steady relationships right now, but they're all secretly romantics at heart."

"Maybe it's something in the Sugar Mountain water," I laugh. "Anyway, all four of us need a break. You know how it is working with family."

"Oh, trust me, I get it." Dakota has four brothers and they all still live and—mostly, at least—work on Sugar Mountain. "Luke and Leo spend half their time bickering and fighting like they're still eight years old. They drive me crazy."

I picture the twins wrestling with each other non-stop when they were kids. Those nights when we all camped out under the stars or slept in a row on the big front porch, they were always rolling around like two little hell-raisers.

It feels strange to imagine my brothers back here now that their lives are so vastly different. Once upon a time we were sun-kissed kids running wild. We didn't care about our skinned knees or our thrift store clothes. We loved the simplicity and the contentedness of the country life, which felt so charmed to us. It was a welcome respite from the rougher edges of our "real" life in the city, where our parents' lives were slowly but surely imploding.

"So, when's the wedding?" Dakota asks. "I can't believe Travis is engaged."

It was big news when Travis proposed to Ruby on stage on the last night of the tour. The internet blew up with replays of the big event and Dakota called me immediately after it happened.

"They haven't set a date yet. But I don't think Travis will want to wait too long. He's absolutely besotted. So's Vaughn. And that's something I never saw coming: Vaughn in love. But I must say it makes both of them a lot easier to keep in line. All I have to do is threaten to tell their girlfriends how obnoxious they're being and immediately they're all contrite. Works like a charm."

I'm mostly joking, but there's an edge to it I hope Dakota doesn't hear. I'm thrilled that Vaughn has found love with a nice girl. Gigi is a country bumpkin and a sweetheart. I've gotten to know her a little and I'm really not sure if she's ever had a mean-spirited thought in her life. She has a purity of spirit that's almost saintly. For Vaughn to fall for someone like that is a wild relief. He's a changed man, and for the better. I no longer have to sweep groupies out of his dressing room every morning or stop strangers slipping pills into his pockets. For Gigi, Vaughn is willing to do literally *anything.* Even reform.

I just hope it lasts.

"What about Kade? Is he still with that girl none of you liked?"

"No, thank God. He just recently ditched her. We're all so relieved."

"Well, it's good he got rid of her, then. But it sounds like you like Travis and Vaughn's girlfriends? You approve?"

"Not that they consult me on these things," I laugh, "but yes. They're both beautiful, inside and out. Even if I have to yell at the boys for being late all the time because they spend so much time in bed, I have to admit they're writing the best songs of their careers. Gigi is really good for Vaughn. Then there's Ruby of course, my newest artist and now sister-in-law-to-be. She's a major talent."

Dakota's silent for a beat. "That must be so busy for you, Rox. Managing both the band *and* Ruby. How do you juggle it all?"

"It's busy," I admit. "It requires a lot of patience and even more caffeine. Plus I'm thinking of taking on two other new artists." I sigh, stretching my neck out and hearing it crack. "I swear I feel like I've aged ten years on this tour."

"Sounds like you definitely need a break. Do you ever get any time for yourself? I mean, when's the last time you went on a date?"

I have to think for a minute, it's been so long. "Um...maybe, like, over a year ago? I went out with that drummer from Austin once, but then we hit the road again. Oh, and there was that sound engineer who basi-cally stalked me but he wasn't my type at all. Kade ended up firing him and threatening to kill him. Anyway, I don't really have time, Dee." It's true. I absolutely do not have time for dating. "There's also the small matter of spending 24/7 with my three extremely overprotective older brothers."

"I hear that." Dakota definitely gets it.

Even before I started managing the band, I'd always avoided getting serious with anyone. Not that I could ever tell Dakota the reason why.

"Well, I know you think of them as surrogate brothers," Dakota says, "but in fact my boys are not related to you at all, and three of them are eligible bachelors. None of them—aside from Tobias and he doesn't count in that way—are in a relationship right now. So you can take your pick."

"Stop." But my stomach flips. I do not want to talk about Dakota's single brothers. "Seriously, I love Luke and Leo, you know I do, but they are not going to settle down any time soon. They have new girls every time I talk to you."

"It's true." I can practically hear Dakota's frown. "They both seem allergic to commitment. Plus, whoever one of them dates is going to have to put up with the other one. The two of them are practically inseparable."

Luke and Leo are identical twins who used to speak their own secret language when they were tiny boys. "Yeah, maybe they could date two girls who are identical twins. That might be the only solution."

"Poor girls, is all I can say." Dakota exhales a pained laugh. "So, I guess that just leaves Nate."

Heat creeps up my neck and warms my cheeks. I've never been able to bring myself to tell her about my secret kiss with her oldest brother all those years ago. I figured it was just a teenage crush and the torch would burn itself out over time.

I guess I'm about to find out …

ALSO BY JULIE CAPULET

I Love You Series

The Obsession Begins (free)

XOXO I Love You

XOXX I Love You More

Love You the Most (free)

Sexy Standalones

Max

Cowboy

McCabe Brothers Series

Hopeless Romantic

My Hero

Arrogant Player

Music City Lovers Series

Nashville Days

Nashville Nights

Nashville Dreams

Nashville Lights

Hawthorne U Series

Lovestruck

Paradise Series

Devil's Angel

Wild Hearts

New York Billionaires Series

Billionaire Boss

Billionaire Grump

Billionaire Devil

Billionaire Romantic

Standalone Rom-com

Beautiful Savages

ABOUT THE AUTHOR

Julie Capulet is an Amazon top 20 bestselling author of contemporary romance. She writes steamy he-falls-first romance with heart, heat and fairy tale HEAs. Her stories are inspired by true love and she's married to her own real life hero. When she's not writing, she's reading, traveling, walking on the beach and watching rom-coms.

www.juliecapulet.com